D1714455

The Lamps of Albarracín

Edith Scott Saavedra

Illustrations by Devora Werchowsky

Dec. 2018
For Gus,
I hope you enjoy
the inter-faith dialogue!
Best wishes,
Edith

Floricanto Press

Floricanto is a trademark of *Floricanto Press*.

Berkeley Press is an imprint of Inter-American Development, Inc.

Floricanto Press
7177 Walnut Canyon Rd.
Moorpark, California 93021
(415) 793-2662
www.*FloricantoPress*.com
ISBN-13: 9781724787514

"Por nuestra cultura hablarán nuestros libros. Our books shall speak for our culture."

Roberto Cabello-Argandoña and Leyla Namazie, Editors

To
Denise Miriam Freudmann Joselson

TABLE OF CONTENTS

LIST OF ILLUSTRATIONS

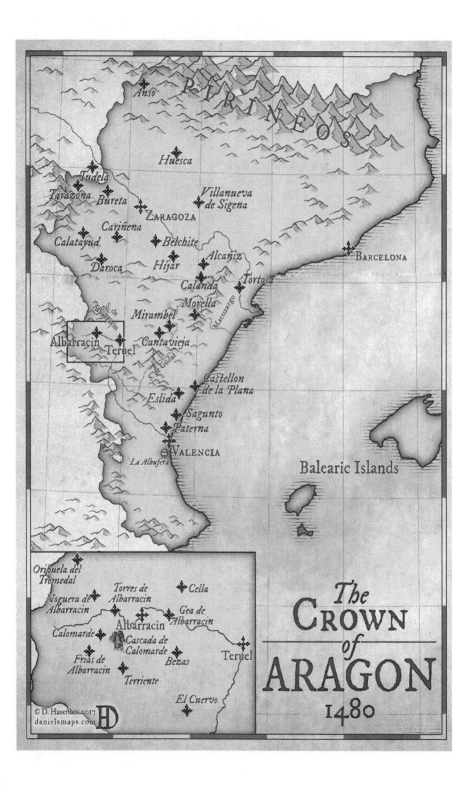

PIRINEOS

Anso

Huesca

Tudela

Tarazona Bureta

Villanueva
de Sigena

ZARAGOZA

Cariñena

Calatayud   Belchite

Daroca   Hijar   Alcañiz

Calanda   Tortosa

Morella

Mirambel

S.ª de Albarracin

Albarracin   Cantavieja

Teruel

S.ª de Gudar

Castellon
de la Plana

Eslida

Sagunto

Paterna

VALENCIA

La Albufera

BARCELONA

Maestrazgo

Balearic Islands

Oribuela del
Tremedal

Torres de
Albarracin   Cella

Noguera de
Albarracin   Gea de
Albarracin

Calomarde   Albarracin

Cascada de
Calomarde   Teruel

Frias de
Albarracin   Bezas

Terriente

El Cuervo

© D. Hasenbos 2017
danielsmaps.com

The
CROWN
of
ARAGON
1480

PROLOGUE

MY NAME, SARA. My crest, the Lions of Judah. Though I left my land long years ago, my heart is Aragonese.

From childhood I remember our festivals, different yet the same. At sunrise on her longest day, Magda lit wicks and set walnuts in wine. She prayed the Christian beads. Summer brought the sunsets of Ramadan. Bronze lamps lit, Arabi the trader gave charity —coins for the poor, sugar cakes for me. Then came the harvest, sweet with peaches from Calanda. At night in my family's cabin we sisters kindled lamps and tied citrons and pears to willow boughs. Our Sukkot, his Sugar Feast, her Solstice. They come to me as one. When I close my eyes in the depths of memory I see lamps and their light.

In Albarracín those were years when the faiths lived side by side. The Christians in their quarter were anchored by the Church of Santa María, Muslims by their mosque, humble and crowded, and Jews by our small synagogue. In Teruel, the neighbouring city, families of all faiths resided on the same streets. On Aragon's old southern frontier, proudly independent, we stood out for our tolerance. Across Iberia, towns as tolerant as ours were far and few.

The Albarracín of my childhood assigned a separate quarter to each faith and there were troubles, but we held together. Our town was a single tree that bore three branches, springing from the shared roots of autonomy, kinship and commerce. Many clans of different faiths were related one way or another. Every day, Muslims, Christians and Jews crossed into each other's quarters on errands that laced us together like a cat's cradle.

My father was doctor to the town, and I was his assistant. How proudly we walked the streets of Albarracín. We tended patients of all faiths as the church bells tolled, the muezzin called to prayer, and the ram's horn called for rain. In those evenings vibrant with bells, verses and the sounding of the horn, how I loved the ornaments of our town. The salmon pink gesso of the houses. Clove pinks coaxed to bloom on balconies. Dragons nailed to doors, to ward off evil.

I was fourteen when King Ferdinand sent the Royal Monarchs' Inquisition into Aragon. For the next five years, to outward appearances I lived in sequence as a Jew, a Christian and a Muslim. Was I a different person each time? No, I was always Sara, no matter who I appeared to others. Though my life was at risk, I learned not to judge my companions by their faith, because the worst and best in all of us is the same. Most importantly, the best.

In 1492, at the order of the Catholic Monarchs, all people of the Hebrew faith were exiled from Castile and Aragon, many thousands. How many lives lost, how many stories gone forever? We need our stories to know ourselves, and the stories of our neighbours of all religions, to understand each other. In the wake of the ships that carried my people to the farthest shores, in the sea of the lost stories of the Spanish Sephardim, mine will survive. A young girl's story of heart and hearth. Above all, an account of the three faiths together.

Albarracín, city of my birth, my beloved town on the hill. My days were lit by your burnished sun and my nights by your oil lamps. Some lamps, we burned in the Synagogue when the third star rose in the sky. Yet there were lamps everywhere, from dusk till dawn, and in the predawn they flickered from every hearth as if each harboured its own steadfast soul. They shone from the quarters of Muslim, Christian and Jew alike. The years of my memoirs, the 1480s, were troubled times for the faiths of Aragon, but we who believed in brotherhood all hoped the darkest hour would be the hour before dawn. These memoirs are also the story of *The Lamps of Albarracín*.

CHILDHOOD

The Year 1481, as counted by Christians

ONE MORNING PAPA rode with Bella and me along the river through the meadows of Torres de Albarracín. It was the season of violets, the first flower of spring in our songs of May, and the Guadalaviar was running high. As we rode into the village we saw a fair in the plaza. Musicians and dancers, savouries and sweets.

Papa often brought me to visit patients, but this time we were placed under the watch of the worthy Widow Astruga. Fortunately for us, she often fell asleep mid-sentence. As soon as she was snoring, Bella took me by the hand and led me from the house.

"Shhh, silly, don't make a sound. Off we go!"

The first thing I did on reaching the plaza, was buy a cup of sweet frothy tiger-nut milk, the drink favoured in legend by King Jaime I of Aragon.

"Please don't leave me alone!"

But it was too late. As usual, Bella was already gone.

I sat on a stool in the shade and sipped the tiger-nut milk. It wasn't *casher*, but I was eleven and naughty when tempted with sweets. In particular I enjoyed licking the froth off my lips, which left them dry and in need of another sip.

The musicians plucked the strings of the mandolins. I closed my eyes. The beats swung me forward, jerked me to a halt and pushed me back again, several times, and I was pleasantly dizzy before they lengthened into the opening *copla*.

"The apple was born green and time ripened it,

My heart was born free and yours captured it."

Every town and village in the Kingdom of Aragon, even the smallest hamlet, had girls who knew how to dance. The girls of Torres danced their sets with grace, it is true, but I was left breathless by the youths leaping in air.

A pair stepped with resolve into the centre of the plaza — and I recognized Bella. She did not strike a pose. She didn't need to. This time as always, Bella was transformed by the soul of dance before she came into view. She leaped into the air, kicked like a gazelle, and landed with precision, over and over in dazzling sequence, from side to side, and front to back and around again, in her soft slippers tied with black laces, her arms and fingers extended. To appreciate our Bella, a man would have to have the soul of an artist, Papa said.

I was still thinking of Papa, when I felt a hand on my shoulder and there he was. We were discovered! But Papa didn't scold. He took me by the arm, and walked over to Bella.

"You were lovely, my dear. It always warms my heart to see you dance."

Naturally, whenever Bella made an appearance she managed to win an admirer. By my tally, she had two dozen swains from Torres to the opposite side of town. One youth in particular had sent a poem that moved my heart. Bella had laughed and told me not to be silly. His people were nothing. I realized she was just practicing the art of the hunt. A blond, blue-eyed, budding Diana.

At home we found Aunt Esther visiting from Teruel. Aunt Esther had brought her friend, Lady Brianda Besante de Santángel. Lady Brianda was married to a wealthy merchant by the name of Luis de Santángel. His cousin by chance also bore the name Luis de Santángel and was the Royal Chancellor of Aragon. We children were required to address Lady Brianda with utmost courtesy. Esther, also wealthy, was designing a gown.

"Bella, I suggest a hoop skirt as curved as the little bell that I keep on my vanity table. Imagine a bell of cut glass, chiseled with quatrefoils. On the over-skirt, we will criss-cross gold and crimson ribbons into stars."

"Stars of ribbon?"

"Yes, the height of style in Seville. Eight-pointed stars, inspired by the Patio of Damsels of the Royal Alcázar."

"And to showcase my best features?"

"A bodice in burgundy satin, with laces down the front, and sleeves of white lawn. What's more, a sash of red silk at your neck."

"To what effect?"

"Love at first sight. We'll tuck strands of silk under the laces, to meet at your breasts in a kiss."

Bella carried at eighteen the most graceful shoulders and neck in Creation. I had reason for envy. When I was a newborn, Aunt Esther came from Teruel to inspect me and found a stripe of silky black hair across my shoulder blades. I had no other claim to distinction.

"It's over the top! Why the fuss?"

"Sarita, marvelous news. Dear Brianda has secured an invitation for our Bella to attend the nuptial festivities of the youngest of the Santángel nieces, in Calatayud."

"If you dance nicely at this wedding, maybe the King's Magistrate, Jaime de Montesa, will notice you. I hear he is a jolly man who enjoys music and dance."

"Never mind Jaime de Montesa, Your Grace, he is old. Vidal Francés, on the other hand, will be quite enough for me."

"Who is this Vidal Francés?"

I was the only one to ask.

"Vidal is a wealthy financier, a *converso*, with an estate in Calatayud. He is known for his collection of art, in particular his tapestries by master weavers from Tournai. All the best girls have made a try for him, but he has resisted. He remains single."

"Maybe you should practice your dances."

"Don't be impertinent. You know I can dance perfectly to any tune, the first time I hear it."

Actually, it was true. I had seen Bella do it many times, and the more people watched, the more beautifully she danced.

Aunt Esther broke in, "Dear, I hear there are many dances from the French Court in fashion in Castile. Modern ones, in triple time. I would love to see you dance them."

"Oh no," I thought, "Never mind the hoop skirt. Bella will want all eyes on her as she holds out her skirt like a fan. She will coax for a dance skirt which flows when lifted on each side, inspired by the Arch of the Peacocks. Time to nip this in the bud."

So I asked, "Vidal Francés, what sort of man is he?"

"Proper and reserved, so they say."

"A pompous bore, you mean."

I couldn't hold it back. Bella annoyed me so.

"What has come over you? Beg forgiveness!"

"A pompous bore?" snapped Aunt Esther. "So much the better. An interesting man has more than one woman. With a pompous bore, our Bella might have a constant husband."

"Enough, ladies." Lady Brianda turned to me. "Are you taught the Torah on a regular basis?"

"Yes, Your Grace, I take tuition nearly every day."

"Your father pays tuition for a girl?"

"Papa sends a tutor for Isaq, but Isaq cannot settle without me. Sometimes he throws things, so I study with him. And so does Reyna. Even though she's young, she sneaks in and sits at our tutor's feet."

"Your tutor, what sort of man is he?"

"We call him Solomon the Aged. I don't know his surname."

"I mean, does he follow the Scriptures?"

"He follows the scripts of a famous physic from Toledo who prescribes apples, beetroot, honey, and onions. I suspect it is mainly onions."

Reyna had joined us. She understood perfectly well — she loved a joke.

"Does this Solomon the Aged focus on the Torah?"

"I steer him off course. I may be little, but I like to hear him discuss the Zohar, especially the Creation bits, lots of things about good souls and the wicked, the Aleph and other letters of the alphabet."

"Why on earth did your father hire him?"

"After giving away his medicines, Papa can pay next to nothing. As Mama used to say, the doctor made of honey gets eaten."

"Esther, I am surprised at your brother-in-law."

"Lady Brianda, Uncle Solomon gave us prayer lamps! Mine is celeste with a rim of deep blue, and Sara's is green — her favourite colour. They fit inside our palms. And from Jerusalem! He is a good teacher, I promise."

Reyna ran to fetch the child-sized lamps and returned with one in each palm, held high. In grace they surpassed Aunt

Esther's bell, with handles like ribbons twisted into half-bows and glazes more lustrous than any glass.

Lady Brianda turned to Esther.

"This talk is entertaining, but faith must come first. The Torah must come before all things that turn young girls' heads."

She stood at full height, suddenly imposing. I kindled the lamps. Their flames reflected blues and greens and the fire in Brianda's eyes as she led us in the evening prayer.

"Girls, you have recited this many times before, but now I want you to concentrate with all your being on every word."

Afterwards, Bella yawned. "I have so much to plan, Sara. I won't be listening to you tonight. Give the guests my warmest regards." She retired to her maiden's bower, where her bed lay strewn with lengths of ribbon and patterns for slippers.

"Bella is planning for the hunt, I mean, her grand entrance. I wonder. How can an unloving woman win the heart of a man?"

"Men always say they want a heart of gold, but in the end they decide differently."

"Why is that?"

"What wins most men is not the good in a woman, but her selfishness. Our Bella will marry the man she wants. Wait and see."

We removed to the receiving room, where Papa had arranged a gathering to hear me recite "The Legend of Count Arnaldos." I was concerned to find our modest salon filled to the rafters. There stood Haim the butcher and his children Judah and Bona, and Jacobo Catorce the pawnbroker with his wife Chaya. Behind them, Aldonza, the old woman who came to milk our goats after our mama died.

My throat was sore, so I swallowed a few times before reciting:

> *Whoever had adventure*
>
> *On the waters of the sea,*
>
> *As did the Count Arnaldos*
>
> *One morning in the spring?*
>
> *Departing for the hunt*
>
> *With a falcon on his hand,*
>
> *He saw arrive a galley*
>
> *Steering onward to the land."*

With each line I shifted my voice from one side of my throat to the other. I reached for my cup of hot water and honey.

At that moment, Reyna climbed up on a dining chair, tossed back her curls, and rang out in a voice like bell chimes:

> *"Then he heard the ancient helmsman*
>
> *Chant a song so wild, so clear*

That it made the sailing sea birds

Poise upon the mast to hear.

Till his soul was full of longing

And he cried with impulse strong,

Helmsman, for the sake of Heaven,

Teach me now your wondrous song.

Here responded the strange Helmsman

'This response I give to thee,

I will never teach this Song

Except to those who come with me.'"

While all faces were on Reyna, I spied our brother Isaq craftily making his way to the door. The worst moment to escape! I didn't want a scene in front of our guests, so I bent low and ran behind them, their backs to me the length of the room.

As I passed Chaya Catorce I heard her say to Aldonza, "No beauty, no grace, and her presence is ordinary. You'd think she would have turned out better, considering who the father was."

"Give a cow a fleur-de-lis, you still get dung."

Stupid women, what were they talking about? At that moment, Carmela, Magda's daughter, came up to me. She pinched my arm.

"Cheer up, Sara, no reason to be ashamed. No one will remember you anyway."

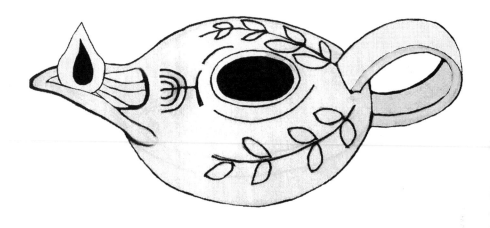

§§§

Uncle Saul was supposed to be at my recitation, but fortunately he was late. Valencia was the principal port of call for his fabric imports, so he was spending more and more time away. At least, that was how he explained it to Aunt Esther. Years earlier, when he had first married Esther, heiress to the owner of the largest house of fine fabrics in Aragon, they had always traveled together.

We waited for him most of that night. Reyna was jumping up and down the front staircase, pressing her nose against the wooden slats of the mullioned window and parting our lace curtains with her fingers. Sleep was out of the question.

Finally, a rapping in the front foyer. Aunt Esther opened the door and in from the dark walked Uncle Saul wrapped in a cloak. She took a step back. She called, "Bella, Sarita and Reyna, come greet your Uncle." We all ran forward to receive him.

Uncle Saul had a time honoured custom of bringing gifts from his travels. This time he was returning from Florence. Each of us had high expectations.

To our surprise he announced,

"Simon, you first!"

Saul's servant gave Papa a large bundle. Soon Papa was undoing layer upon layer of Italian silk scarves, an extravagance typical of Saul. So many layers to unwrap! Gradually, the mysterious object assumed the contours of a child-sized doll, with sloping shoulders and a small waist. At last, into the lamplight there emerged a large, and shapely, string instrument.

"The latest invention in music. The viola of Valencia! I commissioned her for you, Simon. She is played on the lap, with a bow. Five strings, tuned in fourths, and a bridge with a delicate arch that allows you to sound each string separately."

I interrupted, "Look at the neck on that viola. Ebony and ivory!"

"Brother, if she whets your appetite, I have more in store for you from where she came. More comely, and more marvelous to unwrap."

"Papa, may I touch her?"

He coughed. "No, Sarita, later. Your gift is coming. Wait for yours."

"Bella, my niece, hold out your hands!"

Bella received widths of Florentine green and red cut velvet, ample for a dress and slippers. On top, a case of boxwood spilling amber teardrops. No mention was made of the price, which exceeded Papa's purse by multiples.

'Where is Isaq?"

"In his room, with his chessboard."

"I have brought him a deck of cards from France with the latest suits —spades, hearts, diamonds and clubs.

Rouse him now. Tell him it's time for the sweets!"

Isaq's steps were heard upon the stairs.

"Uncle, don't forget Sara!"

"Reyna, how right you are." Uncle Saul snapped his fingers. His manservant knelt before me with a dish and lifted the cover.

On the saucer stood a miniature bell tower of honeyed almond candy. Its base was of dark nougat and its walls of honey brick. Its crenulations, toasted almonds, stood like soldiers round the top.

"A nougat tower! Children, I present to you the Campanile di Cremona in sweet replica. First created for the Sforza nuptials."

I lifted it high. Reyna, befixed, stood on tiptoe.

"A marvel, Saul! Thank you kindly."

"Now, we slice it!"

"So soon?"

"Of course, it's part of the extravagance!"

Isaq rushed in waving a dagger and fell upon the tiny tower. It yielded crumbs of crunchy nougat that barely went round. Saul smiled and moved to command the centre of the room.

"Reyna, are you ready?"

"Yes!"

"Close your eyes and hold out your hands."

From under his cloak, which had been wiggling suspiciously, Uncle Saul swept in the palm of his hand the tiniest of spaniels. She had dark liquid eyes with black rims, fringed ears, a silky white coat, and an exuberant tail.

The spaniel raised her eyes to mine. A collar cinched the ruff around her throat. Its strap of ultramarine blue was stitched with tiny pearls, and from this choker dangled a short pearl strand ending in a pendant of Florentine fleur-de-lis. I caught my breath.

At its heart —a blue diamond!

"I have acquired this pup from a wealthy woman connected to the House of Medici, from whose trading arm I buy the finest woolen. She is what the Italians call a Dwarf Spaniel and descends from the de Medici kennels. Reyna, she is for you, if you promise to share her."

Of course she was meant for Reyna. The blue collar and diamond made that clear. Blue was Reyna's colour.

"She was born in a Florentine palace into the lap of luxury, so treat her well," laughed Uncle Saul.

"She is as silky as a butterfly so her name shall be Mariposa."

Being in the fashion business, Uncle Saul no doubt envisioned the pup as a sort of warm muff for Reyna, with big eyes and a plume. Magda, on the other hand, had ideas of a different kind. No sooner had Uncle Saul and Aunt Esther left the house, than Magda pulled herself up to full height.

"That dog goes out of my house. Now!"

The pup set up residence in the store-room with Magda's son, Jaime, who taught her tricks. Her name soon came down a few notches, to Mari-Paws, because of her talent for rearing up and standing on her hind legs. Fortunately, she grew bigger in stature than is standard for her little breed. Set loose in the pastures with sheep, who towered above her, she proved to be a lion heart. The collar was utterly unsuited and ended up in Reyna's coffer. And that is how a canine aristocrat from Florence came to cavort in the stony fields by the ramparts of Albarracín.

§§§

Isaq would not speak outside the house and the townsfolk thought him a blooming idiot. He cost me many sleepless nights. Papa refused to give him opiates and the only thing that helped was Valerian, which grows wild in our hills.

Pounding it with mortar and pestle fell to me, unfortunately, because Valerian root stinks. As Isaq grew older, Valerian didn't put him to sleep. He escaped to the town plaza where the boys fed him bread. At home bread was forbidden to him, because after he ate wheat flour his temper turned high spirited and then foul.

The day before Passover I went to our market to buy new crockery, recent purchases having fallen prey to Isaq's moods. I already had gone out in the morning for *matzah*, the unleavened bread of our Passover feast. I hoped I wasn't too late, as the sun was low in the sky.

The next thing I knew, I rounded a corner and spied Isaq cramming a bread roll into his mouth with a guilty look. Leavened bread is forbidden at Passover.

"You mustn't eat that bread. Remember the Tenth Plague!" I cried out, to the delight of two onlookers, the Pacheco boys.

Years earlier, old Pacheco had driven into town to sell charcoal and left before dawn, setting the two boys loose. They stole to eat when nature demanded, and sought amusement where they could. Usually they amused themselves with Isaq.

"Remember the Tenth Plague!" they repeated in falsetto, "The last one out of the town gates has the pox!"

Racing ahead, they lured Isaq down the steep and twisting lanes, one after another, further out of town. I followed, winding my way down the streets. They led us past the last houses to the start of the grazing land, with its stony pastures. The chill of night was descending. With the dark hills before us, they paused long enough for Isaq to catch up and yelled, "Off to the races! Home free!"

Under the blackening sky, the Pacheco boys were running at full tilt, hooting and hollering and clearing stone walls with ease. Isaq, intoxicated with freedom, was galloping after them like a yearling trying out his legs. Never before had I seen Isaq run free. A lightning flash revealed the *kippa* still pinned to his head, just barely. How was I going to explain the loss of the *kippa*, much less Isaq? What a disaster!

Then I realized, "he is a boy after all who wants to run with the rest."

Isaq was ranging out of sight. The rocks were slippery and my shins bled. A tiny dog with a plumed tail, gleaming wet in the storm, rushed into view and encircled Isaq. Mari-Paws sprang at him and halted his progress. Jaime came running, collared Isaq, and came my way and took me by the arm. He led us both home.

"You must stop this wandering, Sara. I can't watch you two all the time and this could come to a bad end."

We reached the house late, and scurried in through the back. Jaime set Mari-Paws loose inside to distract Magda in case she was still up. Isaq and I hid in the shadows. We heard Magda's voice.

"The dog is in the house again. I forgot to bar the door."

Out of her alcove came a colossal man wearing nothing but a dark, loose tunic. He peered around but did not see me.

"Hullo, Jaime," the muleteer said affably in Arabic, "put the bitch out, will you, and let's share some herb."

Isaq and I ran upstairs. I brushed the offending breadcrumbs off his face. He sniffled and wiped his nose four times with the back of his hand, from left to right, the way he always did.

The next day Isaq refused to leave his chamber. This upset Papa, who wanted him downstairs for Passover *Seder*. I opened the door a crack, and looked inside. The shards of his basin, saucer and chamber pot were strewn across the floor, glinting in the shaft of light from the window. Here and there, a lonely sunbeam splashed upon on the teal and black ceramics made by Ismael the potter.

Beyond the shards of colour, I spied Isaq's crouching figure jammed between his bedstead and the wall, where once he had fit so easily.

"Come downstairs for *Seder*. Everyone wants to see you."

"You are a moron. Go die."

"You should not eat the bread of the Pacheco boys."

He bridled. "I'm not a slice of bread and I can eat what I want."

It angered him when we womenfolk tied his behaviour to the food he ate or didn't eat. Each day he was becoming more self-willed. He was no longer a child whose behaviour could be explained by his supper.

"Now, now, I will bring you some mint with hot water and soon you will do as you please."

I counted the crockery items to be replaced. Not all was lost —his lamp had bounced across the floor no worse for wear. The fifth lamp from Ismael the potter's workshop in as many months! Rotund, as thick as a flower pot, and its sturdy spout had spikes like teeth. Mari-Paws always growled at it.

"A blessing it did not break. This is the perfect lamp for you."

I smiled my best sisterly smile at its crocodile snout, and turned down the stairs to the kitchen. This time, there was no muleteer.

A few weeks later, Papa arrived home with a gift addressed in a decisive hand to "The daughters of Doctor Simon." I opened it with Reyna pressing up close. Inside was a precious Torah, in green leather and fine binding, with the note: "To my dear young friends. Remember always, the teachings of the Torah are revelations from God. Study every day and we shall discuss when I see you next. With affection, Brianda Besante."

Though Lady Brianda was a *conversa*, she regularly attended the Main Synagogue of Teruel, where she had a reserved seat. She and Aunt Esther, though inseparable, made an unlikely couple, with Lady Brianda, who at birth had been baptized Christian, urging Aunt Esther to practice Judaism.

Over the ensuing weeks, Reyna, seven years old, spent hours with the Torah, reading diligently, helped by what she had gleaned from Solomon the Aged. Even compared to intelligent children twice her age, she could read well and what amazed me was that she read with understanding. I helped her when I could.

One evening, Reyna confided, "Sarita, I am worried. What if Lady Brianda asks that we return the Torah?"

"Why do you worry?"

"Because this Torah has become my friend. I don't want to part with it."

"The Torah is a gift. Lady Brianda will not ask for its return."

"I am so relieved. May I trust you with a secret? Something I can't tell anyone else?"

"Of course, or why would you ask me in the first place?"

"The other afternoon, as I passed by the Torah, I saw a glimmer of light. It was late afternoon and the sun was streaming through the window, but the light was not sunlight. It came from the Torah, a tiny ray of soft gold."

"I think that's how it is supposed to be."

I wrapped my arms round her bony shoulders and sang,

> *"In the sea there is a tower,*
>
> *In the tower, a window,*
>
> *In the window is a girl, who calls to sailors.*
>
> *If the sea turns into milk,*

I will become a fisherman

And fish for my sorrows

With little words of love."

To tell the truth, I began to be worried about Reyna. That was the start of my fear, that she was alone too much and not quite right.

§§§

Unless beguiled by the Pacheco brothers Isaq never did wander the town at random. He would watch in the plaza while the boys and men played chess. The more he tried to blend in, the more he stood out like a dead-white bust with a vacant stare. Isaq caught the eye of Arabi the trader, a long-time friend of Uncle Saul. Uncle Arabi, as we called him, kept a shophouse piled with rugs, saddle covers and, in the back, silk treasures.

One day, two opponents were close to a draw, when Uncle Arabi leaned over and boomed, "You Isaq, make the next move!" To bellows of laughter, Isaq stepped forward and moved one of the pieces. I don't know the game of chess, but apparently it was a well-reasoned move, because Uncle Arabi went to see Papa, and from then on he taught Isaq chess in his store.

After his first class, I fetched Isaq home. He went upstairs meek as a lamb and then gave me the slip. I raced to the plaza where I found Uncle Arabi teaching my brother again, but not chess. Vocabulary! Words that derive from Arabic. I had my doubts. Isaq lost patience with phrases without precise meanings, usually in conversation. Polite talk in the plaza was a nightmare. He would pump his arm up and down, and often I had to lead him home.

"Words that begin with the letter 'a' in the Aragonese tongue tend to come from Arabic," he explained, "such as '*aljedrez*,'" making a gesture towards the chess board at which they sat.

"Not bad," I thought.

"Let's find some more. There is '*almendra*' for almond, and '*azucar*' for sugar."

Also perceptive choices, redolent of Arab sweets. Uncle Arabi and his servant boy Mahoma were well aware of Isaq's sweet tooth.

"Come join us. Let's pick a word derived from Arabic for you, something fresh and lovely. I know, '*azahar*.' Orange blossom."

I thought Isaq wasn't paying attention, as he was staring at the board, but apparently he was. He wrinkled his brow and pronounced, "The flower of the plum tree is called the flower of the plum tree. The flower of the orange tree is logically the flower of the orange tree, and it should be called such. There is no need for another name. Why call it 'azahar?'" My brother had been speaking more of late, and also posing more "why" questions. I hoped Uncle Arabi would answer with consideration. He turned to me.

"Have you ever beheld the *azahares* of Andalusia in bloom under the southern sun?"

"No, Uncle, I have never traveled to the South."

"The buds of the southern *azahares* are whiter than cream and gently curved, and when they unfold their petals reflect the rays of the sun as no other flower.

They are the most resplendent of all."

"The name is from Arabic?"

"We call the orange blossom 'al zahar,' from the word for flower. A similar word, 'al zahara,' means resplendent."

"So, the meaning of 'azahar' is resplendent?"

"Well, the roots in Arabic are different, but in my heart it has always held two meanings, both flower and resplendent.

I laughed, "Then orange trees belong in our paradise, the Paradise of the Three Religions, along with pomegranate trees. Our tutor says pomegranates were the original fruit in the Garden of Eden."

"You are imagining paradise?"

"Yes. Now that we have pomegranates and oranges, I am wondering what tree the Christians would prefer in our paradise, the Paradise of the Three Religions."

"Perhaps the apple," remarked Uncle Arabi with a sly smile, "they carve apples in stone on their cathedrals. And a most remarkable Adam and Eve. You should ask your Uncle Saul."

"Because he knows temptation?"

"Precisely. In any case, I have never heard of such a thing as the Paradise of the Three Religions. What led you to think of it?"

"It is not my idea, it is Reyna's. She is always thinking of things like paradise. It is the sort of thing she carries around in her strange head. She says that we live in the Land of the Three Religions and as our souls are eternal and long for joy, we all should go to the Paradise of the Three Religions."

"In that little head of hers, beneath those curls? I never would have imagined.

You know, we Muslims have many more trees and flowers in our tradition of Paradise, and birds too.

Have you ever seen a Tree of Life?"

"No, Uncle Arabi. The Tree of Life stands in the Garden of Eden, guarded by flaming swords, but I have never seen one."

"We have been designing Trees of Life since the days of the Prophet, perhaps before."

"What sorts of designs, Uncle?"

"A willow, a cypress, a flowering branch. Pull some carpets from the store, Mahoma, so I remember to show them later."

Uncle Arabi and Isaq resumed their play and I stood idle, dreaming of orange blossoms in Andalusia.

"My father was a scholar at heart and named me, his firstborn, after Ibn 'Arabi, the philosopher-poet who lived long ago in the Murcia of Al-Andalus. I fear his choice of name was overly ambitious."

"You are learned in so many things. Chess, geometry, philosophy and surveying. There must be few in Albarracín who know as much as you."

"Albarracín is a small town. It is nothing next to Zaragoza, which in turn pales beside the wonders of Córdoba."

"Have you been there?"

"Yes, once in my youth. My father had business in the south and I was keen to travel. I was no older than you are now, when what is learned stays with one forever.

At that age I was full of daring. My first adventure was to dress as a Christian, in scarlet hose and ankle-high boots. I walked through a so-called 'Door of Pardon' into a church! I think Allah will pardon me because this church was no other than the former Great Mosque of Córdoba, the Mezquita.

In the main hall, pillars in rows curve into horseshoe arches crowned by half-circles, a grove of two-tiered palms. The golden prayer niche, the *mihrab*, once sheltered the Qur'an. It was not designed to face Mecca. Perhaps this sealed its fate, for now it is empty."

"I know of Córdoba. It was the birthplace of our philosopher Maimónides, before the Almohads exiled his family. The house where he was born stands in the Jewish quarter."

"Yes, Maimónides, the renowned scholar, whose teachings are revered by Muslims as well as Jews. Are you familiar with what he wrote?"

"A great deal of writing not intended for the likes of me. He sought to understand the science of the Law of Moses. He taught that the Commandments are divine but the visions of the prophets, except for Moses, were creations of the imagination. This always makes Reyna cry. Our tutor reads to comfort her from The Light of God by our great Rabbi Hasdai Crescas of Zaragoza, who taught that the love of God is enough and there is no need to be rational about it."

"You are learning well, my child."

I turned and saw Papa, who extended his hand to Uncle Arabi.

"If she had been born a boy," laughed Uncle Arabi, "she would soon fathom the mysteries of the libraries of Toledo. But no matter. Your young man is showing fine talent for chess. I spent the morning teaching him fundamentals. He soon will challenge the most seasoned players in the Kingdom of Aragon."

Papa's facial expression was hard to fathom. He looked surprised and not surprised. He coloured noticeably and grasped the hands of the trader with gratitude.

"Yes, my old friend, this son through chess will make you proud. Allah is great and so are His gifts. I also intend to teach him geometry, which can be useful in more practical ways." I caught a wink as he said his goodbyes.

§§§

Our grandfather had prospered by alternating medical arts and money lending. Papa, unlike his father-in-law, was never good at befriending money or lending to those in need of it. To help make ends meet, he took up bookbinding, a passion from his youth. His father had owned a paper mill in the town of Híjar. Books were a luxury, though, and commissions few and far between.

The best thing about being a bookbinder is that you get to repair treasures, the most marvelous books that are hidden about town. The most magnificent volume of all could not be removed from the house of Solomon the Rabbi. For some reason I was brought along on Papa's initial visit, under the strictest warning not to touch. Its frontispiece showed a temple archway flanked on each side by Solomonic pillars and grapevines.

On Friday nights, Papa would spend time with us and ask us questions. Sometimes, I thought he let me speak because

Isaq spoke so seldom, but after a while I decided that Papa cared about what I thought.

One Friday night after we had returned home from the Synagogue and after dinner and songs, Papa was in the mood to ask his questions. He began with my brother.

"Isaq, tell me, what do you like best about our Synagogue, our Synagogue of Albarracín? What is your very favourite feature?"

Isaq always choked on the concept of "favourite." When he was a child, Magda gave him clear choices. Papa should have known better than to ask him an open question — or was he doing it to teach him? With Papa, I could never tell, but Papa wasn't the person who would have to calm Isaq if agitated.

Wheels turned inside Isaq's head. "The parts of the Synagogue equal the whole of the Synagogue. The length is eight *brazadas* and the breadth, seven *brazadas*. The whole of the Synagogue is fifty-six *brazadas* squared."

Bella stifled a laugh. "Isaq, I can just imagine watching you from the gallery, pacing the length and breadth of the Synagogue, counting your paces."

"He doesn't need to," I snarled. "He can do it with his eyes closed."

Papa ignored us. "Well done. I see you have been minding well what Arabi the trader teaches you. Now for you, Sara. What do you like best about our Synagogue?"

"What I like best about our Synagogue, are the two doorways."

Papa knew this was an honest answer. Since early childhood, I have remembered the details of buildings, doorways in particular. But why did I have to blurt this out in front of Bella, who by the hour was acting more grown up? I felt perilously close to being ridiculous, and ridiculed. I jumped to my defence.

"Papa, the doorways of our Synagogue are different from the door of every other building in the town of Albarracín."

"And why is that?"

"Because the parts that make up the whole, to follow on from Isaq, relate to each other and the whole in a certain way I can see but can't explain. In my life, I have seen only one doorway like them, and even that was a picture in a book."

"Which book?"

"The great volume that Rabbi Solomon had open on his table, that evening you brought me on your visit to appraise its repair. The volume was open to, what do we call it, its frontispiece, and there before my eyes was a drawing of the most magnificent door I had ever seen."

"So you are saying that the doors to our humble Synagogue of Albarracín, bring to mind the door on the frontispiece of the Zohar? On the surface, it is difficult to see your point. The illustration shows an ornate doorway and the doorways to our Synagogue are of slight ornamental value compared even to those of the Main Synagogue of Teruel."

"It's not the decoration, Papa, I know there is not much of that. It's the proportions, and beyond that, it is what the doorway leads to, in the spiritual sense."

"That is meaningful, my dear, and someday when you are older we will explore it."

He turned to Reyna. "My young one, what part of Synagogue do you like best?"

"Papa, there are no parts to the Synagogue. The Synagogue is just one thing. Our humble building with its fifty-six *brazadas* squared is filled with joy. I feel it every time. I don't know why people I watch from the balcony shuffle around and talk to each other and sometimes yawn. I want to shout to them, 'this Synagogue is not a building. It is joy. Here, there, everywhere.' Yet they think of it as a building and a plain one at that."

"If you could see it, how would it look?"

"Joy cannot be seen, but if it could, it would be like a light, a splendid light."

"Reyna, the great sages have considered the meaning of life. Some say that the meaning of life is to come closer to God, but how can one come closer if the distance is infinite? Others have said that the purpose of life is to turn towards God, but how turn towards God if God is everywhere? Yet others teach that the meaning of life is to rejoice in God. They explain that the soul of man is the lamp of God."

Papa returned to Isaq. "What do you say to that, my son?"

Isaq pondered for a moment. "The soul of man is like the flower of the orange tree."

I noticed Bella purse her lips, but Papa didn't smile.

"The soul of man is like the flower of the orange tree. They are both resplendent."

"Well done, Isaq, I see that you can apply your lessons very far indeed. Now for you, Bella, my dear grown girl, you can't leave without telling us this. What do you prefer?"

Bella smiled. "My preference is the balcony. And I will share a secret with you two gentlemen." She leaned towards Papa and Isaq with a finger on her lips. "In the balcony we women keep a special set of the lamps of God, to use when the third star has appeared in the sky, and we keep them under lock in a cedar chest, high up where you two cannot reach them."

Having spoken the last word, Bella swept away in her velvet skirts from Zaragoza.

𝓒he Year 1482, as counted by Christians

𝓟APA ANNOUNCED BELLA'S betrothal to Vidal. Aunt Esther summoned the fiercest seamstresses by land and sea. They soon were confecting gowns and intimate apparel to astound Aragon. To the paws of these lionesses Bella sweetly submitted. She was trussed in Brussels lace, smocked in crocheted cotton, and pinned in silver foil across her slender breasts. Pearls were clawed into her tresses. A surprise she wasn't smothered by their lioness breath. My only silver lining was I would see less of her.

Reyna and I had no mind for our lesson, and Isaq, who on principle ignored news of nuptials, was acting more savage than usual. Solomon the Aged did not open the Torah.

"The outer cloth for Bella's wedding gowns has arrived from Florence."

I imagined the great oak table at the Teruel house, spread with white linen to receive the bolts of brocade.

"Reyna and I already know the designs by heart from hearing of them so often."

"Describe each design, and the cut," purred Old Solomon. He hobbled closer on his knobbed walking stick. He also had an ebony cane, but it was pawned.

"Gold silk weave in a honeysuckle design on a ground of floral pattern, inspired by the Mongols' cloth of gold."

Old Solomon cupped his hand to his ear.

"Bella will have two wedding gowns," shouted Reyna.

"The latest fashion. Blue velvet. Pomegranate pattern on silver foil in Ottoman style."

"What did you say?"

"Blue velvet. Silver foil. Stretched tight across the bust."

I whispered the last bit.

He smiled.

"Your slender, pointed breasts will be beautifully presented." Reyna laughed. She mimicked Aunt Esther perfectly.

"Reyna, no!"

"Then why did you mention the bust? He's too deaf to hear me."

"I think he's feigning deafness. No matter. Imagine how lovely those brocades must be, and how soft to touch."

I closed my eyes and saw the bolt being turned against its folds and falling slowly on the table with each turn, a stream of honeysuckle and then pomegranate designs flowing onto the white tablecloth, and somewhere beneath it all, the scent of beeswax.

"Today we will pause our studies and I will tell stories of wonders as in the tales of Scheherazade. Sarita, bring us all something to eat, and we will have our own celebration."

To my surprise, Magda relented to the unusual request, the larder being "closed" as she liked to say, and she returned with a platter of *buñuelos* and a cruet of honey.

"As a boy, I listened at night to the tales of Rabbi Benjamín of Tudela, from his Book of Travel, and his descriptions of the wonders of the East. Such treasures, my son and daughters!"

Isaq grabbed the platter with both hands and crammed fried dough down his gullet, smearing honey on his brow.

"Look, Isaq is raining honey drops." He kicked Reyna but she dodged him.

"In Rome, two columns from the Temple itself, crafted in bronze for King Solomon, which exude tears each year upon the 9th of Ab, and in Baghdad the Great Synagogue, its columns of marble of many colours, with silver and gold overlay and golden letters from the Psalms."

"You've been to Baghdad?"

"Yes. As a youth, I chose to go to Jerusalem, Basra, Baghdad and even the ruins of Nineveh, in the footsteps of Benjamín, only my adventures would be more magnificent than his. He was just a lad from Navarre, after all."

"I am so interested, Uncle Solomon. I want to hear more. Isaq, hand me the tray."

"Talking about yourself again, Sara, and greedy as ever. Who cares what interests you?" I passed around the remnants.

A paltry repast. Pillars with gold overlay and letters from the Psalms set me dreaming of pastries glinting with preserves of peach. Served on linen.

"I set off for the Levant, entered the gates of the Holy City of Jerusalem on a fine steed, and tarried for months, attended by scores of servants.

You should have seen my horse, worthy of King Ferdinand. My hosts greeted me at the gates with banners emblazoned with the emblems of Jerusalem, the Lions of Judah, and spread carpets in my path."

"The Lions of Judah?"

"Yes, stretched tall on their hind legs with swords between their teeth. Vibrant, sinuous lions, each muscle delineated, not like the ones you see on the shields of Christians."

"Like on our family crest. Can you draw me one?"

"Certainly, my dear, if you would bring me one of those sheets of parchment your Papa keeps in his medical office, and one of his fine quills with just a drop of ink. It's a small thing, and he'd never miss them."

"I'm not so sure. From Jerusalem where did you go?"

"I was a young man. Handsome and full of adventure. I sailed the Red Sea and rounded Arabia. I landed at the port of Basra where I prayed at the grave of Ezra the Scribe. In Baghdad, the Great Synagogue. In Nineveh, the tombs of Obadiah, Nahum and Jonah.

From there I wandered east into the vast deserts of Persia. I lived among the tribes with their tents and carpets. Learned their philosophy of life."

"Was it wondrous to live in the desert?"

"At night, the heavens above were like a tent, with comets and stars for loops and hooks. The morning light was a scarlet thread in the East. If I had known you at the time," he winked at Reyna, "I would have returned bearing gifts."

"But you brought us lamps!"

"Of course, dear, of course I did. I meant to say, more gifts."

"What more would you have brought me, Uncle?"

"Let's see. I would have brought you a flower that the Persians call *lale*. That would be a gift worthy of you, my child."

"What is a *lale*, Uncle Solomon?"

"A flower. Like your sister Bella, it brings to mind the words of a Persian poet, 'A graceful chalice filled with wine upon a stem of jade.'"

I felt nauseated at this old man who reeked of onions praising Bella. Besides, he was not supposed to be talking about Bella. He was supposed to help take our minds off her.

"As far as I know, no one has ever planted them in Europe except for the Arab gardeners of Al-Andalus who worked with a diminutive variety. The Persian strains of today are extravagantly beautiful. I must write to my friend the

French baron, to suggest that he bring them direct from Persia to his noble gardens. What colours of *lale* would you like, my dears? I will give you precious bulbs, for you to grow out back in a sunny spot overlooking the river, when my ship comes in."

Whenever Solomon the Aged mentioned his ship coming in, he would stare us in the eyes.

"Blue, if you please, Uncle Solomon."

"Alas, I have never seen a blue one. Instead I propose a Persian nosegay of pomegranate and forget-me-nots, tied in a blue ribbon, which girls no older than you knot into silk treasures with their nubile fingers. And you, the wisest of the damsels under my tutelage, *mi carina*?"

I thought proudly of the pink gesso of our house front, and then of Aunt Esther's designs for Bella.

"Mostly pink, to match our house, if you please, and throw in a few bright red ones, for love at first sight."

"*Lale* pink and red you shall have, smooth and with ruffles, and narcissi, orange blossoms, frilled carnations and muscari, knotted in gold to admire through your own glass window —when my ship comes in."

Later I recounted his promises to Bella, who returned for a short stay, and she scoffed.

"I don't believe a word that old man says, and neither should you. Either of you. In his younger days, he was the downfall of many trusting souls. I don't know why Papa allows him inside our house."

"When am I going to be measured?"

"Measured, my precious, whatever for?"

"My dress for your wedding. And one for Sarita. And, well, something for Isaq. As Magda says, we are the only siblings you will ever have in this life."

"Am I supposed to think of everything? Don't ask me again and don't go pestering Aunt Esther. Go ask Papa. I am sure he will rise to the occasion. Tell him I suggest that he call for Carmela, and don't let her design it because she has no taste."

Reyna stared at the floor. Carmela would require payment in cash or kind. Papa had neither.

"I am sure Carmela will sew you something very nice and next time I visit I will line you up for inspection, just like two dolls and a toy soldier. Won't that be fun?"

Shut in our house on the dark streets of our town on the hill, beset by the winter winds and the crashing of dishes, we needed wonder. It was glorious to fall asleep imagining fields aflame with *lale* in Persia, more brilliant than our roses in summer, and lions by the gates of Jerusalem.

§§§

One winter day Reyna and I slipped away to visit Arabi the trader. I arranged visits in advance when collecting Isaq from class, because there were more sweets when we were expected. In winter, Arabi offered steaming drinks made with syrups. The choices included honey, mint, citrus, rose, sandalwood, or Reyna's first choice, the Syrup of Good Cheer.

Uncle Arabi claimed the Syrup of Good Cheer had been handed down in his family since before the birth of the poet Ibn 'Arabi. I once glimpsed Mahoma preparing it in the yard, a narrow strip, eyed from the wall by a black tom cat. He was up to his elbows in mint, borage and citrus leaves, ground cinnamon, cloves and sugar. None of this was *casher* and we children knew it, but the cups of syrup and steaming water were fragrant and sweet, and not one of us could resist.

Arabi welcomed us to his store with cups of steaming honey syrup. Mahoma served candied fruits.

"Thank you kindly, Uncle. This always clears Reyna's phlegm. She has been coughing in the night."

"Mahoma, pile up some rolled carpets to make a throne. Choose the warmest wool. The red and dark blue."

Reyna presided from her throne of carpets like an Egyptian Jewish princess with ringlets. Her carpet pyramid concealed worlds of patterns and colour.

Each rolled rug formed a passage woven end-to-end with hieroglyphs, or so they must have seemed to the creatures who roamed them. Mid-way up, guarding an opening, perched a grey cat with a slender head and large oval ears. In two bounds she leaped onto Reyna's lap.

"Noor's ears stand tall as top-sails. Where did you find her?"

"A cat such as Noor is not readily found. A cat such as Noor is a treasure. She is a pure bred Tunisian cat from Ifriquyah. They are scarce these days. Her ancestors were crossed with Abyssinian and Egyptian cats, and she does have the look of an Egyptian deity."

"May I keep one of her kittens?" asked Reyna. "She has a nest inside the carpets."

"So she does. Let's investigate."

From their carpet den, two kittens came tumbling. At six weeks old, all tummy and pliant limbs, they landed with ease. Their eyes met and they wrestled, white on black, deep in the wool of a red tribal rug.

Arabi retrieved them with practised hands.

"Well, what have we this time? Green-eyed like Noor! And yes, their ears show promise. Take your pick. The sleek black one, or his white sister with the grey nose?"

I hastened, "No thank you, Uncle, Magda won't allow pets and she likes cats least of all."

"The Prophet adored his cat. To us, they are pure."

Arabi set the kittens down by Noor. She grabbed the black one by his neck and stalked inside the carpet.

Reyna, stifling tears, watched the white kitten knead her claws in yarn.

"See her fine claws. If cats were musicians, how they would pluck the strings!"

"Come, leave them to their mother. I'll recite a poem about a garden of religions. Your comment in the plaza, Sara, brought it to mind."

"Is it by Arabi the Eldest from Al-Andalus, for whom you were named?"

"In fact, it is a verse by the poet Ibn 'Arabi, but first we must have light."

The winter sun shone pale on the store room walls. Mahoma lit ceramic lamps of lustrous turquoise green.

"Slippers for the Peri of Persian lore! Uncle, I've never seen lamps like these."

"Yes, but in the style of Al-Andalus."

As if on cue, Amir, his nephew, took a place between the lamps, holding his lute-like oud. He plucked warm, low notes. Uncle Arabi recited,

> *"O Marvel, A garden among the flames!*
>
> *My heart can take any form:*
>
> *For gazelles, a meadow,*
>
> *For monks, a cloister,*
>
> *For idols, sacred ground,*
>
> *Ka'ba for circling pilgrims,*
>
> *the tables of the Torah,*
>
> *and scrolls of the Qur'an.*
>
> *I profess the religion of love.*
>
> *Wherever its caravan rolls on its way*
>
> *that is the faith and belief that I keep."*

Amir played with abandon, as if in prophecy. His melodies rose in tumult and wove circles round us. Suddenly it was the music of the high mountains. The notes plucked their way across stones and veered into the sky.

Reyna gazed at the lamps with flashing eyes. "Uncle! You promised to show us the Tree of Life this time."

"So I did. Come, let me show you some treasures that are not of the feline variety. Silk hangings, on their journey from Persia to Castile, where they will adorn the walls of a palace.

In Islam, the Tree of Life symbolizes God's promise of immortality in paradise. The Persians have long expressed the longings of the soul in knotted silk o'er traced with flowers and fruits."

"May I plant flowers and fruits?"

"Anything you could imagine in a garden, my Reyna, you can plant in this one, a thousand times more beautiful. It is the garden in the eye of the mind and the heart."

Mahoma unrolled carpets with tree designs. Branches sheltered milk-white doves against a golden ground, their leaves as pale as honeydew.

"Which do you like best, Uncle?"

"Something you have yet to see. The pillars of the *mihrab*. Entwined with vines and flowers."

"The vaulted dome for the Qur'an, as in the Great Mosque of Córdoba?"

"How well you remember. Mahoma, display the twin column Heriz."

Mahoma unfolded a silk hanging. Against a burnished field rose a pair of columns. From the apex of the niche hung a lamp of sky blue. At its heart, a red fire blossom.

"What are the sinuous figures on either side of the lamp?"

"Those are blue dragons. Perhaps they are protecting the flame." Uncle Arabi smiled. "Beneath is a Tree of Life with greenery for Sara."

We all admired the treasure but Reyna said, "This one has only touches of blue."

Blue again. Not even blue dragons were enough. She always wanted more!

"Here is my wish, as in the tales of old. Show me a niche design with a field of deep diamond blue."

Reyna thought she had stumped Arabi, but he knew her better than that.

Arabi ordered triumphantly, "Mahoma, unfurl 'The Sea and the Sky.'

Reyna, this is a masterpiece in the manner of a grand master of the loom in North West Persia. The master of the loom has arranged the colour and texture of the silk so as to image the sea and the sky."

Mahoma released his fingers. The central panel that unfolded showed a niche outline on a blue field.

"Look at it from both ends, children. From the one end we see the pure blue of the sky, and from the other, the sea depth, a deep diamond blue."

Mahoma laid the treasure flat and it was true. The silk seen from one end shone like the sky, and from the other, the depths of the sea.

"Uncle, does deep diamond blue have a meaning?"

"To the Persian grand masters of the loom, deep diamond blue is the colour of majesty and repose."

"And what is the meaning of the lamp?"

"The lamp is the light of the Truth, from the Ayat al-Nur verse of the Qur'an."

Uncle Arabi recited,

"God is the Light of the heavens and the earth;

the likeness of His Light is as a niche wherein is a lamp,

the lamp in a glass,

the glass as if it were in a glittering star

kindled from a Blessed Tree,

an olive that is neither of East nor West

whose oil would shine even if no fire touched it;

Light upon Light;

God guides to His Light whom He will."

We all were quiet except for Reyna.

"Tell me more about the Light."

"According to the philosopher poets of Islam there are several kinds of light —the light of the senses, the intelligence, the soul, astral beings, and the only true Light which is of God."

"Lately I have been thinking of astral beings," she confided. "The first-born children of light are the angels on high, and angelic beings help man in his worship."

"Who benefit most from the light? Let's see if you can answer."

"Those who have remained true to the Lord."

"Yes. Islam teaches that their inherent nature is like pure oil, which will catch fire without being ignited.

For the Godly, this light acts like a 'Light upon their existing light.' It nurtures the brightness of their own hearts."

"Where is the flame of the lamp shown in this carpet? I don't see a flame."

"Amir, do you have the answer for Isaq?"

"The flame on this example is what is called a hidden flame. It is the muted gold that suffuses the main field."

"Children, in the next one, we also will see pillars and flowers supporting a lamp of sorts, a different kind of flame holder."

On cue, Mahoma unfurled a cascade of white mulberry silk. At its centre, among thorns, three pillars of carnelian supported red flowers of an unusual shape. In the centre, on either side of a large fire-blossom, rose stems supporting buds that were half-flower, half-garnet candles. The effect was a glorious *hanukiya*.

"Look beneath the base of the *hanukiya*!" Beneath the *hanukiya* crouched a pair of red-bellied mice.

"Amir, tell our guests the significance of the white field."

"The main field in mulberry white suggests the glass mentioned in the Qur'an."

Uncle Arabi brought us to attention. "My children, now something different. Mahoma, unfold the gold silk."

A cascade of gold silk rippled down the wall. At top centre, two pillars joined in a scalloped arch. From the mid-point of the arch hung a lamp in burnished gold. Within the arch supports, single-petal roses of dark crimson bloomed on silvery stalks flanked by sprays of salmon buds. Beneath the lamp, a floral medallion of burgundy, bursting into lilies and seven-pointed starflowers. A crown bearing four crosses was atop the lamp.

Reyna laughed. "Look what they have hidden in the garden! It wouldn't be complete without them!" Thousands of leagues away, on the far side of the sea, fingers like Reyna's had knotted olive green caterpillars hanging upside down.

"I think they are there to eat the roses."

"But why are there crosses on the crown of the Lamp?" Amir glanced up from his oud.

"Well done, Amir, that is a question, isn't it? Some say this piece was designed for Christian worship, and the other for Hebrew worship, or that the crosses are ornamental, but I think not. I believe these crosses and the *hanukiya* carry a higher meaning.

Two hundred years ago in Asia Minor lived Rumi, the most soulful of Sufi poets, author of quatrains, *ghazals*, and poems beyond form. His family had fled to Anatolia from the farthest corner of Persia. You would have felt at home in his town of birth because it was on a trade route, just like ours. They carried silk on the backs of camels over deserts and mountains. At night round their fires they made swirling music, richer than wine."

"Like the music of the gypsies?"

"Yes, but our gypsies' feet are drawn like magnets to the earth, which they strike and strike again, while those dancers move in a vortex.

It was a land of many religions, more than three, I believe, where different faiths mingled and exchanged ideas. You would be interested that Rumi, a Muslim, used stories about Moses to teach how to love God. He thought Moses a perfectionist. He taught that any words of love will do, if they come from a simple heart."

"Recite a poem by Rumi, Uncle, before we depart."

"Here are the lines I recall,

'The lamps are different

But the Light is the same.

One matter, one energy, one Light, one Light-mind

Endlessly emanating all things.

One turning and burning diamond,

One, one, one.

Ground yourself, strip yourself down,

To blind loving silence.

Stay there, until you see

You are gazing at the Light

With its own ageless eyes.'"

The lamp niches, *hanukiya* and the crosses that we have seen knotted into Persian silk, my children, just might suggest the co-existence of Islam, Judaism and Christianity in paradise. As you have just heard, Ibn 'Arabi expressly included Islam, Judaism and Christianity in his garden among the flames."

The silk dimmed into shadows with the setting of the sun. Mahoma rolled it up. Amir slipped his oud into a satin bag. The spell was lifting. As we walked towards home, I asked Reyna what she was thinking.

"I'm so busy. I have to plant so many things."

"Where? It's winter!"

"In the Paradise of the Three Religions," she smiled.

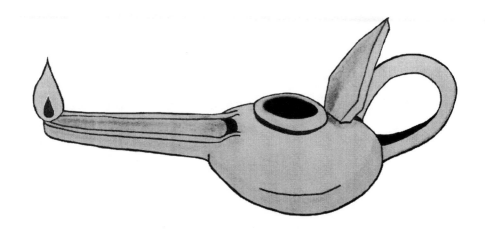

§§§

No lioness attended to our wardrobe except for Magda, who rose to greatness. She pulled from beneath her bed a pillow case stuffed with scraps of white lawn, burgundy satin, ribbon and a length of red silk. Against all odds, for Magda was not a skilled seamstress, she transformed Reyna into a miniature version of love at first sight. The small dress was simplified and at a glance home-made, yet it translated the original sentiment perfectly for a child of seven. We twisted ribbons of scarlet and burgundy round her ringlets and in her mind Reyna was ready to be received at Court.

Not so for the rest of us. Though Magda put her heart into it, all we could do was trim my best dress at the neck and wrists with left-over Brussels lace. Skimpy and unconvincing.

Isaq vowed to hide under a large hat. I told him his only conceivable role in the wedding party was court jester and for days he ran about the house acting like one.

Bella lined us up for inspection and banished us from the nuptials! I accepted her sentence philosophically.

"It's not seeing you as a bride that I'll miss, it's the marzipan figurines and the crullers."

"That's part of the problem, my glutton."

Truth is, they captured my imagination more than all the pomp and circumstance of Aragon.

"The Church of Saint Paul in Zaragoza is most fashionable these days and soon will have altarpieces painted in the Flemish style."

"Good for you. Will you be married by a Christian priest?"

She gave no answer.

"Perhaps you may visit after the wedding."

The night after the wedding, Reyna asked, "Do you think Bella converted to Christianity before her marriage to Vidal?"

"That's the concern of Bella, and Vidal's family. She lives in their circle now. Why should it matter to you?"

"Why should it matter to me? How can you say that, Sarita?" Reyna broke free, wrapped her arms around her knees, rocked back and forth, and wept. "What's this world coming to?"

That was one of Magda's expressions.

Reyna could be such an old lady sometimes. She alternated between very young and old. Mama wrote in a letter eight months after her birth that this daughter was an old soul, very knowing, who had lived many lives on this Earth before. Whatever she was, she made my heart ache.

"That was Bella's decision. Let it go."

"I can't let go. She is my sister." Reyna still rocked back and forth.

"She says it is all the style in Zaragoza, to convert. The wealthiest and best-connected families are doing it."

"But what about the Synagogue, Torah and my beloved Shabbat?"

"Bella says that Jaime de Montesa, the King's Magistrate, a converso, is convinced he can have the best of both worlds, as he puts it. On the Shabbat, his table is spread with a cloth of the most exquisite white linen, and he spends the day in his study, reading the Torah. On other days, he is the most powerful magistrate in the land."

"What about his kitchen?"

"His kitchen and vast cellars are staffed by converso servants."

"Does the Jewish community accept him?"

I had my doubts, particularly about the Rabbi and his family and those close to him, but I did my best to assuage Reyna, who at that moment needed rest more than worries.

"I think so. His daughters still pay visits to their lady cousins and are received into their chambers. The magistrate himself is much sought after as a guest at Jewish weddings throughout Aragon."

"Because he is a royal appointee?"

"Yes, and a fine dancer, and he likes to have fun. He is the life of the party."

"So Bella's conversion is not as grim as I thought?"

"Well, we can discuss it later. Jaime de Montesa and grandees like him do not think it endangers their observance of Hebrew rites. They should know best, as they have royal appointments and watch what goes on at Court. At least it does not isolate Bella socially, to be a conversa. It would not even surprise me if some day she is known at Court."

"For all that you say, it still saddens me."

"Me too, but now it is time for you to sleep."

I held her in my arms and sang,

"In Castile, there is a castle.

Its name is Roca Frida.

The castle is called Roca

And its spring of water, Frida.

Its base, it is of gold,

Its parapets, fine silver.

Between the crenulations

There shines a sapphire gem

As brilliant in the night

As by the mid-day sun.

Inside there lived a damsel,

Her name, Rosa Florida.

Her hand was sought by seven counts,

Three dukes of Lombardy."

But Reyna did not sleep, nor did she seem to like the ballad. She pulled away and settled at her dressing table by her blue lamp. As I watched, its flame unfolded into a many-pointed star rimmed in azure. I stared. The lines of the star did not waver and its blue light shone steadily.

She cradled a doll that had belonged to Bella. "Sara, the castle is built wrongly. *'Its foundations shall be sapphires, and its battlements, precious gems.'*"

Reyna opened the lid of her cedar chest and lifted up the strand of Mari-Paw's collar, the pearls gleaming like miniature full-moons linked in a row.

"Do pearls come from the sea?"

"Yes, from sea creatures with shells. Uncle Saul calls them molluscs. They are not clean food to eat, but inside them, pearls are found sometimes. In the seas of Arabia, divers swim down deep to bring them up."

"Uncle Saul brought them from Florence?"

"He says the pearls are brought from the East to the city of Venice, where the pearl markets are. The pearls are traded in halls larger than this house, in gleaming mounds on long tables, sorted by size, colour and lustre. Bella told me that the Duke of Burgundy has a rare cloth of gold completely embroidered with pearls, and George of Bavaria wears pearls on his hat, worth more florins than we can count, and as for the Princess of Poland, her headdress is completely overlaid with the finest of pearls."

"It's lovely to think that fashion comes from the sea. So many treasures. Did Uncle Arabi tell you of the time he first saw the Mediterranean?"

"Tell me."

I grasped her tresses and started combing her hair.

"He was about my age now, on the road to Valencia. There was a steep rise over the sierra. He didn't have a mule to ride —he had to clamber along on foot, behind the pack. He was tired and gasping for breath among the reddish rocks of that mountain range, grateful for the shade and scent of the pines, when suddenly in front of him far below lay the Mediterranean, diamond blue, stretching to the horizon where the sea meets the sky."

"Like in the Persian silk masterpiece with the two shades of blue?"

"Precisely. Once he saw the sea for the first time, he realised there is so much more to the world than he could ever imagine."

"Yes, the sea is a great marvel."

"Let me think of a song, about molluscs and kings."

Reyna didn't need to learn stanzas from Magda any longer. She had grown adept at composing her own, curious verses.

> *"Neither conch nor limpet,*
>
> *No creature of this sea.*
>
> *Tell me, little mollusc,*
>
> *Whose is your treasury?*
>
> *The Temple is His castle,*
>
> *Few mortals see my shell.*
>
> *I bring you blue for tassels,*
>
> *And joy to Israel."*

She stopped, and hugged the doll in her lap. I guessed her thoughts —she was thinking of the next generation, wishing that Bella would give up her courtly ambitions and raise her family the Hebrew way.

"I would trade all the pearls in Venice for just one *chilazon*," she said addressing the doll.

"Reyna, Solomon the Aged says that the mollusc of the sacred blue dye was lost to our people at the time of the Exile. Since then, all prayer shawl fringes have been white. Why worry about it anymore?"

"We have treasured the *chilazon* for generations, and we must treasure it always, for its blue is similar to the sea, the sea to the sky, and the sky to the Throne of Glory."

She stifled a cough, thrust the pearls into the coffer and decisively shut the lid.

"She's just a child herself," I thought, "sick and alone, and with caring for Isaq I can't attend to her enough. I recall Aunt Esther saying, 'what this child needs is a mother —and a father, too.'"

"Make a home for the *chilazon* in your Paradise of the Three Religions, in a beautiful blue sea."

"I think I will, Sarita."

My hands worked through her hair with a comb of boxwood inlaid with tortoiseshell. I loved her curls, so firm. Each strand had the pattern of its waves finely etched on it. Against my hand, her tresses glowed like dark honey in the candlelight, like the honeyed sworls of the tortoiseshell. And when that tortoise started swimming towards me in the sea I closed my eyes, battling sleep.

"I'll include the tortoise too. After all, Hermes made the first lyre from a tortoiseshell. Maybe the sea gave us music."

Reyna took the comb, kissed me, and climbed straight into bed. In an instant she was rolled up in her coverlet, facing the wall, her dreams her own.

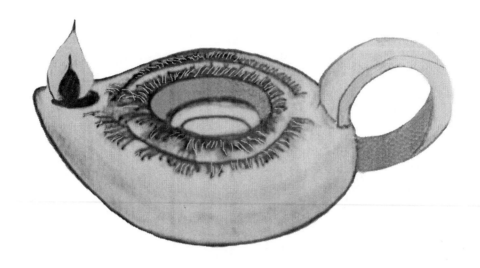

§§§

Reyna and I received an invitation to Vidal and Bella's mansion in Calatayud facing the Plaza de la Jolea. We breakfasted on one of her terraces. Bread rolls, hot from outdoor ovens! Honey of a thousand flowers, from the nearby hills! I helped myself to the jar a few times. Bella eyed me critically.

"Today I will have a visitor, a lady of rank. You know, I always do my best to act my station in life, but she is the authentic item."

"What do you mean?"

"Lady Miriam has money, rank and elegance. On her father's side, she is a distant relation of the grandfather of King Ferdinand."

"Truly?"

"Yes. What's more, she is related to Jaime de Montesa, the King's Magistrate, who as you must know is the highest-ranking judge in Aragon. She is spending the summer with her friend Lady Leonor, the royal magistrate's daughter, at their manor house at Bureta to escape the unhealthy humours in the city."

"She is coming here to visit today? Bella, you amaze me. Tell me, is Lady Miriam a conversa?"

"What sort of question is that? I don't rightly know. In society these days it is all one and the same. Her parents certainly were born Jewish."

"How about Lady Leonor?"

"You impertinent child. What did I just say? Lady Leonor was baptized at birth. Her father, a very powerful man, also was baptized but observes the Shabbat. Promise not to mention religion."

"I promise. Why is Lady Miriam coming here?"

"I think she is curious to see our Reyna. I have spread word of her ringlets which curl so naturally that there is no need to wrap them in strips of cloth, not to mention her spiritual tendencies. Speaking of Reyna, where is our pet? This afternoon, she must be at her most beautiful."

"Reyna? I don't know. I haven't seen her today."

"Go search for her, will you, while I refresh myself."

The staff and I searched the house, gardens and stables, but there was no sign. I hurried to a broken cistern, hidden by grapevines, where Reyna would toss pebbles to see if it held water. Peaceful, except for some startled frogs. I noticed the shadow on the sundial. At this, my heart quickened. I left off searching just in time to tidy my hair.

When Lady Miriam arrived, we saw that Bella had an unexpected visitor, Lady Leonor de Montesa herself. For Bella, this raised the stakes considerably. She ushered us into one of the formal salons.

We settled ourselves in chairs of gilded Cordovan leather, stamped with coats of arms, which Vidal had commissioned to match the coffered ceiling. Under our feet were the brindle cowhides of Aragon prized by the French kings, and overseeing our proceedings on the far wall of cedar wood was a figure of Saint Erasmus of Formiae rendered in yellow and black silk by the master weavers of Arras. Saint Erasmus was supplicating God on Mount Lebanon with crows circling above.

Lady Miriam, dressed in yellow satin and velvet from Brabant, impressed me in particular. Her face was shaped perfectly, like the finest of apples, her jawbone strong, her cheekbones prominent, and her eyes pleasant. Even her forehead and brows had a pleasing symmetry. On top of this, she was tall (perhaps a touch too tall) and carried herself with natural grace. She had a charming smile, which conveyed interest in others and satisfaction with herself.

Lady Leonor de Montesa, who must have passed fifty, was dressed in voided black silk velvet patterned with silver wire thread. Like her father the King's Magistrate, she was of medium height with an oval face and dark eyes. She stood as straight as the palms of Jericho and her appraising glances intimidated Bella.

"How fares your esteemed husband, Vidal?"

"Very well, thank you kindly. He and I have returned from a visit to Naples, where we saw the latest masterpieces. Vidal has promised that a recognised artist will capture my likeness. The question is, a portrait in oils or a marble bust?"

Vidal enamoured of our Bella? Marriage is one thing, but a portrait? Sounded serious. Aunt Esther's prediction made manifest.

What was worse, she had been memorising lines from Vidal, which made her sound smarter than she was.

"The artists in demand are painting luminous likenesses in delineated detail, with powdered colours mixed in oils. Of course Beatrice of Aragon, who married the King of Hungary, had her likeness sculpted from marble about ten years ago, and marble busts are still in style. I have to make up my mind."

"I have never heard of Princess Beatrice. Is Naples part of Aragon?"

"Yes, ever since the days of Alfonso the Magnanimous who gained dominion over Naples and Sicily."

"What news of the dynasty?"

"In Naples, the infant prince, Alfonso of Aragon, was born last year. He is a bastard, but an advantageous marriage is on the cards, no doubt. A precious child, with golden ringlets and immense green eyes, similar to our Isaq at his age."

"Many ships ply the waters between Valencia and Naples," added Lady Miriam kindly as she waved a fan of patterned parchment.

"In Naples the sun is tempered by breezes among the myrtles. Springs erupt from the earth steaming hot, and you can soak overlooking the sea. The locals serve pastries and refreshments."

"So they have myrtles? So fragrant! Papa says that three drops of myrtle oil in a cup of wine cures infections of the lung and the bladder."

The ladies smiled and Bella shook her head, but I persisted.

"Pray tell me of their pastries."

"Poached pears with lemon syrup and candied citron. Always with cinnamon. On sponge cake called Pan di Spagna. The syrups and fillings make them moist. Delectably moist."

A practiced hostess would have taken the hint and served moist Calatayud sponge cakes.

"Anise biscuits, My Ladies."

We nibbled at the small flat rounds, sandy with aniseed. There was an awkward silence.

"Dry, compared to the Neapolitan pastries of my fancy."

Too late I bit my tongue.

Lady Miriam swallowed a morsel and reached for wine. "Come to think of it, Leonor, I do wish we had gone abroad this summer."

Bella glowered at me.

"Leonor and I have been in desperate need of amusement in the countryside, so yesterday we called in Zahara, a fortune teller. Have you heard of her?"

"Yes, Your Grace."

I received a withering glance from Bella whose eyes said "shut your mouth, my precious fool."

Why stop when I had their attention?

"Our dear friend Lady Besante de Santángel in Teruel told us that when her young daughters lay on the verge of death, she summoned Zahara, who said that if she promised to observe the feast of Yom Kippur each year, her daughters would live. This Zahara also knows how to predict the efficacy of medical treatments by spattering hot oil in a pan."

"My dear child," laughed Leonor, "this fortune teller is not of the Hebrew faith. She is a gypsy."

Bella smiled. "Aren't they all named Zahara?"

"You have a point. In any case, this Zahara has a reputation in our circles for telling the future. All of our friends have consulted her recently. They say she can see hundreds of years ahead, and she also receives messages from the dead."

"They all do that, too," rejoined Bella.

"Zahara was escorted into the sitting room of my private quarters at Bureta," put in Leonor, "watched by my trusted servants, I assure you."

"Did she have a crystal globe?"

"No, to my disappointment. She produced cards and told me to select some, and then she turned them right side up."

"What did she say?"

"She said I would perform a good deed in the eyes of God, and that my name would go down in history for it. She saw a Biblical tree and a sacred flame." Leonor stifled a yawn.

"What do you make of that, Lady Leonor?"

"Nothing in particular. I think she was grasping for things. I am very hard to 'read,' you know. They all tell me that."

"And you, Lady Miriam?"

"You won't believe it. My lifeline extends far into the future, and many sons and daughters will survive me, and their children will also survive, for many generations."

"You don't say."

"Wait, there is more. 'One of your descendants will be almost as beautiful as you, but she will not be Aragonese. She will be from the North. She will marry the heir to the Crown of England and Wales, and give birth to a son, a blond Crown Prince.'"

"The Crown Prince of England and Wales?"

"Yes, and the lamest thing, is that his name will be Jorge. What a dull name to come up with for a prince, if you are a gypsy inventing things. How about Ildefonso?"

"Surprising," I said, for lack of anything better.

"Not surprising at all," Bella hastened to correct me, "you certainly stand as tall as any queen, Lady Miriam, and your face and figure are better than any alive today, I dare say, including the English one."

"They say she is homely, with pockmarks and bad teeth."

Actually, I didn't know for sure if there was an English queen. Worse, I was boring the guests. Lady Miriam was eager to see the object of her visit.

"Where is that darling doll of a sister of yours, Bella, the one with the curls, who speaks with angels?"

As if on cue, a servant entered with Reyna in tow. She was dressed in love at first sight, streaked with mud, and bits of straw poked out from her frizzled curls like errant hair pins.

"Reyna," cried Bella, "where have you been all this time?" She turned to the servant, "She was supposed to be washed and changed first."

Reyna broke out, unheeding, "Oh Bella, Sara, my ladies," here she gave a curtsy, "you will never guess what I found."

"Tell us," urged Lady Miriam.

"I was in the dovecote with the pigeons."

"In the dovecote?" gasped Bella.

"Yes, collecting their eggs for the cook to put in the *challah*."

"She doesn't use those eggs for our *challah*."

"Oh yes she does, I watch her in the kitchen. She sells the hen's eggs to feather her own nest, she says. We make sure the tiny eggs don't go to waste, but the doves' nests are hidden all about the dovecote. We don't know if they are fresh."

Lady Miriam discretely laid down her biscuit.

Bella winced. "Go on with your story."

"Anyhow, it was dark in the dovecote, and peaceful with the cooing of the doves and the smell of warm straw, so I fell asleep."

"So that's how you went missing," I interjected.

"When I woke, I got busy checking all the nests. My dearest pigeon, however, is a clever mother bird. She's the large white one with her wings splotched with caramel candies."

"What did the mama bird do, my child?"

"She made her nest up so high I could scarcely reach it, I had to climb on a bale of hay and stretch my hands in the air and grope about for the nest. When I lifted it, it was heavy! Too heavy for eggs to be inside, but it was silent, and still. 'Oh no,' I thought, 'perhaps there are dead birds inside,' and for a moment I hesitated, and the entire nest fell with a thud onto the straw floor. At once, I recovered myself and peered inside. Ugh! It was all black!"

"And then?"

"My eyes became accustomed to the dark and I saw pairs of shiny black eyes with dark rings around them, and shiny black beaks looking at me sternly, as if to say, "you naughty girl! Why did you drop our nest?"

"How many were there?"

"I think there must have been eight baby birds, and their mother bird would make nine, of course."

"I am no expert on birds, but that's too many for one nest. The cuckoo, for example, deposits an egg in the nest of other birds, but only one."

Reyna ignored me. She turned to Bella imploringly.

"May I keep them?"

"Certainly not. Just for you, I will permit those infant interlopers to stay in the dovecote where their mother will feed them. If it weren't for you, I would evict them."

"Perhaps they will grow to be rooks, or sooty grey pigeons, like the ones that infest Zaragoza's Plaza de la Seo, the city square. Those birds are not clean.

Bella is right, Reyna, it is best to leave them where they are." Lady Leonor was firm.

I tried to imagine the Plaza de La Seo in Zaragoza, a grand expanse with dark storm clouds of dirty birds.

"Please, let me keep them. I will take them home in a little box. We will make a dovecote out back by the storeroom and the thistles." Bella lost her colour.

"Nonsense. Enough said. Maids, take her for her bath at once, and burn those clothes." She turned to Miriam and Leonor.

"My dear friends, I apologize for her waywardness and appearance."

"I haven't been this well amused in some time. This is better than Zahara and her tiresome predictions."

"I am going now, Bella. I am due at the Synagogue to give the oil for the Shabbat lamps." Lady Leonor took her leave, followed by Lady Miriam.

Bella sank into her chair. I could see she was angry, and dangerously so, because Bella was not someone to cross. There was no use pointing out that Ladies Miriam and Leonor had been mightily entertained. She was convinced that Reyna had entertained them well enough, at the expense of her own reputation. In my opinion, Bella had made enough gaffes of her own.

The dovecote and kitchen were put off limits, the cook dismissed for lining her nest, and Reyna's frock sent to be burned though she did plead for love at first sight. Reyna herself took to hiding in the laundry.

She and I departed for Albarracín a few unremarkable days later. I was disappointed, because after the talk of the thermal baths of Naples, I had hoped Bella would take us to the hot springs outside Calatayud, at least to bathe our feet.

Upon arriving in Albarracín, Reyna ran to Papa and settled in his lap. Naturally, she told him of the eight birds with eyes with dark rings round them, like our Mari-Paws. Would Papa ask Bella to send them? Please, while the weather was still warm and they could survive the journey? She would ask Jaime to make a travel box, just for them.

Papa was thoughtful. He did not commit himself, nor did he say no. The weeks went by till it was nearly our New Year. Papa brought out the ceramic seed box we all knew from childhood and prepared it to receive seeds. Reyna planted barley and delighted in tending the slender shoots which would be hers till their solemn harvesting on the Day of Atonement.

On New Year at morning service, Reyna was chasing small boys whose locks the rabbi had not cut. I was happy to see her act like a child. She quieted to the murmur of the prayers. From a seat in the balcony, I gazed upward. Oil lamps, rings of light swinging on fine chains, brightened the synagogue. The chanting of the cantor circled near the ceiling, then descended and descended till it came to rest on the sturdy "amen" of the men present. In the stillness, though we knew when to listen, the burst of the ram's horn took us by surprise.

On the eve of Sukkot, its wondrous voice sounded again, this time through the streets of our quarter. There was drought and the men were calling for rain.

Papa joined them.

"Bring us willows, Papa, we need more."

"Bring us rain too, but make it wait till later!"

All day we had braided wreaths and fastened onto them citrons, pomegranates and pears from Aunt Esther. This time, she also had sent some precious twigs of myrtle. It arrived without flowers. Most years the only myrtle twigs we saw at Sukkot were kept inside the Synagogue.

Papa trotted home with more bundles of willows. Their twigs resisted our hands as we trimmed. The next night we lit our oil lamps and dined under the boughs. Reyna and I admired each fruit, marvelling at its majesty from below.

"I prefer the pears. They take shape in the lamp light."

"I prefer the citrons. Though their life is short, they are splendid."

Her words made me shiver. Bud, blossom, fruit, all splendid —then silvery mildew, a birthmark at first, then the rind struck to dust, then nothing.

"Don't be sad, Sarita. This is the season of our joy. I have so much to harvest, and it is not too soon. I feel Mama sometimes by my bed."

"I don't, when I stay with you at night."

"That's because she is not there for you."

72

"Time for sweets."

I squeezed her hand and led her visiting from booth to booth. All the women wanted news of Bella. I embroidered the finer points of her gowns, bed clothes, dinner linens, and finally, her intimate apparel. It was fortunate that Reyna had sought refuge among the laundry girls in Calatayud. Her narrative of the first signs of Bella's pregnancy gave satisfaction all round, and we were plied with overripe peaches and sugar.

Reyna also was fêted over the success of love at first sight. Of course, the frock had not been burned at all. The head laundress had sent it to her niece, who debuted it at a wedding outside Calatayud. Since then, it had inspired copies on girls at festivities up and down the countryside. Though the ribbon stars varied, all of them featured a chemise of white lawn and red silk or cotton around the neck, "in the style of Reyna." I gave her a hug.

"Did I behave like a good big sister this evening?"

"The best. I didn't miss Bella, and those converso cousins who used to hang about."

"You don't miss her at all?"

"No, but I do miss those birds."

I spoke with Papa, Papa spoke with Ismail the potter, and on the first night of Hanukkah, a new *hanukiya* graced our table. In a tray-shaped nest, they sat all in a row —eight ceramic nestlings, with two black eyes, a pointed beak for a spout, and a wick in the centre.

"Like the birds in the nest! With the spaniel eyes of our Mari-Paws!"

Black circles round their eyes extended to where their ears would be. If we could see the ears of birds.

"They have lined their eyes with kohl, the naughty things," laughed Magda. "Those eye rings make them look decadent."

"They will stay in line. Look at their mama!"

At the row's end, a bird of ample proportions watched over the rest.

"Thank you, Papa."

He smiled from across the table.

"Aunt Esther's *hanukiya* is made of bronze." Magda wasn't entirely pleased, but no one paid her mind. "And one of the birds, the first in the row, has defects."

"To the contrary, that one is the most beautiful."

"What do you mean?"

"Ismael's son insisted on making it for us. He is four years old."

Reyna was delighted, and Papa's smile was growing wider than I had seen in years.

On the final night of Hanukkah, Papa adjusted the pegs of his viola from Valencia and drew his bow in a delicate arc, sounding each string separately. Magda droned, "*They worked and worked their needles, the daughters of the King,*" which is such a yawn, but we drowned her out, so she sang instead:

"One little candle

Two little candles

Three little candles

Four little candles

Five little candles

Six little candles

Seven little candles,

Eight little candles for me."

This song, as everyone knows, has its own set of dance steps and hand claps which are heard just once a year. In the centre of the circle of dancers, Reyna clapped the rhythm and danced all the steps, as graceful as could be, by the flickering lights of her eight little birds.

The Year 1483, as counted by Christians

IN APRIL CAME the Feast Day of Purim. Magda, Reyna and I spent the early morning making Haman's Ears. We kneaded the dough and cut it into half-moons which we then pinched in the middle and fried in hot oil. The dipping syrup was made of honey and lemon juice.

I had built up a prodigious appetite the day before, on the fasting day of Queen Esther. Boiled eggs and parsley after dark, with sips of wine proffered by Papa, had not been enough to get me through the night comfortably. In other words, I was hungry, which made me grouchy, and sad to say, I began to protest.

"In Teruel, Aunt Esther always bakes proper cookies with a filling of dried apricots and lemon, and I am certain Bella oversees the baking in the oven, as it should be, of all sorts of cookies for Purim, with sweet fruit fillings."

"I am not your Aunt Esther or Bella, and with the chores I have to do, I am not going to set about baking."

"Magda, I know today is Purim and you are busy, but I feel you could make more effort with the cooking, at least when you are not so busy, you know."

Magda turned her back to me.

"I can't help thinking that if our mother were here, she would bake us proper cookies."

There was silence from Magda. While her back was turned I started surreptitiously eating bits of dough, and the more I nibbled the hungrier I became. When Magda noticed what was going on, she thought a while.

"Sarita, I have some treats to send over to my cousin who lives past the river. Why don't you do the delivery and return in time for the festivities? You may take Mari-Paws with you." This was tantamount to a bribe. I looked inside the basket. It held two small skins of wine, and two dozen Haman's Ears, still warm.

"And be sure to bring Isaq."

I went upstairs to Isaq's room. He was hunched over the chess board playing a game against himself. I shrugged and came sneaking down the stairs behind Magda's back.

"Just one thing more," added Magda pleasantly without turning her head, "be sure you are not recognized by Aldonza, the old hag with the big mouth who lives by the ramparts. She'll get hold of your goodies one way or another, I assure you, because that's how she earns her living. She never takes a step without profiting."

"I'll be on my guard. I promise."

Magda nodded. "Here, put this on and cover your head, and Jaime is going with you of course."

Magda handed me a hooded cloak fashioned from red wool that Bella had never wanted.

"Pull down the hood if you see her and conceal the basket inside your cloak."

April was a glorious month on the banks of the Guadalaviar. The river, fed by melting snows in the Sierra, was running high. I lagged behind Jaime and turned my head in time to see a dipper dive into the water and raise a pearling foam. Soon the shallows would cradle hatchling newts.

But my reverie was brief. Walking toward me along the river path —Granny Bigmouth!

"Long live Queen Esther, if it isn't Sarita! How you have grown. Why don't you ever visit me?"

In all my life, it had never occurred to me to visit Granny Bigmouth.

"I milked the unctuous nectar of your infancy. With my own hands from the teats of she-goats. Like Zeus and Amalthea."

Funny choice of words. Magda always said Granny did milk the goats, and our family too while she was at it.

"And how is my dear Magda? What strangers you have become!" She was coming closer, nose first, and pushing up against me. Under my cloak, pressed to my belly, the fried dough felt warm.

"My eyes aren't what they used to be, but my olfactory organ tells me you carry, close to your tummy, Haman's Ears and red wine."

"Granny, we must not tarry. Don't you know? There are bandits roaming about."

"Bandits? What bandits? I do not know of any bandits."

"The Pacheco brothers."

"The Pacheco brothers need their noses wiped, and so do you!"

I fumbled for a handkerchief. Quick as a fox she thrust her hand into the folds of my cloak seeking the goodies. Mari-Paws landed a bite on her ankle. I sprinted away, laughing.

Her words came on the wind, "Daughter of your mother! A cold sore will eat you!"

I ran past rye, onions and lettuces into a farm courtyard. Jaime pointed me to the back entrance of the house beyond. He walked away to visit a friend.

The moment Jaime was out of sight, I heard "Psssst, Sara, it's me!" The whisper was urgent.

I didn't want to step inside, because I had bathed specially for the Feast of Queen Esther, and I was proud of my meticulous nails. The storeroom was dark and heaped with piles of straw and farm implements, redolent of hay with a hint of chicken shit. A frightened hen ran past.

Concealed behind the hay, Jusef Pacheco lay miserably on his side. His right hand gripped his ankle.

"It's good to see you. Jesus, this hurts."

"What happened?"

Jusef didn't answer. I rolled my eyes at him.

"I suppose you flew here on the wings of a huge bat, like the sorcerer Esperpento in the fairy story?"

Jusef lowered his voice and began to speak in Hebrew of the kind heard in remote hamlets. He used archaic words here and there. I wondered where his parents had come from, probably far out in the mountains.

"I was rifling the fold for hens at night when I took a false step in this blasted straw. You are a doctor's daughter. Can you look at it?"

I set down the basket and looked at his ankle.

"It's a bad sprain, nothing worse. You are lucky. In two weeks, you will be going about as good as new."

"In two weeks?" He stared at me incredulously. "How am to I lie in this hay crib for two weeks?"

He had a point, but that was his problem. I had not got him into this mess.

"Where's your older brother?"

"He's gone down to the Sierra. He says there are opportunities there."

"What have you been eating?"

"I have been sucking raw eggs, the ones that don't hatch, but they are covered in chicken poop, what else, and I am sick of them."

"Do you know what day today is?"

"No."

"Today is the Feast of Queen Esther."

"Until I was ten, we lived with a roof over our heads in the Sierra and our mama used to fry us Haman's Ears." He was fighting a sniffle.

"Where was that?"

"Out past Crow's Peak."

I shuddered. That was really the frontier, a place Papa had described as wilderness. Why on earth would families live out there and what sort of hob did she use? Then I reached into the basket, pulled out one small skin of wine and a dozen Haman's Ears, and handed them to Jusef. There was still a skin of wine and half the fried dough left for Magda's cousin. She would never miss them.

He sat with his arms around his bounty, looking wolfish. "I can't pay you, now or ever."

"That's all right. Just remember to return the favour someday to Sarita, the doctor's daughter."

I took careful steps through the straw, stepped out into the fresh air and went on my errand with Mari-Paws running behind.

Jaime was immersed in conversation with the farm manager, about how to make money in the Sierra. I fell asleep. When I awakened, they were still talking and it was nearly dark. Then I remembered —the Feast of Queen Esther! I was going to arrive late for the children's frothy drinks. My favourite was hazelnuts and pine nuts simmered with cinnamon and whipped to a thick foam. Jaime had not intended any harm, he just forgot as it was not a feast day for him.

We retraced our steps, past the rye and lettuces toward the river that was running high. The air was chill and I wrapped myself in my red cape. I was humming the refrain to Purim couplets,

> *"Long live you, long live me, long live all the Jews,*
>
> *long live Queen Esther who gave us such pleasure."*

As the sun sank further, my throat felt dry and I stopped singing, and at that moment the musical intonations of the muezzin sounded across the hills. In the lengthening shadows, his familiar cadences were reassurance that all was right with our town on the hill above. At that moment his voice seemed to me a part of all our tomorrows.

That night after our festivities, I spoke to Papa about Jusef, hiding in the storeroom with a sprained ankle.

Papa smiled sadly, "If I attend to him, then he's found out. He'll mend. That ankle of his is the least of his problems."

"I wish you could have heard how Jusef speaks. His Hebrew sounds so antiquated. Why is that?"

"Sometimes that happens when a community lives in isolation for a long time. Where is he from?"

"Out beyond Crow's Peak."

"Beyond the vineyards of Crow's Peak is wild territory, which I am sad to say is known chiefly for its bandits."

"I like to think his people were Hebrew slaves who escaped from the Romans and whose descendants have been hiding up on the frontier for a thousand years."

"As much as the history of our people interests me, I am not venturing there to find out."

Then I told Papa that I had given away half of the Purim basket to Jusef.

"Sara, the world stands on three things: study, worship and deeds of loving kindness. You have done the right thing, from the heart."

§§§

Midsummer dawn touched the hilltop with rosy fingers that crept down the streets, set aglow the salmon gesso round our balconies and stoked the petals of the clove pinks. Through our slatted windows summer arrived in stripes. Inside, Magda was ready at the hearth. On her longest day, she rose before dawn, lit her lamps and set walnuts in red wine. The walnuts would have magic power forever. This dawn enhanced the potency of every potent thing.

"Midsummer morn! Don't lose a ray of sun, take Reyna now."

"Will you braise the spring hens without me?"

Magda braised spring hens for midsummer dinner. She called them her pullets of Saint John. An ancient tradition, Papa said. He seemed not to mind.

"Browned on all sides, with thyme, salt and chives. Now go, the two of you! No time to waste."

"You just want us out of the way so you can pray the beads. Time for the chaplet's five sets of ten."

"True enough, you little wag!"

"Hand me some aniseed, and remember to bake us cakes!"

I wrapped Reyna in a blue shawl and led her to our overlook high above the Guadalaviar. Seated on a rock, she held her hand below her breast, and waited.

A yellow arrow darted from the thistles. The goldfinch perched on her finger and tilted his scarlet head. He trilled freely, and added a sequence of bells, before closing with a "cheer." He lowered his head to her palm, and cracked a few seeds before darting away.

The old moon waned. Soon Reyna and I watched rise above our mullioned window the slenderest of outlines sliced by a celestial scimitar. The *hilal*. I saw it again, stencilled on a sky of grey when we went out to the thistles at dawn. From the mist the goldfinch darted and perched confidingly on Reyna's finger —but for the first time, she coughed during its flourish of bells. The finch took flight. She cried and scattered the aniseed. I brought her inside, and was heating the kettle when the knocker sounded.

At the threshold, announced by our guardian dragon door knocker, stood a fine youth. His turned-up slippers and Persian turban were yellow satin, his kaftan lilac and gold.

Who was this gallant at our door? Mahoma the Youngest! Normally the humblest of messengers, he was outfitted from Arabi's store of silks, for this first day of the tenth new moon —

the feasting day of Ramadan. Standing before us with a plume in his turban, he shone with the confidence of a caliph's son.

"Happy Eid to you both, from Arabi the Trader."

Mahoma the Youngest handed me gifts of the Sugar Feast —a bronze lantern, sugar cakes, and a flagon of Teruel ceramic filled with Syrup of Good Cheer.

Reyna clapped with delight at the treats —small pyramids of ground sugar and almonds, scented with rose water, sized to toss into the mouth. Their name —*azuquaque* —was also a mouthful.

"And Happy Eid to you and yours, with special thanks to Uncle Arabi."

Mahoma the Youngest went quickly on his way, with coins from us for the poor. He had risen well before dawn and prayed at the mosque. This morning would be busy with deliveries, followed by a grand luncheon to serve at Uncle Arabi's home.

I lit the lantern and poured steaming water into a cup thumb-deep with Syrup of Good Cheer. Reyna expertly popped a sugar cake into her mouth.

Perhaps the sugar tickled her throat because the cough came back. It echoed through the house.

Papa summoned me. The door to his study was ajar.

Inside, in an ancient clay lamp shaped like a swan he stored a medicinal supply of the oil of myrtle. In the doorway I inhaled its essence —a hint of camphor, then an insistent bouquet, an ineluctable sweet blossom still a mystery to me. Reyna and I had never seen myrtle in bloom.

"Good morning, Papa. Lovely fragrance. Reyna says the myrtle is the flower of the Garden of Eden."

"Has she been reading the Zohar again? Too much for a girl's constitution. Does her harm."

"It does no harm to dream of a flower in a garden."

"You do her harm each day, taking her out into the damp. Her morning rambles must stop. Keep her indoors."

"How she loves the finches, merry at the thistles, their gold robes blown with dew. Besides, blue thistles are salubrious."

"Chaffinches are not charms and thistles are not a tonic."

"Goldfinch. She is befriending one of the birds. He is learning to perch on her finger. Papa, how sweetly he sings for her."

"Goldfinch, chaffinch, chiffchaff. We have been down this path before. Nine ceramic birds are enough."

Papa shifted in his seat. I thought he loved birds, even ceramic ones —the *hanukiya* of nestlings and the swan in his study. I thought it was a love they shared. At moments like this, I felt I didn't know him at all.

"I want Reyna to pass the summer with Bella. She is in decline. The air is better for her there and they have servants to help."

"Do you want her out of the way for some reason?"

"I am planning a modest trip with Saul. It would be better if Reyna were with Bella."

I glowered with disapproval.

"Saul as my brother has my best interests in mind. Recently he has brought to my attention the advantages of marriage." Considering how Saul neglected his wife, poor choice of words.

"A wife is always a wife but a daughter is only a daughter."

So that was it. He was determined to deposit Reyna with Bella for an extended stay but it would not be easy. He knew nothing of her disastrous performance a year earlier, with Miriam and Leonor.

"Papa, let me go first, to discuss the matter with Bella."

"Saul and Esther are departing soon for Zaragoza, on a sales trip, and Esther can stop by Calatayud on the way."

"When are they leaving?"

"In a fortnight."

"Let me go with them, Papa. You see, last summer, Bella was not pleased with Reyna. It's not that she did anything wrong. Her manners were too provincial. Let me smooth this over with Bella."

"Normally I would not entertain this, but for Reyna's health, I will speak with Saul now."

I arrived at Bella's mansion on Wednesday and was sent home the next morning like a parcel she wanted out of the house. This is how it happened.

Uncle Saul and Aunt Esther did not stop to visit Bella. They set me down at the front door, and were on their way. A footman opened the door and a lady attendant received me. I noticed at once that her dress was more elegant than mine.

"Do not remove your cloak. My Lady will receive you directly in her sitting room. Your valise will be taken to your quarters." With that, I was swept upstairs.

On a Flemish tapestry, noblewomen presided at a loom flanked by lionesses. In front, my sister presided in red satin. I noticed that despite the recent birth of her son, her figure was perfect. She embraced me cordially —a promising start?

"My dear, I have a gift for you."

"A gift?"

"Of course. We are sisters, after all. In the old days, we always understood each other so well."

Forgive me, but at that moment I recalled Bella kicking me under the table at *Seder* whenever I said something to Papa that went over her head.

"You naughty girl, you gave us no notice of your arrival. What could we do in a week's time? My seamstresses were already hard at work on the robes for my commission.

More on that in a moment. Here, Sarita, is the gown that they have worked up for you."

Bella extended her arm toward a girl in the shadows, who came forward with a silk summer frock —coral pink with an organza neckline and sleeves of soft green, the bodice trimmed in a finger's width of bronze satin. The green sleeves stole my heart.

"Hurry up and try it on. Just as I thought, the colours suit you, though you are thinner than I expected."

"There have been troubles with Isaq."

"Hush, say nothing of that here. Let my girl dress you, and I will tell you of my latest success. In Aragon, working on commissions from Zaragoza to Daroca to Teruel, there is a promising painter in the Flemish style, by the name of Miguel Ximénez. He is looked upon with favour by members of the Royal Court. The rumour is that he will soon remove to the Court itself.

Of course, it will not surprise you that my poise and grace are known from here to Zaragoza and beyond."

"Certainly, Bella, no one carries herself as well as you. I have always seen that."

"Last month, Master Ximénez requested an audience with my dear husband. He explained that he has received a commission to paint an important piece, and he sought Vidal's permission to paint a portrait of my person, for inclusion in the large tableau."

"What did Vidal think of this?"

"The request was unusual, and had Ximénez been any other artist, Vidal would have dismissed him. But there were two unique considerations.

Once Ximénez arrives at Court, my portrait will be seen by the Queen. My person will not fail to impress. You must see the significance of this. And my Vidal, of course, appreciates my extraordinary beauty. He always says I am his first and finest piece of art, the crown jewel of his collection. Why not record me for future generations? This appeals to me. It is a way to secure a piece of immortality, if you see what I mean, and concretely, much superior to Zahara the Gypsy's insubstantial predictions."

I understood at once. Bella's ambitions should not be underestimated. This was her bid to outplay Miriam's royal hand in the centuries to come. Absurd, yet her vanity prevented her from seeing it.

"What an inspired idea. Is the painting here?"

"Of course not. However, Master Ximénez has completed a small portrait of my face, in oil, as a study, and charcoal cartoons. The cartoons are in his studio, but the portrait is here with me.

Come over to the window, and notice our glass panes which I myself ordered to be refitted."

Her maids threw wide the brocade, and the summer sun poured onto a small canvas. At first the sun bounced off the oil paint and I saw nothing, but then I discerned a face and shoulders, and Bella shone in all her glory. No disrespect intended. The truth is, the face in the portrait was very beautiful, and the portraitist had understood that the power of attraction lay in her poise and the grace of her neck. I recalled Papa's words, only an artist could appreciate Bella.

I couldn't help thinking, "I hope this portrait does not end up in the private chapel of some unknown gentleman, to sweeten his moments of holy contemplation."

"Why the silence? You have no idea how grand the final piece will be. Vidal estimates its cost at 8,450 *sueldos*."

"Because you are so very riveting, Bella, so lovely."

Bella gave a knowing smile.

"Master Ximénez assures us that its purpose will be secular, for the burghers of Salamanca in one of the guild halls there. As proof of this, he is already painting studies of a dozen prominent members of our community. Vidal has confirmed it."

"Don't be so sure."

"Don't be so smug. If you could sit for a portrait in your new frock, you'd jump at the chance. Tell me the reason for your visit."

"Reyna is not well. She has coughing fits."

"Since when?"

"Since forever, but lately they are worse."

"Go on."

"Papa is worried for her. He thinks our town life is not conducive to her recovery. And the upsets weigh on her."

"The upsets?"

"You know, with the crockery."

"How often?"

"Every day. Papa thinks that a stay with you would help her. She loved it so when she was here. She has spoken to him many times about your doves."

"What you ask is impossible."

"But why? She is your sister. He says she is in decline, and he has treated many such cases. Papa asks this of you. Our mama would have wanted it also."

"Don't invoke my mother, thank you, when you have no inkling of our situation," she whispered. "Come, sister, I will show you the grounds."

We walked past garden beds of blue and yellow — borage starflowers, hyssop, and fennel with its feathery heads. Beyond the hearing of the staff, she confided, "Grandfather Francés is putting this mansion up for sale."

"For sale?"

"Queen Isabella has a favourite, a man of the worst sort, by the name of Torquemada. Torquemada convinced the Queen five years ago to create a Royal Inquisition and send it into Castile. Terror reigns among our people in Seville and Córdoba. So far, it has been limited to Castile. The question is, whether King Ferdinand will be persuaded to expand the Inquisition and send it into Aragon."

"What do the monarchs have to gain?"

"They have everything to gain —unity, power, and wealth. Persecuting conversos unites Old Christians behind the monarchs and enriches the royal coffers with the property of convicts. In Aragon, it would weaken the localities in favour of the Crown. My father-in-law is a forward-thinking man. He prefers to sell this property now, in case the King decides to send in the Inquisition and prices fall."

I crushed sprigs of fennel and recalled the lines from King Rodrigo's Ballad, "*Yesterday, I was King of Spain, today not of a town; yesterday, towns and castles, today I have none.*" Only in our case, the monarchs were growing stronger, at our peril.

"I entrust you with our secret, for the ears of Papa only. You must promise to tell him out of range of the servant."

"I promise."

"If the tide does not turn soon in our favour at Court, the Francés family will be emigrating, and we will go with them."

"Where? Navarre?"

"Bother Navarre. We are going somewhere where life is a hundred times finer and the sun is more resplendent. Salonica. You do know of Salonica, don't you?"

I nodded. Since when was she expert in geography?

"Grandfather Francés has business ties there. His financial empire is such that arrangements can be made to transfer money, even to Salonica. His partners assure us that the families of our elite are already arriving."

She sounded so grand when she pronounced the word "financial," our Bella who never had a head for numbers and ridiculed Isaq's paces. Come to think of it, she was never much for languages, either. I imagined Bella standing straight as a rod, issuing orders to servants wearing turbans, in a thick foreign accent.

"Will you have to learn a foreign language?"

"No, our own tongue should suffice, at least at the start."

"Take Reyna with you."

"Again?"

"Take Reyna with you on your voyage to the East. Just for a year, if you must. Being at sea will do her good, and Uncle Arabi says the weather in the Levant is most salubrious. She would live her dream of an adventure on the sea. How she dreams of the sea! Remember how she recited 'The Legend of Count Arnaldos' when she was several years older than your Jonah?"

"I love Reyna as a sister, but do not mention her in the same breath as my Jonah. Jonah, for your information, is the first born heir to the fortune of Grandfather Francés. And, as everyone knows, a girl is a blessing, but boys are better, and my Jonah is in a category by himself."

"Papa says that in her condition, Reyna cannot withstand the house in Albarracín for long."

"Sara, you must remember that our places are different now. Give my love to Papa and to Reyna.

Maybe your fortunes will take a turn for the better and you will visit us in Salonica. You know we will always receive you with open hearts and the prodigious generosity of my husband's family."

I was led away in the silk frock, berating myself for donning it to assuage Bella's insecurities and for choosing the wrong things to say at the wrong time. Upon reaching my quarters, I was hungry, but there were no refreshments to be seen. Just like our old Bella, I thought, this is why Magda never allowed her to attend to Isaq.

Papa's instincts had been correct. Aunt Esther would have done a better job of advocating for Reyna. She and Bella had always understood each other. I drifted into an agitated sleep, in which a portrait of Bella kept moving its lips inaudibly till I distinguished two words in a Greek accent, 'prodigious generosity.'"

Before dawn I was startled awake by a rapping at my door. It was the chambermaid. "You are advised to rise at once and prepare for your journey home."

"My journey home?"

"Yes, you are to travel with the second footman and the old nurse to Jonah. This will inconvenience My Lady, not to mention the nurse herself, who is too aged for such adventures." She eyed me with reproach. "You depart within the hour."

"And breakfast?"

None had been arranged. A trifle. I had a matter to settle before I left, in my own way. On the table was my green lamp. I lit it and prayed, "All who thirst, go to water. Harken, and your soul shall live."

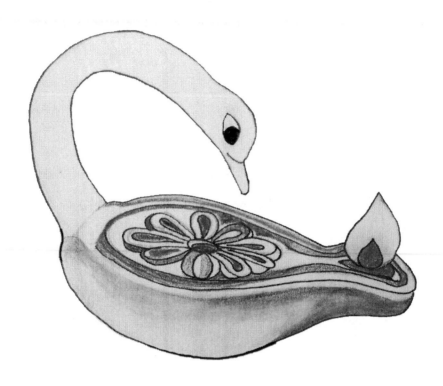

§§§

About that time, I decided to test Solomon the Aged on his purported knowledge of other religions. If he had traveled to the Levant, he would know of them. I waited till the lesson was nearing its end and the old man's mind had started to wander.

"Uncle Solomon, is it true that long ago, in the Levant, there was a land where people of different religions lived and worshipped?"

"Indeed, there have been more than one. For example, in the days of my youth, Persia was a land of tolerance. In my travels, I arrived to find ancient Nineveh in ruins, with hamlets springing up here and there, but not far away, in the city of Assur, the Synagogue of Obadiah was open to worship, and many more in Baghdad. So, as for your question, be more specific."

"There was a poet, Rumi, who taught that the lamps are different, but the Light is the same."

"Well done, Sarita. Who taught you this?"

"Arabi the trader."

"I see. Arabi continues to surprise. Go on."

"Uncle Arabi taught me that two centuries ago, the poet lived in a town where Muslims, Jews, Christians and people of different religions lived side by side and discussed faith with each other. My question is, what were those different religions? In your travels, did you come across them?"

"In Anatolia, where Rumi lived as a grown man, were Zoroastrians. Further to the East, where Rumi was born, there were some Hindus as well. Rumi wrote of them in his poems."

"Have you been to Anatolia?"

"I visited there once, as a young man. Anatolia, my dear, is a land where the cypress climbs, the yellow rose opens, and the nightingale sings. The narcissus whispers of the iris. The willow listens to the stream. The beauties of Anatolia, as I recall, are scented of roses and basil."

"Uncle Solomon, I am speaking of matters of the spirit."

"My daughter, so am I. What is your question?"

"Did you encounter the religion of the Hindus, in your travels?"

"In my travels across Persia, I met a Hindu once as I was walking a stretch of barren land. We walked together as brothers of the road. He hailed from far to the East, across the River Indus."

"Did you converse?"

"In Persian, by the campfire till it burned to embers. As in the poems of Rumi, the Indian and I understood each other better than many neighbours do."

Solomon the Aged paused. "You should live to see dawn in that desert. The night wanders into the sands and day rises red as candlelight."

"Is the River Indus very far, from Persia?"

"Do you recall the story of Maimónides' brother, David, who traded in gemstones? He set sail to India and perished."

"Yes, but David did not sail from Persia. Maimónides lived in Egypt. Is India far from Persia?"

"The ancient Macedonian emperor, Alexander the Great, pressed his armies across the Indus River, the farthest he ever traveled from home, but he fell ill with fever and died. The Hindus inhabit lands beyond the ancient realm of Alexander the Great."

"What was he like?"

"Alexander the Great? Come now, don't exaggerate. He was before my time. I am not that old, you know."

He fingered his cane, the good one.

"I mean, the Hindu you met in Persia. Did he wear a turban?"

"To think of it, no. He was bald and bearded, and wrapped in a white cloth at the waist. 'One Light' doesn't mean we look or dress the same." Solomon the Aged paused. "But then, I learned something interesting. The Hindu described how he prays, and how his human soul relates to the Light. What he described was not so different from what I have gleaned from our great spiritual teachers of Toledo."

Isaq leaned forward. He had been listening, in his way, all along. "Rumi equated the Light of Islam with the Light of Judaism, Christianity and also those other religions."

"That is correct, Isaq."

"It means, that the Light of the Jews is one with the Light of the Hindu who was wrapped in the cloth."

"Logically, if this were a problem in geometry, you would be right. However, this is a weighty question, which is beyond me to answer, at this late hour and even more so since your Papa has engaged me to teach you Judaism in the Talmudic tradition.

The shadows outside are lengthening. It is time for me to depart, my children, in search of warmth and refreshment."

Saying this, Solomon the Aged exited the chamber with remarkable agility. I followed him to the landing, where he gestured to me. When I was alongside, he quickly pressed three *sueldos* into my palm.

"With thanks for your many kindnesses, the apples and honey."

"Has your ship come in, Uncle Solomon?"

He laughed. "Not my ship, my dear, by any means. You might say, a pallet."

Solomon managed a pirouette on his stick, and scampered like a spider down the stairs to the kitchen. I found him there later. He was seated, which was unusual. Stranger yet, he was slurping up an entire casserole of trout cooked in wine — Papa's Shabbat wine! It was not the wine to accompany the recitation of the *Kiddush*. It was another of Papa's Shabbat wines, the finest of white wine from Valderrobres, fragrant of fruits and prepared according to our own traditions. Whatever had Magda been thinking?

Our dear Magda, not noticing me, was singing an old pastorela popular in her youth, and she warbled:

> "Gentle lady, gentle lady
>
> Lady of lovely appearance,
>
> 'My bare feet are in the grass,
>
> Awaiting this pleasure while others rest.'
>
> Hence comes the squire,
>
> Prudent and courteous;
>
> 'The words that she told me,

Were all words of love.'

'I am as white as paper,

My blush is blended with the tints

Of the rose on the bush,

I have the neck of a heron,

The eyes of a sparrowhawk,

Slender pointed breasts

That are straining to burst my tunic.

Well, what I have under wraps

Is a marvel to behold."

I decided to put an end to this recital before the next two lines, "Taste, Squire, this body, this body seasoned to your pleasure," an invitation without par in her store of songs. I started to ask Solomon what had happened to his regimen of apples, onions and beets, but Jaime pulled me aside.

"How dare you let that old goat come down here and ogle my mother?"

"Jaime, he is not ogling your mother. He is too lame and too old."

"You should know by now that age has nothing to do with it, and if he comes down here again, I am holding you responsible, for the wine and more."

Jaime had a point. What was strange was the way old Solomon was looking at Magda. I felt he knew her from before, and that might have explained the reappearance of his ebony walking stick. With his "pallet," he must have redeemed it from Jacobo Catorce at the pawn shop for the occasion.

Past midnight, I returned to the kitchen to prepare quinces and honey for Isaq, who had awakened hungry. There sat Magda, by the light of a lamp that shone on her wrinkles, singing to herself an ancient couplet from Al-Andalus.

"Come, man who casts spells. A dawn with such vigour, when it comes, asks for love."

§§§

The next day dawned on tears in our kitchen. Upon discovering that the Shabbat wine had ended up in a casserole with trout, Papa dismissed Magda forever.

Papa was lax to a certain point, which sometimes I used to my advantage. Sometimes he was lax by necessity, other times by habit, and also, I had come to conclude, by his unwillingness to face unpleasant things.

Nevertheless, Papa immediately drew the line at desecration of the wine for our Shabbat. That is the word he used, desecration. To Magda, a scant cup went missing and besides, she never touched the wine. Solomon had helped himself. I think this was supposed to address the desecration argument, as she knew only Jews can touch the Shabbat wine, but Papa didn't cede.

For the rest of the day, Magda cried and banged things about in her room.

"Just think how hard I worked to care for you all these years, raised Bella to be a lady, me the pillar of this household, and now this. As for you, Sarita, I have always been a mo-mo-mother to you! *Guayas, guayas!*"

Among the flotsam that came flying from Magda's room were broken bits of furniture and utensils that she had stored away towards old age.

"Where are you going?"

I felt growing alarm.

"To live with my Carmela," she huffed. "Where I am going is a much better home than this, with all the comforts. I will live better there. No more cooking and cleaning for me."

She wagged her finger in my face. "Carmela has her own servant girl now. Father Solís has her installed in a decent house, I mean, she is set decently now. Oh bother what I mean. I don't care what you people think anymore."

I never trusted Father Solís. There were so many rumours. The worst involved Azizah of the beautiful eyes, when she was an adolescent. Azizah, Uncle Arabi's cousin, was from a wealthy mudéjar family that had converted to Christianity. Although her parents had arranged a church baptism in her infancy, she was not observant in the Christian way and preferred the Muslim rites.

As her baptism had been entered into the church registry, Father Solís treated her as a member of his flock. Many times he told her she looked like the Virgin. It was rumoured that he beguiled the young Azizah into sitting for an artist at a property some distance from town, something to do with a sketch for the face of the Holy Mother. He promised she would be home before nightfall, as her parents would never have approved, but the artist took till dark and in the end she was led away to sleep in the stable.

That night something bad happened. Azizah always had been fearful since, prone to crying fits at the oddest times.

After her disgrace Azizah was forced to marry and her husband never accepted Mahoma as a baby. That's why he went to live with Uncle Arabi for his keep. As Arabi's houseboy, Mahoma led a commodious life compared to most of the boys in town named Mahoma, and there were many.

Magda's broken heart affected me profoundly. On the other hand, Papa's disappointment did not affect me at all. I wondered if Solomon the Aged would get his just deserts.

Papa did not dismiss Solomon. He appeared the following day as usual, perhaps a touch less jovial than his normal self. I think this was not fair of Papa.

Perhaps Papa thought that boys will be boys, even very old ones. Or perhaps the problem was Isaq's reputation for throwing things, or the times he ran about waving a knife, or the scanty wage Papa must have paid for tuition.

After Magda left, Papa and I spread word that we were seeking a housekeeper. No lines of applicants formed at our door. The sole candidate to present herself was old Granny Bigmouth, known in her youth as Aldonza, the widow who lived by the ramparts and had tried to grab my basket.

I had finished cleaning the hearth and thought it looked good, when Granny Bigmouth let herself in through the back.

"Good day, my love, I have come to put everything in order." I was left speechless by the intrusion.

"Such a mess that Magda left! You'd think she would have been a better housekeeper. No pennyroyal to repel fleas!"

"We don't have fleas in this house."

"Always useful to have plenty on hand, pennyroyal." She squinted at my person. "Especially for poppets like you."

Pennyroyal was the herb of choice for ending pregnancies. I suddenly suspected that the rumours were true —Granny was a procuress.

"Just look at that hearth. It hasn't been cleaned properly in years and it smells of fish. Fish are good for your brother, aren't they? Show me where things are kept, and I'll start at once."

My suspicions aside, her audacity annoyed me. She was busying herself in our kitchen, when I hadn't even discussed hiring her. The prospect of playing out our domestic dramas for Granny Bigmouth to spread about like the town crier did not appeal.

"Granny, thank you kindly but there is no need for your good help. We have engaged a young girl who is arriving shortly."

"Girl? What girl? I haven't heard of any girl and I know all of them. From where?"

"She is coming from Noguera de Albarracín, from the esteemed household of Baruch Astruga. She needs time to make the journey," I fibbed.

"No worries, I'll have things nicely in order before she arrives."

"See here, Granny, there is no money to pay you. None at all. I need to leave now and lock up. Papa's patients await."

"Well, you'll regret this, I'm sure. Whenever you come round, you know where to find me." I had to lock the door myself to get her out.

My first challenge was to put meals on the table. I mastered a cabbage and chickpea stew —with beef, bay leaf, anise and sugar when we could afford them.

This is what I prepared during the week, most often without the beef but always with a simple salad. On Friday mornings, I shopped for chickpeas and cabbage again for our Shabbat stew scented with cumin, the same as families prepared throughout Teruel.

One morning after a month of cabbage and more cabbage, there came a knock at our door. Susana entered. She was young and straight of back, with impossibly slim hips. She promised she could cook fish-and-cheese casseroles with her eyes shut. I should have spent more time questioning her, but instead I spent my time presenting our household in the most normal light possible. Susana certainly had all the right answers at hand.

"I have a brother and he isn't quite like other boys his age. He has tempers. Do you understand?"

"Yes, Doña Sara, I love boys and understand them. I helped raise my three brothers after my mother left us. The youngest used to fall down in fits and foam at the mouth."

"Often?"

My medical curiosity was getting the better of me.

"Every day, almost, and still does, after Father beats him, sometimes with his hand and sometimes with the hard part of the shoe."

"Where does he hit him —what part of the body, I mean?"

"Usually the butt, sometimes the head."

"He hits him on the head?"

"Only when he's drunk."

"Can you go to market, cook and clean?"

"Yes. I did all that and more for my last family in Gea de Albarracín. They had five young ones and their mother, you know, she was always expecting, vomiting and taking mint in hot water. I did everything for them."

"What did you cook?"

"The boys, they liked couscous."

"Your employers were Muslims?"

"No, Doña Sara, they are Christians. They attend Mass."

"We are Jews, you are aware of that?"

"Yes. I was born Jewish myself before being baptized in the name of the Father, Son and Holy Ghost, though we don't mention it. The rules of your home will be familiar. I won't mix meat with milk, or touch pork, or light the fire on Saturday."

Come to think of it, I should have checked this before letting her into the kitchen. I missed the old days, with Magda, when there was order to our lives and whatever happened, happened within safe parameters. I specified her wage.

"That's more than I was making in the village. What you offer will be fine for the first year, anyhow."

Over time, it became clear that Susana managed by conserving her energy. The least possible work got done to keep the household going. Nor was she fastidious, except with her person. The dirtiest and stickiest corner of the kitchen was where she retired with her individual plates. When she went out, however, she made sure she cut a fine figure.

To be fair, Susana did understand boys. Nothing Isaq did ever fazed her. She befriended him, handing him coveted treats and sweets when I wasn't looking with growing frequency till they became his sustenance. She took his tantrums with perfect equanimity, keeping secure in the kitchen when dishes were flying upstairs, which was as it should be, come to think of it.

Maybe it was the loss of Magda and her ministrations, or maybe the onset of Susana's sweets, but soon Isaq's door was almost always barred and he began splashing water from his basin in his chamber. At lesson time, Solomon read the Torah aloud outside his door, leaning on his walking stick, hoping that Isaq would listen.

Once, at lesson time we found his door unlocked and I told him we would open it. My green lamp sailed diagonally across his chamber and hit the door frame. It broke. I moved forward to collect the pieces, but Isaq shouted at me that they were his.

I confided to Solomon, "Isaq is trapped in rage. Anger can lead to Hell. I fear he has no future. I fear his life will end up, as the poet once wrote, like *'a plate smashed into countless shards.'*"

The old man replied, "Remember how Samuel ha-Nagid starts that verse, Sara," and he recited in Hebrew,

> *"I gaze at the sky and stars above*
>
> *And down at earth and the things that creep on land,*
>
> *And in my heart I consider how their creation*
>
> *was planned with wisdom in each detail."*

"Reality takes on emotional value when recognized by *Da'at*. Isaq's journey is different from yours. Don't keep him in with the womenfolk. Send him outside with the men and his life will take on meaning. You will see."

§§§

Before bed, Reyna was talking about Susana.

"I don't think that Susana is a conversa, after all. I think she pretended to be, to get hired."

"How can you tell?"

"Every day in the kitchen there are so many details as she calls them that she forgets or overlooks. I think she doesn't know. Magda's hair was always pulled back and covered, with not a strand loose, when she cooked. I am finding Susana's hairs in the food."

"Me too. She brushes her hair in the kitchen. Magda would faint."

"The worst thing I ever saw her do, was cut her own fingernails in the kitchen and let them fly and land on the floor. Everyone knows that nail cuttings must be disposed of properly, and hands washed afterward!"

"That's disgusting. What is bothering me, is that she never goes to the butcher, though she somehow manages to do everything else. I have to do it, always at the last minute, even if Papa instructs me to tell her to buy meat in the morning."

"Well, that isn't much. We don't eat meat often."

"The point is, she has a way of making things go the way she wants. Isaq is devoted to her but I don't see her doing him any good, quite the opposite."

"I know a way to test her."

"How?"

"Are Mother's garments still in the trunk?"

"Reyna, you wouldn't."

"Yes, I would. Mama wouldn't want our home being run this way. Here's my plan. We offer Mama's old cloak to Susana and see if she takes it."

"Don't you think that's extreme?"

"No, it is a *mitzvah* of sorts, if you think about it.

Susana is always cold. She won't suspect a trick, and if she takes it from us, that settles it for once and for all. Mama always used to teach Bella, 'Never wear the clothes of a dead person.'"

"Speaking of Bella, she will kill us if we give away Mama's clothes without asking her permission."

"But Bella is rich now."

"Yes, and being rich has just made her worse. What's hers is hers and what is ours is hers. Anyhow, if she ever asks for the trunk, we can pretend it was lost."

I brought the trunk down to the kitchen and turned the lock.

"What's that?" queried Susana with interest.

"Oh, some clothes of my mother, who died years ago. I am checking to see what's here. Look at them, they are still fine."

I held the cloak up to the light. The merino wool was still intact except for a sprinkling of holes here and there, mostly in places no one would notice.

"We don't need it anymore, do we, Sara?" chimed in Reyna. "Would you like it, Susana?"

"With pleasure." Susana snatched it, then withdrew to the alcove in case we might have second thoughts.

"Well, that settles it," announced Reyna when Susana was well out of range.

"It settles nothing."

"Why not?"

"Because, she has yet to wear it. Maybe she intends to sell it at market."

"I think she will wear it. You know how much pleasure she takes in her appearance."

So it came to pass, on the next Sunday evening, a drab and misty night in November, that old Magda was walking down the street, turned a corner, and had the shock of her life.

"Mama, what is the matter?" Carmela found Magda returned to their doorway instead of at church. Mass was a regular part of her week, now that she lived with Carmela.

"I need a rest, my heart is not good and my mind is worse."

"What happened?"

"As I was walking towards church, a figure came out of an alley in the gloom —it was Orovida, gone these five years or more, perfect from head to toe, with that lovely figure she had in her youth. No one else ever had such slim hips. What's worse, she entered the Church of Santa María by the side door. What can this mean?"

"It means that it is wrong to play tricks on people. That wasn't a spectre. That was Susana dressed head to toe for

Christian Mass in the best Shabbat cloak of Orovida. Sara must be up to something."

I know this transpired, because the next time I saw Carmela in the market, wrapped in a bright new shawl, she pinched me hard on the arm. "May jaundice seize and blindness smite you."

§§§

"Papa will dismiss you today, Susana."

Reyna had been instructed not to say anything, but she went ahead, candid as usual.

"What do you mean?"

"You are sloppy, and lazy, and tell lies."

I nudged Reyna, but it was too late.

"You are behind this, Sara. I will not forget. May you be eaten by a giant blister!"

Papa dismissed Susana with an air of authority seen only in medical matters. I was glad to see her go, but Papa worried me.

"Sara, I have left too much to you. It is time for me to take charge of the situation."

"If it's the cooking, you won't face a tureen of cabbage stew every day, I promise."

"It is far more than that. It is time I take up Saul's offer to travel to Valencia. Our home requires a new foundation both practical and spiritual —the divine energy of *Shechinah*. I am off to seek my future wife. If all goes well, we shall return in three months."

"We." So much depended on that word. I wondered what woman Saul had in mind for Papa and what man she had in mind for herself. Saul would present Papa to her with the same flair with which he had unveiled Mari-Paws. The esteemed doctor, personal physician to Luis de Santángel, in turn first cousin to the Royal Chancellor!

"Keeping house and caring for Isaq will be work enough for you. I will bring Reyna as far as Teruel, where she will nest under Esther's sheltering wing. She's only a daughter, but she might console Esther for the loss of Aaron, their son, a fine young man gone these ten years."

Only a daughter? It ran deeper than that. Papa had never known what to make of Reyna. Despite her angelic curls, something was distancing about her, unlike Bella, Papa's girl. In any case, she adored her aunt and uncle, and it was mutual.

Esther and Saul soon came to receive our youngest. He enveloped her in a bear hug and called her Saul's precious girl. Lady Brianda had come with them. Esther said that Lady Brianda had taken a personal interest in our education.

With Reyna by the hand, Aunt Esther climbed the stairs to collect the trunks. They were a long time up there because Reyna didn't want her coffer with her treasures as she called them, including Mari-Paws' pearl collar and pendant, to go with the valises. She was insisting on hand carrying it.

In the meantime, I settled Lady Brianda as best I could, offered her some wine and raisins and apologized for the simple reception.

"Don't apologize. There are many girls in my prayer sessions in Teruel who have much less. You may not be aware, but many of our community live in poverty."

"I thought Teruel a wealthy city."

"Saul and Esther do not live like the rest. Do you still say your prayers?"

"Yes, Your Grace."

"Which ones?"

"Those for dawn, mid-day and evening when the first star appears, the one they call the Star of Venus."

"This morning, how did you recite the morning prayer?"

"'Blessed is the light of day and our Lord who sends it.'"

"That's acceptable so far, but it's just a start. What next?" Her intense gaze was unsettling.

"Nothing, not today, Lady Brianda."

The truth was, I had been so focused on Reyna's imminent departure that I had neglected my prayers.

"And what would your papa say to you if he knew?"

"Papa would say that study, worship and acts of loving kindness are the most important in life, and that in my case, worship is what needs extra work in terms of where a girl my age should be on her life's path."

"Can you tell me why worship is important?"

"The sages have taught that the soul of man is the lamp of God, but I have never grasped it. Reyna does. She intuits it, but not me. She said when she was a small child that the Synagogue is not a building, it is joy."

"Rarely is a person born with that gift. Most of us have to cultivate our understanding to arrive at that level of insight, and there are higher levels still. It is through prayer and meditation that God becomes tangible."

"Can God be a constant presence?"

"If you work at it with your heart and your soul. It is best to have a mentor and someone your own age with whom to share your journey. As the Talmud says, learning is achieved only in company. When you come to Teruel, I will see to it that you attend my prayer sessions, which are attended by women and girls. We meet in my own home. We do have girls your age, and to participate in prayer with us would bring you farther spiritually than you can imagine, in tandem of course with regular attendance at the synagogue."

I nodded. With her forceful personality, I could well imagine her leading prayer and study sessions.

"What are the prayers you recommend?"

"It is not a matter of recommending prayers. Besides the blessings, as you know, we have spontaneous prayer, standing before the King of Kings, and the declaration of faith. I always worship in Hebrew and expect you to do the same."

"May I ask you another question?"

"One more, my dear girl, I must rest before continuing on my journey."

"Is the God of Judaism and Christianity the same?"

"You are requesting my personal opinion, I presume. In my view, Christianity has many gods. The Christians won't admit it, but it is a problem for them. Their philosopher monks spend lifetimes coming up with explanations how 'there be one God in persons three.' The Father, the Son and the Holy Ghost. Beyond these, they have many others —the Virgin Mother of God, and the saints."

"Is the paradise of Judaism and Christianity the same?"

"My child, I said one more question, not two. If you wish, write to me in Teruel and I will answer you."

Aunt Esther entered the room, wiping her brow. Her crocheted handkerchief fell to the floor.

"I have met my match in this niece."

"What's the fuss over Reyna's coffer?"

"I thought she was concerned about losing the pearl collar and pendant, but no, it's the *hanukiya*. She fears it might break en route so she is insisting on carrying it herself inside that chest of hers, wrapped in a linen cloth. The chest is missing its key and her hand carrying it will only raise the risk."

"Have you found a solution?"

"Yes, it will be carried in his own valises by Papa Saul."

The words "Papa Saul" cut into my heart. They made it sound so final, as if I were losing her. But when Reyna joined us a short while later, I did my best to sound positive.

"This isn't good bye, my dear. It is just for a short while. Aunt Esther has invited me to come visit and Papa promised that we will soon."

I enclosed her frail arms in mine.

"Dear Sara, I promise this is not our last hug. There will be two more."

Before I knew it, they were gone.

Papa, though absent on his travels, was true to his word. Isaq and I rode to Teruel. We lodged with Aunt Esther and Uncle Saul at their home in the fashionable district by the Zaragoza Gate. It was regal, as always. Dinners were served on their oak table, fragrant of bee's wax polish under white linen. Aunt Esther's salt dishes were of silver and glass. While eating, Reyna and I took care to sit up straight. She often seemed lost in thought, gazing past the colonnade to the courtyard black in the night beyond.

Reyna had new colour in her cheeks, though she seemed as thin as before. Certainly, no effort had been spared. From the kitchen with its broth-pots and ovens, the cook sent up bouillon and partridges with herbed stuffing. The best physicians sent phials of tonic. The consensus —rest was required for her overactive mind. The brilliant child was forbidden to read.

Uncle Saul said a resounding "no" to Lady Brianda's prayer classes for girls. Lady Brianda appealed to Esther, and Esther appealed to Saul, and then went over his head to Rabbi

Simuel, who did nothing for marital relations. We young ladies stayed home.

At the Festival of Lights, the dessert bowls held crunchy Muscat raisins and dates in paper wrappers from Uncle Saul's travels. Goblets shone with a luminous rosé scented of strawberry. Aunt Esther set on the table Reyna's *hanukiya* of birds. Next to them her own *hanukiya* glimmered in the dark. Behind its lights a bronze plate rose like a fan punched with cut stars, projecting flickering stars high onto the wall.

We sang "Eight Little Candles" and Reyna clapped the beat, but no one stood up to dance. Lady Brianda, the guest of honour, and Uncle Saul were at odds. Uncle Saul wanted to relax and savour the festive evening.

Saul had not even invited Lady Brianda —that was Esther's doing. Lady Brianda, backlit by flickering stars, looked stern. She turned to Reyna and me.

"My daughters, these are troubled times. The monarchs are persecuting conversos. How are you coping in spirit? Are you strengthening your worship and your faith? Sara, you answer first."

"At night, Your Grace, I do what I always have done. I review my actions over the course of the day, to think on the good I have done and also the bad, how I have helped others and how I may have hurt them. Then I resolve to learn from this for the next day. After that, I recite the *Shema* and fall asleep."

"That is good as far as it goes, but I believe more is necessary in these times. I shall discuss this presently."

Then she turned towards Reyna. "And you, my daughter, how are you coping and growing in spirit?"

"With all the troubles and sorrows, I am spending more time in my garden."

"Your garden?"

"Yes, in my Garden of Eden. I think of it as The Paradise of the Three Religions. It is planted with trees and flowers like the Tree of Life, and each day I plant more flowers and fruits, to share joy."

"Whoever taught you such a notion? Was it that old tutor, Solomon?"

"No, Your Grace, I have always thought thus, for as long as I remember, only now with the troubles, I think of it more. It is the Garden of Eden as it was before the Fall of Adam. Jews, Christians and Muslims share this tradition so I call it the Paradise of the Three Religions. I believe it exists today."

"It exists today?"

"Yes, because the present is eternal. Everything that ever existed exists now, only we can't generally see it. I myself have sensed it only a few times."

"Don't make up grandiose tales, Reyna. They become no one and the young least of all."

"When you sense the eternal present, it is not grandiose but infinite and intimate. When your own time comes, you will see."

Reyna lifted one of Aunt Esther's cruets and rubbed olive oil on her hands. We girls often did this at night, but at table it was forbidden.

"Reyna, mind you manners."

"I was thinking that we are both like the oil of the olive that gives radiance. I have burst into flame without being ignited, as the Qur'an says, but my light is small. Your flame will burn high and be a beacon for centuries."

I clasped my hands. Reyna's oddest statements had a way of coming true.

"Your Grace, the Paradise of the Three Religions is a garden where souls from the three religions exist in harmony. Expressing joy in God is slightly different for each of the three but the joy is the same. Whenever I learn of more troubles, I plant more flowers and fruits of each kind, to help the souls share joy. But mine is an inward flame. Yours is outward."

"So the souls of different faiths share the same paradise?" asked Esther.

"The lamps of Albarracín all light the same path. The individual is as nothing next to God, who is infinite.

When the individual is nothing next to God, salvation is not the goal. The reason for being of every soul is to rejoice in God and to burn with His Light."

"Sara, what do you have to say to your sister's preoccupations?"

"I think that these days, the most important thing is to honour the Law of Moses, believe in the revelation of the Torah, and trust in the coming of the Messiah.

Other than that, I don't think too much about the resurrection of righteous souls, or a heaven that is like a physical home. Maimónides advised us to look forward to the earthly coming of the Messiah and not to worry about something we can't fathom."

"Sara," insisted Reyna, "I think if you reconsider Maimónides you will see that I am not far off what he said about immortality. He suggests it might be the collective contemplation of God. He means everyone."

"Saul, what is your view of paradise?" queried Lady Brianda, acidly, as Saul had been joking with his manservant and chatting with Lady Brianda's husband.

He smiled. "As I always say, there is no other heaven than the market of Calatayud."

"Saul, that is not appropriate to this company and moreover I assume you intend it ironically given the poverty among families of that community. Calatayud is more and more a society divided between the rich and the poor."

She turned to Gonzalo, the converso servant who was serving more helpings to Uncle Saul. "What do you say to this, Gonzalo?"

"You are quite right, Your Grace, entirely right. It is just as you said. There is no other paradise than being rich and no other hell than being poor." At this, Isaq burst out laughing.

I feared this might have repercussions but Lady Brianda kept her composure. "My girls, I have guidance for each of you. Reyna, you first."

Reyna sat at attention.

"'*Blessed is He who planted trees in the Garden of Eden.*' According to the Talmud, thirty trees. Do you know what happened next?"

"Yes, Your Grace, the Earth did not properly heed the commands of Hashem and the trees did not grow as intended. The trees were imperfect."

"As the trees were imperfect, so is our earthly realm. Each of us has the power to change the world for the better. To lift it higher. This Divine Gift has potential if we put it to work, which, dear one, is not done by dreaming.

Sara, you made a good start saying we must fulfill the Law of Moses. Remember the story of the shepherd named Moshe. He stood in the desert at Sinai, wondering at the light and warmth of a flame that seemed to be feeding on a hedge of thorns, though it did not consume the hedge. In these times of turmoil, we Jews must burn bright with the fire of our faith, with a fervour that enlightens us. Now let us recite together the *Shema*."

I thought perhaps Uncle Saul wouldn't want to be led in prayer by Lady Brianda, she being a woman, but he went along. The evening ended on a harmonious note. A few days later, when it was time for good-byes and farewell hugs, there were no strange comments from Reyna. It was impossible to know that over the next year things would change so much.

The Year 1484, as counted by Christians, Part I

IN JANUARY, PAPA arrived home from the outskirts of Valencia with the surprise of all surprises and the foundation of all bliss. Her name was Dueynna, she was Valencian, and Uncle Saul had found her for Papa. Such a woman! Saul had completely outdone himself —and done me in. She would have power over Papa all his life.

My enemy had eyes of jet, full coral lips, and black ringlets that fell in cascades. These were strong lustrous ringlets that could break the teeth of any comb. What others might have faulted was her nose, which gave her personality. Papa looked humbled even to stand beside her.

"Dueynna is to be your new mother. She is descended from the ancient and venerable Jewish community of Valencia. The refinement of her person is surpassed only by her knowledge. Learn from her and better yourself in every way."

What a choice of words. Dueynna might have her way with Papa, but her being my mother was out of the question. I was glad that Reyna was away in Teruel with Uncle Saul and Aunt Esther, and did not have to wake each day to face this woman, newly installed in our house.

The day after she arrived, I rose well before dawn. I intended to escape early to the market, with Isaq in tow, when Dueynna stopped me on the landing.

"Sarita, there will be no more of this going about town with your brother. You have grown tall and are attracting notice. A girl like you is not senseless of these things, and I can only surmise that you are using Isaq as an excuse to go out."

"What am I to do, stay indoors all day?"

A childish response, but I knew my game was up.

"Coins are scarce and you are old enough to assist. You will help embroider the trousseaux of the Santángel girls. At least, the fastenings, seams and hems."

"It isn't seemly for me, the daughter of Simon the Doctor, to be a seamstress. Everyone knows that to take measurements of another woman is a mark of low status."

"You will not be taking measurements, or going to others' homes. I will arrange for sewing to be brought here."

"Honestly, you overestimate my abilities. I wasn't even good enough for stitching Bella's dressing gown. 'Sarita, you bungler, you are fit only for my backside,' she used to say so charmingly."

"Can you think of something better?"

"Yes, as a matter of fact. For years, I have been in charge of preparing Isaq's powders."

"So? He is one boy, just one. A business needs lots of patients, and patients need more than what you prepare."

"Perhaps, but many in this town suffer from sleeplessness, poor appetite, nerves, and ill humours.

If you consider Papa's patients, I would say these are among the most prevalent complaints in Albarracín, and the most enduring."

"I have raised the idea of charging his patients for tonics and such, but he refuses."

"There's the detail. I am not suggesting that Papa make his patients pay. I suggest that we sell to patients who return for more tonics. These sorts of maladies persist like the bad grass that doesn't die."

"So, the idea would be to sell remedies for nervous complaints, which you would prepare, from the confines of our home?"

"We would need a trustworthy messenger, and I know the one."

I was thinking of Mahoma, taciturn and money-wise. He would work on commission until he found something better.

"You will keep accurate accounts. I know how to read them, so don't indulge in fancies of *sueldos* for yourself."

Within the week I discussed my hiring needs with Mahoma. Mahoma said he was not available. He was exploring some opportunities outside of town. However, he could help.

"I know the one for you, if you promise to pay me a percentage of what you make." Negotiations ensued.

"Twelve percent, my best offer. You pay the runner from that, not me."

He considered this with a practiced air. "So be it. I know the one for you. His name is also Mahoma."

"Another Mahoma? Shall I call him Little Mahoma?"

"Actually," he lowered his voice, "he was born the eleventh of eleven children. His father must have saved the best name for last. He named him Abenámar."

"As in the song? How comical. I suppose he is the most honest young man in town."

I recited one of the latest romances,

> *"Abenámar, Abenámar,*
>
> *Scion of Moorish lines,*
>
> *The day that you were born*
>
> *Portentous were the signs.*
>
> *The waves becalmed at sea,*
>
> *The moon waxed full in the sky.*
>
> *The Moor born under such omens,*
>
> *Must never tell a lie."*

Mahoma shrugged. "His father died soon after, and his mother had the sense to call him Mahoma instead, but that is not his true name."

"What's the point?"

"The point is, I am one of the few people who know his name. Arabi told me."

"Uncle Arabi knows the secrets of everyone, even the innocent."

"Once I reveal to Mahoma that I know he is Abenámar, I have unlimited power. Imagine what the local boys would do with the name Abenámar. They would taunt him without mercy from every heap of rubble. He is very conscious of his image, that one."

"He had better be reliable, Mahoma. I am planning to obtain from Uncle Arabi pure opium, for relief of the most serious pain. Every dispensary in Aragon would pay a fortune for Uncle Arabi's opium. It's the best."

"Opium? Maybe that requires a higher percentage."

"If you raise your percentage, there won't be any business."

"All right, then. The deal is done. I will bring him on board in the morning. You may call him Mahoma the Younger, as he is several years my junior."

"Do you mean Mahoma the Youngest? Of course I know him. He's Uncle Arabi's junior messenger."

"That makes me Mahoma the Eldest."

One never knew if he were joking.

§§§

It was the month of May, when lovers enlist in the service of Cupid. In the Christian quarter, eligible lads had serenaded their "May maidens." In our house, marriage hadn't changed Papa much. He went on the same as before, except that Cupid's arrow had pierced him stupid and there was nothing to be done for it.

Dueynna rearranged her ringlets and dressed to favour her figure. She launched a season of lengthy visits which, to my relief, took her out of the house. I knew she meant to impress when she told me to fasten the gold chain that held her locket. On top was a design of interlocking grapevines worked in gold and silver.

"Dueynna, was this a nuptial gift?"

"From your father? Hardly," she sniffed. "This is my own family heirloom from the days when the Jewish jewellery smiths of Valencia were the finest in Iberia."

"Perhaps from your beau of times past."

This was beneath her dignity. No reply.

"Where are you going, my lovely Jewess, in finery so well composed?"

Lyrics from an old song —about a woman whose lovers met untimely deaths.

"To visit Chaya Catorce, and then out to dinner with Simon. Mind your own business and your chores."

As soon as she closed the door, I recruited Isaq. He was craving bread.

"Let's meet Magda at the market in the Christian quarter. Today, you may buy whatever you like. Yes, dear brother, forbidden bread."

"You still owe me for Passover Eve. You stole my bread."

"I didn't steal it."

"You made me drop it, same thing."

"That was years ago."

"So what? Still a selfish idiot."

"Fine. I'll buy you a nicer one. A yeast roll the size of your fist, moist with fruit syrup. But you have to spend the day with Magda and me."

"What fruit?"

"Cherries from magnificent trees watered by the River Grío of Tobed. Near Bella's place."

He walked so fast he led me running across town. At the edge of the market, at a stall that sold charms, we found Magda.

May was the season of roses in Albarracín. The vendor came with her broad-handled basket laden with pink and white flowers. She lifted stems heavy with half-blown buds. Beside them were lilies with freckled petals, curved into lips.

"These will be perfect to scent our amulets, our lockets of the soul."

"Sara, don't touch! Mind what I tell you, the white lily is the Christian flower of death."

"Magda," scolded the flower vendor, "the white lily is a symbol of the Resurrection of Jesus Christ, Our Lord, and also the Virgin Mary."

Magda whispered, "The white lily is the flower of Old Christian funerals, and only they understand why they parade their dead around the streets in fancy boxes."

I raised my finger to my lips.

"A casket should be of simple pine. At death all of us ride the narrow boat."

She must have had a premonition. We turned a corner and walked into a funeral procession of the well-to-do.

"You know that I am now a Christian, but to me their most horrid custom is how they bury one person on top of another and then take out the bones and put them back in again."

I ignored her.

"Imagine how interred bones must smell under the church floor."

"Magda, let's think of something else."

"No burial in the church for me. Mark my words! I don't want to lie under those suffocating tiles. I want to lie in virgin earth, in soil neither turned nor struck, in the meadows outside town."

The procession enveloped us. Magda grasped my hand. I was envisioning the roses in the vendor's basket. Anything but this.

"Never lie abed when a Christian funeral passes by your window. You must jump up, and remain standing while it passes." She shouted over the mourners.

"Why?"

"Never mind why, just do as I say. You don't want to end up dead, do you?"

Before I could smile, I felt eyes upon me.

I had heard rumours in the market that tied Father Solís to our Magda before I was born. I found them hard to believe. Father Solís was looking our way and he wasn't looking at her but at me. It was as if he saw something in me, something he recognized, and not for the first time.

"Come home, Magda. We have to go now. Isaq ate a loaf of wheat bread this morning and his good mood is wearing thin."

"I'm sorry. You know I don't like Dueynna."

"Her victim today is Chaya Catorce. Chaya may be the wife of a pawnbroker, but she answers only to the Rabbi's wife. Convincing Chaya of her Valencian superiority will take all day. Then she and Papa are going to dinner. I don't expect Dueynna home till late."

"I don't know why he married her in the first place. She is from Paterna, and everyone knows that a Petenera brings bad luck to men. The worst luck. The kiss of death."

"I thought the Peteneras who bring bad luck are from the south, from Almería."

"As I always say, bad luck is bad luck, wherever it is from."

"Magda, will you come home with us?"

"Jaime is in town for a few days. He lives up in the Sierra now, where he earns his living."

"Then he will come too, and we will sit round the hearth, as in the old times."

That night by the hearth, the fire already low, I was pounding Valerian root and trying to ignore the foul smell. Magda lit the kitchen lamps she'd used throughout my childhood, thumb-sized casseroles with spouts pinched from the clay. She set about rinsing greens for chard with garlic sauce.

"Magda, I am nauseated from Valerian root and garlic. Tell us something to sweeten the room, tell me a memory from when you were fifteen."

"The peach harvest in Alcañiz, the best in all Aragon! I was gathering fruits at the break of day, the moment when the nightingale sings his last and the *calandria*, our lark, replies. How well I remember, a youth came and whispered 'the finest peach of Calanda does not compare to you.'"

"Now, a song."

"It would be a pleasure, my daughter, to sing to you again. Perhaps this is the last time. I am getting old, Sarita."

"Just like our Magda," I thought with affection, "as exaggerated as always. She looks fine to me."

It was a mistake to encourage Magda to sing. She started on the longest ballad in her repertoire, the Ballad of Melisenda and Count Ayruelo. I ignored the first half, which was just the warm-up anyhow, until the mid-point, when our heroine's ardour for Count Ayruelo burst into flame.

Melisenda leapt from her bed, as naked as when her mother bore her. She threw on a white tunic and ran among her damsels, slapping them awake, asking what she should do for love. The eldest, an ancient woman, replied that the time for love was now, because if she waited till old age not even the most rapacious of men would desire her.

So intense was her passion, that when apprehended leaving her home Melisenda stabbed her father's guard to death. She opened wide by magic the doors to her beloved's castle. Face to face with the alarmed Count, she told him she was a Moorish girl from beyond the seas. He recognised her voice.

Speaking of voice, Magda always saved her best singing voice for the last lines of the song, and she warbled the closing in glowing tones:

> "He took her fine hands and led her away,
>
> And beneath the shade of a laurel tree,
>
> Of Venus is their play."

I decided to tease Jaime.

"Next month is Midsummer Night. Whom will you take up the mountain under the myrtle boughs, Cristina?"

Cristina had her eye on Jaime since she was thirteen. Maybe somewhat of a dishrag, but our standard was Bella.

Jaime laughed. "I haven't found anyone good enough for me, not just yet anyhow." He lowered his voice. "I am saving money. These are uncertain times."

"From your work in the Sierra? What do you do there?"

"From the city of Cuenca to our Sierra de Albarracín, the trade route traverses mountain ranges. The tallest has claimed many lives. Frías is the first Aragonese village with a water supply on the way to Teruel. That's how I earn my money most of the year, selling sundries to muleteers."

"Everything they need?"

I was thinking of my medicinal powders.

Jaime blushed. "Well, not quite. For refreshments and company of another sort, there is an inn up the road at Calomarde. It is not a place for you."

"Is that it, Jaime? Do you keep your sweetheart hidden up in the Sierra?"

"Sarita, the Sierra is sliced by canyons strewn with boulders. Tossed by the Devil in a rage. His footprints are cloven in rocks. In the winter, snow blankets the pine forests, and at nights wolves steal sheep and bandits do worse. It is no place for a sweetheart."

"Are you sure there are no myrtles for a bridal bower? Myrtle in bloom would be best, with the fragrance of Paradise."

"You are forever the dreamer. Juniper switches for witches' brooms, more likely."

"Witches' brooms?"

"In the Sierra, we don't need legends about girls with fancy names like Melisenda. We have our own legends about witches."

"I'd like to see the village of Frías. Perhaps I could sell medicinal powders and ointments."

"To the muleteers?"

"Why not? They must finish their crossing with sores and bruises."

Jaime frowned. "There are many reasons why not. The muleteers have their own brotherhood and it is an alliance of thieves. If you ever travel with them in your retinue, remember they are known for their lust and cunning, and as a rule they are not to be trusted, with your secrets, your goods or your person."

The thought of lusty muleteers must have inspired Magda, for she started singing again:

"*Count Claros, Count Claros*

Lord of Montalván,

What a lovely body you have,

For doing battle with infidels!

Thus responded the knight,

Such answer he gave,

I have my body, Madame,

To make love to women.

If I should have you tonight, Madame,

The next day in the morning,

If I should not kill one hundred Moors,

May they send me to die.

Hush, Count, hush

Do not sing your own praises,

He who wishes to serve the ladies

Always speaks this way,

And upon entering battle

Has well-worn excuses.

If you don't believe me, Madame,

You shall know by my deeds.

For seven long years I have loved you.

At night I do not sleep,

By day, I find no pleasure.

You have always known, Count,

How to make burlesque of women,

But let me go to the baths,

To the baths to bathe,

And then do with me as you will.

Responded the good Count,

Such answer he gave,

You know well, My Lady,

That I am a royal hunter,

When I have prey in my hand,

I can never let it go.

He takes her by the hand,

To a lush bower they go,

And in the shadow of the cypress,

Under the roses,

From the waist up they give sweet kisses

And from the waist down,

As man and woman, it is done."

Magda stared into the fire and I kept on talking to Jaime.

"I can mention this to Dueynna. Jaime, if we can convince her that there is better money to be made, perhaps she will let me go to Frías to try out my business idea."

"Where would you stay?"

"Frías has a Jewish community of a dozen families. There will be a worthy widow from whom I can rent a room. Perhaps Isaq will come with me."

Jaime hesitated. "The muleteers are a rough lot, raised on the road. They do their dealings in Arabic and they do not conduct business of your sort with women. If these were ordinary times, I would say no.

However, these are not ordinary times. Our lives are more uncertain each day. In times like these, we all need money. I will serve as middleman."

"There are troubles in Castile. You live near the border. Is it safe?"

"The city to watch is Zaragoza, from what I've heard. There is none of that where I stay, on either side of the border. Not even in Cuenca, according to the muleteers."

I resolved to approach Dueynna with my plan. To my relief, she approved, deciding she and Papa would go to Teruel to visit Esther and Saul. Isaq agreed to my plan so quickly he surprised me. He wanted to depart at once and Mahoma the Youngest sang, "Isaq can't wait and his bread won't bake."

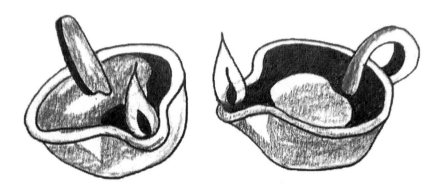

§§§

We stayed in Frías for two weeks. Jaime lived in one of the narrow houses leaning upon each other in rows. The rows ran the length of the village, more or less. His was the second house from the end, facing the trail that sloped down out of Aragon and away to Cuenca. In this corner of our kingdom were millstreams, waterwheels, and caves. From Jaime's house, I could see caves along the rock face. I wanted to climb rocks and visit a cave, and asked him every morning. Jaime said the rock was too slick. This went on for days, till Jaime had an idea.

"There is a waterfall up the road near Calomarde, Sara. Let's have an outing tomorrow."

"I'd love to, Jaime. You are so dear to be thinking of me! Who will make up the party?"

"You, Isaq and me, and one or two dogs, and, maybe someone else."

"Who else?"

"Cristina."

"I see. Glad to hear it. It's time for progress on that front."

"Time to feed the dogs," blushed Jaime, backing out the door. I pursued him.

To keep him company Jaime kept two dogs. Mari-Paws helped mind the sheep out back, and a fat hound occupied the hearth.

"Who's that?"

"That's old Galgo. He is a master of escapades which take him many leagues. Last month a neighbour found him roaming in Terriente and hauled him back.

His prodigious nose is bigger than his stomach. He claws his way into storerooms, eats half his weight in Serrano ham, and vomits."

I shuddered on two counts, the vomiting and the ham, both of which I found revolting.

"He's not coming with us on the picnic tomorrow, is he? What a bother to keep him on lead, and he'll ransack the food."

"We have a solution." Jaime fetched a collar and a leather lead.

"Oh no!"

I glanced at the old glutton who watched me with morose eyes.

"Yes. He may be a glutton but his nose is better than the others. We need him as a sentinel."

"And who will take the lead?"

Jaime whistled to Mari-Paws. She came running, scooped up the lead in her mouth, and led Galgo outside. The old dog was proud to be led.

"She'll lead him to the waterfall and back, and if he tries to wander off, she will bring him back. As for letting him eat, forget it."

The May morning dawned warm and clear. Cristina met us at Jaime's house. She managed some shy smiles while making herself useful. She even polished up Jaime's hearth. Not the way to shine, in my opinion. There wasn't much to do, because we planned to go to the inn for their picnic basket. For Isaq and me, I brought along our own satchel of *casher* treats, prepared by the widow.

From the inn, Jaime returned with a basket of roast hens with lavender flowers in the stuffing. Also, round loaves of country bread, almond nougat, and wine. How could Jaime afford such bounty?

"I'm so happy to come along," announced a jovial voice behind me, and when I turned, there was Mari Pilar, the inn keeper's daughter. Her bust was the envy of all the girls, and also her jet black hair. She wore a white chemise pinned with crimson ribbons.

"Poor Cristina," I thought with a glance of sympathy in her direction, "your hopes for Jaime are pinned on this picnic."

Jaime drove the mule cart past Calomarde to a marsh and helped us down. From there, a trail led to the falls. We made a festive party, with Jaime and Mari Pilar bedecked with flower garlands followed by Mari-Paws leading old Galgo and then Cristina, Isaq and me. Even Isaq had spring in his step. Distracted by the scent of deer, the dogs disappeared into the golden gorse, keeping Jaime busy.

We walked along the margins of the forest. Inside, elms and pines held up the heavens. Woodpeckers drummed on boles of oaks and owls slept. Fawns watched us from the bracken.

"Papa Simon has patients on the main road. He says there are more bucks on this ridge than men in our congregation."

"I don't know about that, but this ridge is known for its deer," Jaime said with pride.

"We've arrived late for the first gifts of Flora. When did the flowers open?"

"By March, the narcissus, and by April, the violets."

I closed my eyes and imagined the forest fringe spangled with wildflowers —narcissi with their six-pointed stars, and the violets of the May songs of the Sierra. As I opened my eyes, a breeze came up. Butterflies fluttered in all directions. It was late spring, the days of daisies of Arab verse with their hearts of gold.

"Next year we will bring Reyna. A pattern for her garden."

Jaime smiled. "Here she doesn't have to imagine paradise. In the Sierra of Albarracín we have blooms for every creed."

Isaq kicked a stone into the wildflowers. "I didn't come to pick daisies."

"I meant that Reyna would find inspiration for her spiritual garden."

Too late, I remembered it was impossible to put Isaq off track once he was focused on something.

"Maybe I care and maybe I don't. That's not the point. Where are the fly-eaters?"

"What?"

"The boys in town told me that plants in the Sierra eat flies. They wait for flies to land and close on them. You can see the flies dying inside. Sometimes their legs stick out."

"You mean, the fly-trap plants," corrected Jaime. "Those grow only in the quaking bogs. Those bogs look solid but quake under your feet. They lie hidden in the oak and ash forests of Orihuela del Tremedal. You won't find any here."

"Then I've come all this way for nothing and it's all your fault."

"You can hunt butterflies. Jaime will teach you."

Isaq sulked.

"The Apollos are the lords and the Celestes, the ladies-in-waiting. At night their queen, the silky green Isabelina, wafts among the pines with moths for bodyguards."

"Save your stories for yourself. Whenever you open your mouth, you waste my time."

Jaime intervened. "Isaq, you and I will find something else to do, just us men."

"I'll search for spiders. I've seen a nasty one, mottled like a nutmeg, with legs as long as my thumb."

Mari Pilar and Cristina set a rustic table. Stones from a mill, long abandoned, served as trestles. Jaime was scaling the silver limbs of pear-trees and called to Isaq, but my brother stayed below clutching a hand of cards. They slipped free and flew with the wind. Beyond the leaves of pears fluttering like inverted spades I caught a glimpse of living water.

"Don't fall into the river, Sara, you're supposed to be watching me."

The river sparkled over pale gravel and its mosses flowed like mermaid's hair. Bedazzled, I advanced into the stream. Silver minnows swept over my feet. Long-legged insects darted about, steeds for water sprites. Blue flax flowers waved from the bank. I slipped and sank to my knees.

Isaq counted paces round the orchard and shouted his measurements up to Jaime. His temper steadied. The words of Solomon the Aged occurred to me, "Let him go with the men." Perhaps open air and someone to serve as a brother was the answer.

I was wet but contented, lying on my back and looking up at the green pears in the foliage. I recalled the Feast of Sukkot. I was about to bite into the peaches and sugar of my memory —spherical fruits of creamy yellow from Calanda, when Mari Pilar burst into song:

> *"Let them talk all they want,*
>
> *Let them know what they know.*
>
> *The tree with no pears,*
>
> *Has no pears to bestow."*

She leaned fetchingly beneath Jaime in the branches, scooped up a wormy pear, and threw it at him. It landed just north of his member. Feigning annoyance, Jaime shouted, "Mari Pilar, do you think you're the king's daughter? Keep your pears to yourself."

Jaime jumped to the ground and sang with more vigour than poetry:

> "*The apple was born green and time ripened it,*
>
> *My heart was born free and yours captured it.*"

It was the song Bella had danced to in the square years ago. On signal, Mari-Paws stood up on her hind legs and danced, her round eyes trained on Jaime's face. Not as graceful as Bella, but the dog had rhythm.

Over our laughter Mari Pilar exclaimed, "One of our roast fowl has gone missing!"

Galgo looked at me with mournful eyes. Everyone laughed except Isaq. Then Zephyrus blew from the west, and thunder sounded.

"Follow me quick," said Jaime. We trampled banks of blue flowers. On a log, a greying he-otter grasped a trout and chewed fast, tilting his neck to swallow. He paid us no mind. Pelted by ice we arrived at a cliff with chiselled steps that led up the rock face —steep, wet, and sized for our feet.

"What good luck, Jaime. A ladder in the rock! Did the ancients hew these rungs and rundles?"

"Don't be silly. The miller."

"The miller?"

"Steps to the new mill. Hurry!"

We climbed to the crest of the rock. Below poured the waterfall, its waters churning over boulders in three cascades —aqua, white and tourmaline green in the hailstorm. Jaime stepped sideways along a ledge behind the cascades, grasped onto the roots of yews and dropped from sight. A cave! We landed at its foot and were buffeted by curtains of hairy wings. The bats flew out into the storm. We wiped our faces.

Light trickled down from the clerestory. Jaime was at the back. I moved next to him and arched my eyebrows at Cristina. This picnic was supposed to be her chance.

"How? I can't, not here," mouthed Cristina. She stared at me like a startled doe.

Mari Pilar bounded over. "If it's all right with you, Sarita, I'll take your place." She knelt next to Jaime, pulled from the basket an ample woven shawl, and draped it over them both.

The rest of the party dozed off, the cave smelling strongly of wet dog. Galgo's eyes trembled beneath their lids as he dreamt of rabbits. Cristina and Isaq sat with their arms around their knees, facing in opposite directions. As a courtesy, I feigned deafness to the lively sounds coming from beneath the shawl, devoted myself to scratching Mari-Paws behind her ears, and nibbled the last of the nougat till the rain stopped.

THE INQUISITION

The Year 1484, as counted by Christians, Part II

I RETURNED FROM Frías in late May without money to show for my business scheme. Jaime had been right. The muleteers were tight with their coins and spent them at the inn. Just past dawn I was standing in the lane polishing the forged iron on our front door, starting with the knocker shaped like a dragon which guarded our house, when Mahoma the Eldest walked by.

"Where are you heading so early?"

"If you must know," he lowered his voice, "I am headed up to the hills beyond town. Deep under the mountain lies an ancient tunnel."

"Buried treasure! Uncle Arabi told me what the Berber emirs gave their wives in the days of the taifa. Silver flasks for essences and perfumes. Bring back one for me."

"Be serious. Once upon a time, it carried water."

"An aqueduct? Underground?"

"Yes. Abandoned for a thousand years, but according to Arabi the trader, our people knew all its entrances."

"But why?"

"Hiding places might prove useful. These are uncertain times. Also I want to learn how to build things like tunnels, waterwheels and windmills. I will be a prosperous man. No more sweeping storerooms for me!"

"Have you started exploring?"

"This week, I will go to the top of the ridge, to survey the hills in the direction of Cella. I will bring you no gold nor silver, not even a dinar coin —but you shall have news if I hear any."

A week later, deep in the night, I heard pebbles striking my balcony. I opened the shutters, and spied him standing in the shadows.

"Sarita, this is important. It has nothing to do with waterworks. I saw something. Something you and your people need to know."

"What?"

"I was surveying the hills above Teruel."

"Your surveying took you as far as Teruel?"

"Why not? Anyhow, as I was inspecting the place, a man rode up to the gates of Teruel on a fine steed. His party was made up of executioners who carried weapons and nooses. He demanded admission. "

"To Albarracín?" I said, testing him.

"No, you are not listening, Sara. This is important. He demanded admission to Teruel."

"You were really there?"

"Yes. He blew a horn, which I could hear from the hill. The guards at the gates of Teruel held him back! A member of the town council arrived in haste, and then another. They spoke there for the longest time, for hours."

"That does sound odd, Mahoma. Have you seen the likes before?"

"The guards at the gates let most everyone pass except for highwaymen, and contraband too, for a percentage."

"What happened next?"

"He tried to gain admission, but they wouldn't let him pass. By the day's end, he turned round his horse and rode back up the road, followed by the executioners. He kicked his spurs and made a big cloud of dust, as if to show his displeasure."

"Did you sneak into town?"

"Of course. The town square was abuzz. The man's surname is Solibera or Colivera or some such, and he claims to hold the title of Inquisitor on the authority of King Ferdinand himself. He says that the Royal Monarchs have created a New Inquisition of their very own, independent of Rome and the old Inquisition that he says was a bunch of do-nothings.

The town council told him he had no proof that he was an Inquisitor sent by the King. Solibera or Colivera or whatever his name, now roosts at a monastery up the road. That crow has not flown."

"Why would the King of Aragon send an emissary of the Inquisition to Teruel, here on the old frontier? Teruel's town charter laid down rights to home rule centuries ago, with special privileges. The King and Queen reaffirmed these on their visit just two years ago."

"That was then. This is now. Times are changing."

"What is the word in the plaza?"

"'The devil is afoot and at the gates.'"

"But what does this mean for us?"

"The New Inquisition is coming to start the same horrid troublemaking it has started in Castile and Zaragoza. Burning 'heretics' at the stake!"

"People have been burned alive in Zaragoza?"

"Yes, offered up as sacrifices by this so-called New Inquisition and the Inquisitor who was sent there, Pedro de Arbués. He and Solibera are comrades in arms. This is the start of dangerous times for everyone in Teruel."

"Papa says the Tribunal of the Holy Office has its sights on conversos who secretly remain faithful to Judaism. Baptised Christians only. It has no jurisdiction over persons outside the Church."

I bit my lip. Mahoma the Eldest had been baptized at birth.

"The town council knew that Solibera was coming. Gonzalo Ruiz had attended the assembly of Aragonese parliaments, and warned them. The members of the town council are acting as one united city with one wall, in defence of all the faiths. But who knows how long they can hold out. We are all in trouble, sooner or later."

"If you promise to come here and tell me, once a week, what you see and hear, I will pack you food for one day's journey."

"Including what I discover in the hills, the waterworks?"

Every madman with his theme.

"No, Mahoma, not that. The stranger, Solibera, at the Gate of Teruel."

"Agreed, but I can't be here every week like clockwork. It takes me a while to walk to Teruel. If I'm lucky, I hitch a ride. By the way, is there payment for me?"

"Next time. Mahoma the Youngest has just started work."

"You are going to have to manage his services, and be sure to pay me, because between us I am considering moving on to more lucrative activities."

"How's that?"

"One day I was praying in the mosque of Teruel when I overheard that the widow of Abdalla Abenyez was hiring messengers. I went looking for her house. It is in a row of prosperous homes near the Zaragoza Gate, next to the house of a Christian notary."

"Yes, Aunt Esther and Uncle Saul live in that very same row, and their home is a small palace."

"I started thinking, this house in such a central location must be worth a fortune. Just think of all the *sueldos* that change hands at a sale of property like this. So I checked around. I learned that her husband had been represented in the purchase transaction by a Muslim agent and the sale was transacted in accordance with Muslim law. I'm thinking I should find work in conveyancing instead of construction."

"You'll need an apprenticeship somewhere. From what Saul tells us, there's more conveyancing going on up north, in Huesca. Talk to Arabi the trader. In the meantime, use your time on the aqueduct to greater profit."

"How?"

"Take Isaq, who is capable of counting paces with his eyes closed. You will get twice the work done, and I will pack bread and cheese for the week."

"Just once, as a trial. I'll come tomorrow before dawn. If he's not ready, I won't wait."

Isaq joined Mahoma on his rounds to Teruel. He never told me what he saw, but Mahoma confided that the city held a night of revelling. The town council built in the Plaza del Mercado a platform and a huge bonfire. Amid carousing and roistering the men of Teruel pitched stones at the stake. Thus they would punish the Inquisitor if he dared pass through their gates.

§§§

Once again I was called ominously to Papa's study. Papa and Uncle Saul were both waiting. That was unusual. I wondered what the reason could be. From the expressions on their faces, it was serious.

"Sit down, Sarita. Uncle Saul, through Luis de Santángel, has something to recount. It concerns a certain portrait reportedly painted of your sister Bella. You visited her at Calatayud so we have called you to see if you can confirm first-hand the existence and details of the portrait. This is a most sensitive topic with potential repercussions for us all, so your discretion is required. Understood?"

"Understood, Papa."

"Saul, her discretion and her words are to be trusted. You may proceed with the account as related to you."

This was not the Saul of capers and gifts. He looked stern.

"A portrait was painted of your sister by a rising artist from Zaragoza. Did you learn of this while in Calatayud?"

"Bella showed me a small study of her face and shoulders. She said the final work would be much grander."

"Did she mention its purpose?"

"She assured me the portrait would not be for church use. We had a discussion about that. I didn't want the episode to end badly."

"Did she tell you the intended destination and purpose of the work?"

"Not exactly. She was coy. It had something to do with a municipal guild hall. She said the proof of it, was that burghers of the Jewish community had their likeness sketched as well."

"You are certain that you saw the study?"

"Yes, Uncle Saul, I am. What's more, it was an excellent likeness. She was so proud of her dress and jewels. She had a burgundy dress and black snood designed for the occasion."

"Listen with care to what I am about to relate, and if any detail contradicts your knowledge of the history of the piece, let us know. Feel free to interrupt me."

"Yes, Uncle."

"Bella's portrait was brought to the Royal Court, where it was much admired."

"What happened?"

"The canvas at once caught the eye of a very important personage, Tomás de Torquemada, the Grand Inquisitor. Word has it, that the Grand Inquisitor ordered the canvas to be brought to his private study, where he placed it facing his writing desk. That evening, alone, he lit a candelabra and contemplated the woman on the canvas."

"What did he see?"

"You know better than we do, Sara. You saw the study and undoubtedly noted your sister's dress and adornment. You can imagine better than we what the Royal Inquisitor saw. I leave it to you and your thoughts. I do not wish to know."

"Why not, Papa? I remember it well."

Papa shook his head. "It is a blight on our family's name. Since ancient times, the honour of a married woman is paramount to us. You know that. Bella's vanity must have got the better of her. To permit herself to be portrayed so recognizably and in such a voluptuous manner, is in itself a grievous betrayal."

Saul resumed. "In the morning, his Eminence assembled his clerics.

'What is the title of this work?'

'Jesus and the Adulteress, Your Eminence.'

'What does it depict?'

'The meeting between our Lord Jesus Christ and the fallen woman brought to him for judgment by the Pharisees, as related in the Gospel of Saint John.'

'Who are the men standing behind her?'

'Pharisees, Your Eminence.'

'Is the artist to be found at Court?'

'Yes, his name is Miguel Ximénez. He trained under the Maestro Bartolomé Bermejo, and he is recently arrived from Zaragoza.'

'Bring him to me.'

Miguel Ximénez, interrupted at his paints, was brought before the Grand Inquisitor.

'Did you paint this canvas?'

'Yes, Your Eminence.'

'Who is the woman who posed for you? I assume she is your mistress.'

'No, Your Eminence. She is the wife of a wealthy converso from Calatayud.'

'What is his name?'

'Vidal Francés, I believe.'

'Is his wife a Christian?'

'I don't know, Your Eminence. I believe she was born to a Jewish family from Albarracín. Her name is Bella.'

'Of course, the beautiful, original Eve. This woman, this adulteress, is a living, breathing threat to our Christian men and their God-fearing souls. Scribes, verify the personal particulars of Vidal Francés and his adulteress wife, and add their names to our confidential list for the upcoming autos de fe in Zaragoza.'"

Here I interrupted. "But Bella, Vidal and baby Jonah were thinking of departing for Salonica. Have they left?"

"I believe so, with the Holy Office at their heels. But the Grand Inquisitor is a determined man. He is likely to burn them in effigy."

I fought back tears. I had spent my life sparring with Bella, and now I saw we were on the same side. She needed help. I hoped with all my heart they would make it to Salonica and that young Jonah would survive to start a dynasty.

Saul continued, gravely. "The Grand Inquisitor turned once more to the artist. 'What is the intended purpose of this piece of art? I am tempted to have it burned.'

'Your Eminence, this piece is intended for the Royal Monastery of Saint Mary of Sigena in Huesca, to help teach chastity to the nuns and show that Jesus has love in His Heart.'

'The painting may be preserved, but for its intended purpose only. Remove it at once from sight, and keep it well covered while in transit to Huesca.'"

That same artist was painting an altarpiece at the church where Bella was married. I could keep quiet no longer.

"Bella was hoping that her portrait would attract attention at Court. She told me so. She told me the portrait was sent to win the favour of the Monarchs if fate allowed. She hoped the King and Queen would see the sincerity in her face.

Uncle Saul, you taught me that most Christian church-goers cannot read so the artwork in their churches serves as a kind of teaching material. You said it serves an instructive purpose."

"That's right, Sara."

"Placing this painting in a church teaches not that Jesus has love in his heart, but instead that our lovely Bella and others like her are adulteresses. Maestro Miguel Ximénez is a sign painter for the Inquisition."

"There's more. The next day, the Grand Inquisitor showed the portrait of Bella to King Ferdinand and Queen Isabella, to demonstrate the religious orthodoxy and artistic power of the painter newly arrived at Court."

"What did the monarchs say?"

"As of the second day of May, Miguel Ximénez has been appointed Royal Painter to Ferdinand the Catholic King."

That night in my bed, I closed my eyes and tried to imagine the scene of the Grand Inquisitor inspecting the portrait of our Bella, alone in his chamber. Papa had used the word voluptuous. I had never thought of Bella quite that way and my imagination started to take flight. Yes, Papa was right, but how did he know to use that word when he had never seen the sketch of Bella with her pose, clothing and jewels? I closed my eyes to imagine the scene.

The Grand Inquisitor approached the canvas with the candelabra in his hand, closer and closer, examining each detail. The woman that is Bella stood with a dancer's stance, her long neck erect, her face tilted to one side. Her fine, fair hair fell in waves down her neck and her eyes, a blend of gold, blue, and green, were averted. He moved the candelabra down to her breast. Her neckline of silk, suggestive of ermine, was flecked with arrows. He moved the light higher, to her neck. A choker of intertwined links as black as jet cinched it provocatively. He moved the light a bit higher, above her forehead, revealing a black velvet snood trimmed in gold braid. On the face of the snood shone an oval stone of amber with a liquid centre, ringed by cabochon diamonds, staring like a third eye. Yet most extraordinary of all was her long, slender neck, voluptuous in its perfection, yes, asking to be kissed. He pressed his hand to his robe and blew out the lights.

§§§

One night in October I lay dreaming that I was fashioning a lamp from clay. The lamp was perfectly spherical but as I admired my handiwork, shooting stars struck it. Upon impact each burst into a different colour. Soon the damp clay was pocked with craters of blue, green, peach and yellow.

"Isaq, my brother, this is the perfect lamp for you!"

I woke to a shower of stones at my window. I rolled over and tried to ignore them. The stones hit their mark on my shutters, again and again. What persistence. I roused myself, opened the shutters, and peered out into the dark.

It was, of course, Mahoma the Eldest.

"Go away, Mahoma, it's late."

"Go wake Isaq. I have been trying to rouse him for an hour."

"Isaq? At this delightful hour of the morning? Whatever for?"

"We have a date with Amir, on the ramparts."

"You have what?"

"A date with Amir."

"Now? To do what?"

"It's not your concern, but if you must know, we are going in search of Aldebarán."

I thought, not another escapade in the Moorish quarter. "Who is Aldebarán? I've never heard of him."

"Sara, Aldebarán is not a person. Aldebarán is a star, one that glows with the light of a ruby, and this is the best time to see it."

"But why the ramparts? This town is on a hill. Can't you see it from anywhere?"

"Too many questions, and my time is short. Will you go wake Isaq or not?"

"I'll try, but he might not come. He always decides things on the spot."

So I went to Isaq's chamber and woke him gently. He sat up, rubbed his eyes, and leaped from his bed.

"Why didn't you wake me before? Now I am late and it is all your fault."

"How can it be my fault if I didn't even know about it?"

"Mahoma, bring Isaq home before dawn. If Dueynna finds out about this, we are out of business. Understood?"

But the two boys were gone. By his bedside, Isaq had left a sheet of parchment. It read, "My sister Sara."

"My sister Sara is a blooming idiot. She thinks she is so good. She deceives herself. With deception, no soul remains untainted —purity is ephemeral, for fair is foul and foul is fair. Life calls for both. I am alive only when I am outside this house."

I didn't sleep all night, fretting over Isaq's safety, and also the judgment he had passed on me. Why did I care? And did Isaq truly believe that man's darker nature must be expressed? The Talmud teaches us to follow the ethical path.

It was nearly dawn before Isaq returned. I was worried sick.

"How was the stargazing?"

"All right. We spotted Aldebarán where Amir had said it would be."

"Was it red like a ruby?"

"It was small. I was hungry. There was food."

"You were gone for five hours. What were you doing up there on the ramparts all that time?"

Most boys his age would have dismissed this as a rhetorical question. Isaq had never learned to dissimulate. Or was he pretending to be simple?

"We were eavesdropping."

"On the ramparts at night?"

"Yes, on a secret meeting of the municipal council of Albarracín and allies."

"Impossible. Isaq, stop talking nonsense. It is dangerous nonsense."

"Not for us men. You know there is an area along the ramparts that is avoided at night."

"Yes, Granny Bigmouth says there's a ghost up there."

"I will tell you our secret. Amir through mathematical computations predicted a point on the ramparts where all sounds emanating up from the front of the house of an eminent official should be audible. He says it is the working of physical laws, called a sound chamber. The Arab scholars of old knew all about these."

"But why did the boys want you along?" Isaq was known to be clumsy.

"To walk along the top of the ramparts in the dead of night counting the exact number of paces to the location as predicted mathematically. We couldn't carry lights."

"What did you hear?"

"Someone on the Teruel municipal council, I think the name was Ruiz, has sent a defiant missive to their Royal Majesties refusing entry to their new Inquisitor.

He has written that he would sooner cut off his right hand than betray the conversos of Teruel."

"What happened next?"

"There was much talk. It was hard to discern. Then a loud voice rang out over the crowd, 'our leader means well but he has no power before the Crown. The Archbishop of Zaragoza is the bastard son of King Ferdinand the Catholic King. He is a teenager and does what his papa tells him to. The Inquisitor will enter the city gates of Teruel within months, mark my words, and soon will be causing as much sorrow and trouble here as in Zaragoza. As things stand, soon all of us in this room will be left without hands.'"

"Go to bed, Isaq, and promise never to speak of this to anyone."

Isaq shrugged and slammed his door. I was proud of the town council of Teruel —defying Their Royal Majesties and the Inquisitor, to uphold our rights —and very proud to be Aragonese no matter what might come next.

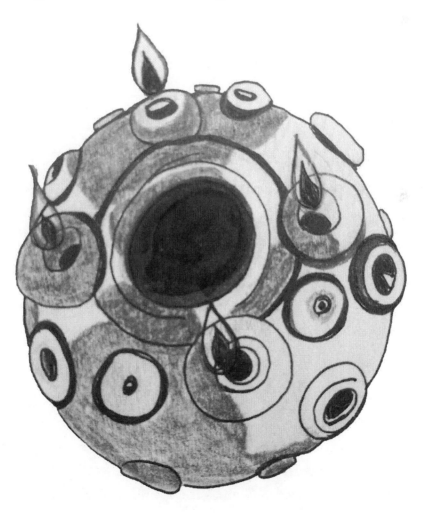

The Year 1485, as counted by Christians

JANUARY WAS COLD and dry. The entire town had a hard cough without broth to treat it. One evening as I was rinsing some almonds and heating our dinner —I recall distinctly we had chickpeas, three eggs, a few stalks of green chard that hadn't frozen, pine nuts, and "widow's crumbs" fried with garlic —there was a rapping at our door. It was Mahoma the Eldest.

"Arabi the trader has sent me. Leave off your cookery and come anon. Azizah needs you."

"What's the matter?"

"Azizah, as ever, is a-swoon."

"What brought it on?"

"Him again. Solís, the curate, surrounded by his informants. He is everywhere these days and the sight of his cassock gives her a fright. I have told her many times not to leave our part of town. She has been out in the cold for an hour."

"What is she doing in the cold?"

"Sitting in the mud, helpless, with gawking children. Our women couldn't move her and called on me. She may be my mother, but truth be told, couchant in the mud she reminds me of a cow. Can you come help? I would be grateful."

"Yes, this sounds like my sort of work. Let's see what I can do."

Azizah sat on frozen ground. The subtle beauty of yore with eyes of the Virgin had aged into a massive woman. Her eyes were open, not quite focused but staring straight ahead, her cheeks the colour of ashes, and her face had acquired the expression of a death mask except for the despair that coursed beneath like the river's own currents.

Children of all sizes were milling round. I needed to find a way to disperse them —I, Sarita, to whom no one ever listened, much less obeyed. Then the image of Lady Brianda came to mind —her voice, her presence, her force of character. With nothing else to help me, it was worth a try.

I appraised the group —about twenty children. The largest of the boys were taller than I, but they could be managed. My biggest worry was Xemci, sister of Mahoma the Youngest. She was a blue-eyed girl with blond hair under her headscarf who could toss the bar farther than most boys. From her rooftop she called her family home from the fields as surely as the muezzin called his faithful to prayer.

"I am Sara, the medical doctor in charge. I have been sent by the esteemed Doctor Simon and Arabi the trader, to take charge of Azizah."

Of course, this was against the law as I was not licensed, but who cared. My voice sounded strong! A hush fell over the crowd of children.

"I tell all of you assembled here to spread this message: Azizah will be cured in one hour."

Why had I said that?

"But first, you all must do as I say. Boys, go to the hillside and dig Valerian root. Fill two baskets and deliver them by nightfall to Arabi the trader."

After tussling among themselves, a small army of boys moved off toward the river. The bigger youths led the way, leading a cavalry mounted on poplar branches.

"Girls, Azizah will not be able to cook tonight. Go home and prepare her fritters —borage crisps drizzled with rosemary honey."

To my relief, Xemci rallied the girls to help Azizah. So far, so good —but why had I announced she would be cured in an hour? Fortunately none of them would be present to see if my cure took effect.

Fatima, Azizah's niece, a girl of fifteen who had inherited the same ethereal eyes as her aunt, had stood by her. She was pale and fighting back tears.

This would not do.

"Fatima, stand at the other side of Azizah for the next hour. You must listen to my every word, say what I tell you to say, and do what I do. Do only what I do. Understood?"

Everyone had tried telling Azizah what to do, and it had not worked. Then the insight came to me. The Azizah we knew and loved would have to come out of wherever she was, the way a cat climbs down from a tree —at her own pace. "One hour" was meaningless.

The only time that mattered now was the time Azizah needed to mend. The one thing I vowed not to do, was to tell poor Azizah to do anything.

I pulled from my basket a soft shawl, big enough for two. I snuggled up against Azizah and wrapped it round our shoulders. Perhaps the warmth and contact would help. She did not pull away, a good sign. I then produced a brass dish which glinted in the cold, setting sun, which held dates, each one stuffed with a blanched almond.

I said in a loud voice to Fatima, "Try these dates, they are the finest Medjool from Gibraltar and they melt on the tongue."

I made sure to pass the dish to Fatima in front of Azizah, right under her nose.

"How does the date taste, Fatima? Say it is delicious and pass the dish back to me!"

"It is delicious."

"Pass it back. I have the most tantalizing surprise in my basket, an assortment of exotic dates that Uncle Saul brought us from beyond the sea, each variety finer than the last and labeled with paper. Everything wrapped in this basket is a marvel to the tongue."

Back and forth we passed the brass dish, first with Sayer dates, all soft and syrupy with brown and orange flesh, and then Ftimi dates from the palm-fringed oases of Ifriquyah. Next came Deglet Nour from Libya with centres of light gold when held to the sun, and Mozafati, dark, creamy and deeply sweet, beloved of the caliphs of Persia, the ancestral home of all dates. After that came Amir Hajj from Baghdad with their delicate skin and delectable flesh, and more and more dates till I poured a flask of the biblical date wine of Nineveh. And offered the dark brown sugar dates of Arabia and the golden-amber dates of Yemen or whatever dates Benjamín de Tudela might have eaten while sailing the Arabian Sea.

We had reached the twentieth passing round of the dish, when Azizah bestirred herself, moved her hand and put a date in her mouth. She said nothing, but after a few moments sighed and moved to rise. Though she was heavy, together Fatima and I walked her to the home that they shared, where we put her to bed.

I didn't want to leave Azizah yet, not in that dark room. Fatima kindled her lamps. Each had a spout like a long foot laced with green stripes. Alit they glowed like slippers with lights on their toes. As the magic lights danced, Fatima changed into her tunic and lifted the lids off Azizah's henna pots.

"Whatever happened to Mari-Paws? We haven't seen her in the longest time. I adore her."

Azizah would not have allowed such talk, as Islam teaches that dogs are unclean, but Azizah was asleep.

"Jaime took her down to Frías."

"Is it true, the story they tell, that Uncle Saul brought her home one night, wearing a collar with pearls, a fleur-de-lis pendant, and a tiny blue diamond?"

"Yes, she was wiggling under his cloak."

"Tell me the truth, the pearls were really the irregular ones we Muslim girls use for our necklaces and hair ornaments, what we call *aljofares*."

"Not at all, Fatima, they are perfectly spherical pearls that Uncle Saul purchased from a Venetian pearl merchant in Florence. Reyna and I always thought they looked like small moons linked in a row. He brought the diamond from Florence also and it truly is blue."

"If Mari-Paws were mine, I would not waste her on the sheep. I would bathe her every week, comb her silky white hair, fasten her jewels round her neck, and carry her about with me all day."

"She'd nip at your earrings, jump free and run off, a thousand times," I laughed. "And besides, your faith does not permit dogs. Maybe a cat would be better."

"Sing me one of Magda's songs. We girls all know that Magda knows the best songs. She is like the storyteller of old." Fatima winked.

Word of Magda's songs had spread among the Muslim girls!

"Uncle Arabi told Amir and me that there used to be a storyteller in the town square at sunset who retold the old legends in Arabic. We don't have one anymore, thanks to Father Solís. He drove out of town the paternal grandpa of Abenámar, I mean Mahoma the Youngest, who ended up mending shoes in Gea de Albarracín. Uncle says we used to have a minaret too, but a church was built on the site."

"Fatima, his grandfather told of the minaret built here by the emirs of Banu Razin. They brought in craftsmen from Córdoba. Elegantly tall, of ochre sandstone. Toward the top of the tower, in ochre and teal, a set of *mihrab* columns interspersed with windows and above an arch of mosaics. It was as though a great stone carpet had been inlaid with green tiles, and displayed from the top to reflect the sun. From the summit of Albarracín it could be seen for miles round."

"All we have left is a neighbourhood mosque, with a front as plain as any other."

"Here's a poem that Solomon brought back from Persia:

'If one day on a Minaret

Your eyes in robbery you set,

Dig a deep pit with room inside

Where you can fit your prize and hide!'"

"I can't laugh at that one. I think the Church did a good job of burying our minaret. Sing me a song, Sarita, one of Magda's best, you know."

I tried hard to think up a song worthy of Fatima, but after her mention of Father Solís the only ballad that came to mind was menacing and salacious, which after all was what she wanted:

"A Christian came to my chamber door, with intent to deceive,

In Arabic he spoke so well, his words I did believe.

Me, I was Moorish Moraima, a marvel to behold,

'Open the doors, my Moorish maid, may Allah guard your soul.'"

At that instant, a gust snuffed out the flame of the oil lamps. Their wicks emitted threads of smoke. In the half-light, in her tunic, Fatima shuddered. I lowered my gaze.

"Why are you painting yourself with henna?"

"I am imagining myself a bride. Let me paint your ankles, they are so nicely tapered."

Fatima painted me with vines and blossoms, and a burst of dots. I sang her a line in Arabic.

"Round your ankles, bracelets swirl like doves at dawn."

"Fatima, excuse my Arabic, it is awful. Solomon the Aged taught it to me. He says the song is from Egypt."

"No worries, mine isn't much better. My dear Papa is always telling me to improve my Arabic but I have no mind for it and I don't see the need —unless he ships me to a wealthy husband across the seas, with striped silks and a font of rose water of Isfahan in his harem."

"And creamy curd with honey syrup and cinnamon?"

Azizah made the best in Albarracín.

"Sarita, I'm hungry. Let's eat the dates."

I smiled. We had started Azizah's treatment with twenty dates in the dish and ended with nineteen. Fatima had followed my instructions to the letter —which meant she had eaten none at all.

"The dates all were from the same sack at the market, weren't they?"

"Yes, the cheap ones."

In fact, they were tough dates from the Maghreb, papery brown and yellow, and shrunken like dead wasps.

"Those? Their pits can break teeth!"

"Well done passing the magic dish, Fatima, you are very clever when you need to be. You could master Arabic before setting sail. Let's enjoy our reward."

I passed the dish of dates to Fatima and together we dispatched them with precision as Azizah snored. Those chewy dates from the sack, with blanched almonds, were sublime.

§§§

One morning in March, Papa called me to his study, enquired after my health and wellbeing, and handed me a letter. It was from Reyna.

"Dearest Sister,

I have terrible news. Inquisitor Solibera has made his grand entrance into Teruel. No one resists him anymore. He 'excommunicated' the entire city last summer, which outraged the Christians, and our town leaders fought back successfully. Then the soldier Juan Garcés de Marzilla threatened to lay siege. He's been named captain of the city and he dismissed the town council. Leading converso families are fleeing, our community expects an expulsion order, and Uncle Saul says it is time for us to leave, too.

This morning Lady Brianda came to call and I overheard her talking with Aunt Esther. Aunt Esther was urging Lady Brianda to leave Teruel with us. Lady Brianda replied, 'This is no time to retreat, Esther. This is the time to stand firm. I will guard my community with a flame in my heart.'

Aunt Esther said, 'Brianda, I have one request: come with us now.'

Lady Brianda replied, 'Esther, I have one request: stay with me and defend our faith together. There are almost no Jews left here. We need you. '

I don't know what happened next, but Lady Brianda left the house with her head held high and Aunt Esther was crying. Imagine, Aunt Esther crying! I never thought I would see it in my lifetime. What is this world coming to?

By the time you receive this letter, I will be on my way to Navarre. Uncle Saul is taking Aunt Esther and me. We leave tomorrow, by way of Tarazona. How I dream of seeing the Synagogue of Tarazona and the Torah scroll with a silver crown! But we'll have no time. The Inquisition is already there.

We will bid farewell to Aragon and cross the frontier. Uncle Saul says he has a home for us in Tudela with a big hearth and logs on the fire. We cannot carry much with us, Sara. I am sad that my *hanukiya* of nesting birds must stay behind. Uncle Saul says that when times are more certain he will send for them.

I want them stored in a truly safe place so I implored Aunt Esther to allow me to take them down to the cellar. She said Uncle Saul didn't want me to go down there because of the damp but I insisted so that I will know exactly where to find them when we return.

The cellar really is vast. I found a crawl space under the supports that should be safe even from earthquakes though I'm not sure we have them in Teruel. Anyhow, I moved my blue lamp about in the darkness, and chose a place for my birds.

Papa says there always has been a Jewish community in Teruel and always will. There on my knees in the cellar I wondered what the future would hold. What if it is too cold for me in Navarre, and I don't come back? What if none of us comes back? So, I wrapped up the *hanukiya* birds ever so carefully in their chest and folded a cloth over them. I said, 'My little birds, if I don't return, may you rest for one hundred years, and be awakened by a child holding a light.'

I hear them calling me, dear Sara. I am going now.

Kisses,

Reyna

Your little sister who loves you very much."

§§§

The church bells of Santa María were calling insistently. It was the Christian Feast of Easter and Dueynna was in bed with a headache. I wondered if her nerves had more to do with a packet she had ordered from a well-known woman doctor in Calatayud. From a single whiff, I knew what was inside. As handed down by Rabbi Yehuda Harizi of blessed memory, an aromatic blend of cinnamon bark, citron, galangal, tamarisk and a dozen other ingredients. Also, a costly sachet of mandrake granules.

What a surprise that Dueynna, childless at her age, had ambitions in this direction. She soaked the mandrake granules in white wine, changing it daily. Every nine days, when she thought I wasn't watching, she drained the flask, and added musk and grey truffles. She pounded these into paste, and made a ball. I knew what came next — she inserted it inside.

Dueynna had been carrying around a mandrake egg in her secret place for months. By this time, anything was possible, or perhaps the symptoms were wishful thinking on her part. As for me, I was fifteen years old, shut up in the house, and springtime made me rebellious.

I entered Papa's medical office, uninvited. He was repairing a book and signaled to me not to speak. When ready, he would invite me to touch the calfskin and parchment. Not this time. I broke the silence.

"Papa, I have overheard talk at the butcher shop. In Grandfather's day, after the Disputation of Tortosa, Pope Innocent issued an edict announcing the 'temporal closure' of our Synagogue of Albarracín, which he had no right to do. Whatever 'temporal closure' meant, half of our congregation fled to the Church of Santa María, which the bishop enlarged to receive them. Those were scare tactics.

Now that the Inquisition is in Teruel, something's afoot. The Church of Santa María is building new pews. The lumber is piled in their workshop. For families they expect to receive from our synagogue.

That lumber is part of a larger scheme. They are planning to close us down!"

Papa went on with his work.

"Haim's son Judah says that something dreadful is going to happen. Worse even than in Grandfather's day, worse than ever before!"

"I am surprised at you, interrupting me at my work without being summoned, only to tell me something I know more about than you. Is that why you tarry at the butcher's — to visit with Judah?"

"This is not why I am here. Solomon the Aged needs you."

"Solomon the Aged has been evading my services for a decade. What makes this day different?"

"He hasn't held down food for two days, he is spitting up, and his skin looks waxy. He is calling for you, Papa. An old fox knows when his time runs out."

Papa and I walked through the streets of our quarter, past walls of salmon red, round twists and turns and under arches, into a warren of lanes. At our approach, cats disappeared down alleyways. Those were dark days for cats. They were being trapped, and burned as Satan's consorts and sometimes flayed alive.

We stopped before a hovel and rapped at the door. It opened abruptly. I was hit in the nose by a swinging broom of rosemary and cilantro, fastened to the knocker. The herbs were tied up in a swag to repel witches.

I rubbed my nose to make sure it wasn't bleeding.

"Papa, there must be some mistake."

"Sara, prepare yourself."

I followed Papa Simon up the stairs, with foreboding, to the garret rented by Solomon the Aged.

The litter on the floor was worse than I feared — wizened apples, onion skins, and clods that I hoped were beet roots in decay. The stench that filled the room was of something worse, as if frightened cats had been shut up inside. But there were no cats, no cats at all. Solomon had not been reaching the mark at his chamber pot.

"Note the pungent odour of the urine. It has diagnostic value," whispered Papa. I fought not to gag.

Solomon extended his hand. "Simon, my esteemed doctor, it is a pleasure to see you. I have a trifling problem, you see," and he winked at Papa. "What goes down won't go down, and what should go down, comes up." Solomon spat into a handkerchief that was stained black.

Papa made a gesture to leave the room. I waited for a short while downstairs, where he joined me.

"It is time to notify our Rabbi so he can communicate with the Head Rabbi in Toledo."

"Solomon says he has family in Toledo, but Bella says he is an impostor."

"Why are you so quick to take her word, when you bridle at everything else she says? Disrespect is easier than respect, in particular at your age. To lack respect clouds the perception of truth."

"I am sorry, Papa, but Solomon the Aged has looked like a buffoon, hunched over his ridiculous stick, ever since I was a girl."

"If he were a buffoon, how would you have learned with him so much of the Torah, the Talmud and the writings of Maimónides?"

I had to admit he had a point.

"In the words of Simon Ben Zoma, who is wise? One who learns from every man."

I was becoming annoyed, and so was Papa.

"I promise you, Sara, every person alive has a gift of some sort that you do not have. Even Carmela."

"Carmela?"

"Yes, your feelings toward her have been evident for years, and you think I don't notice these things. But have you seen how she excels as a housekeeper? Carmela is not the point, just an example of what I am trying to show you."

I said nothing. How could he say this to me?

"As for Solomon, who for years has taught you patiently and done his best to keep you in good humour, which is not easy, in his dotage you are laughing at him not with him. As I have told you many times, gratitude is one of the most important virtues and also the most difficult to cultivate."

"I'm sorry, Papa. Do you believe Solomon the Aged has family known to the Head Rabbi of Toledo?"

"I have it on excellent authority, our Rabbi's own, that Solomon was born into one of the wealthiest families in all Iberia, albeit a maternal branch, who trace their lineage generation by generation back to King David. He completed four years of religious training, which ended abruptly following a dispute with his teachers."

"He told us that he travelled to Jerusalem."

"Yes, where by all accounts he was accorded the welcome of a prince. Later he left for Basra and Baghdad, and then wandered the deserts of Persia. He returned to Iberia years later bearing Persian treasures to sell to the richest families of Castile."

"Without much success. Poor Solomon. Is he going to die soon?"

"A blockage such as his takes its time before it kills. Try to see him every day if you can, and make him comfortable. He may take sips of water, but no solid food."

"Perhaps honey with hot water, or narcotics?"

"Yes, Uncle Arabi's recipe. Also, clear broth. You will do a good job with a dying patient and the experience will prove useful because, my dear, maladies vary from one to the next but everyone dies. You have the makings of a doctor yourself."

Papa lowered his voice. "The man is ashamed of the smell in the garret. Bring him my pomander filled with scent. It is the one pleasure left to him. Always remember the importance of respect."

Solomon died at the end of summer, when the field hands were threshing the wheat. In a pewter pomander I brought basil and attar of roses for one last breath of youth, but his eyes had dimmed, his soul already passed through. It was the day after the running of the cattle through our quarter, and the widow poured floods of water from each garret window, in her eagerness to release his spirit and distance herself from death.

The fasting day of Yom Kippur I prayed in the balcony of our Synagogue next to Bona, Haim's daughter. In the old days, when we were very young, we had been allowed to run about in the vineyards and groves in woven slippers of esparto grass, nibbling on grapes and olives. No longer. We sat lady-like indoors observing the fast in the stifling heat.

Perhaps all my life I had been more generous in my actions than my thoughts. I wanted to change in the coming year. I wanted to believe in the goodness of others. As the heat intensified and we wiped our faces with a damp cloth I held to the hope of becoming a more trusting person in the eyes of the Lord.

Trust! What a time and place to aspire to trust! Everything the Inquisition did, destroyed it. But we are not without help in mastering our lives. I placed my trust in the Lord, my confidence in Him.

§§§

Autumn returned with more bite than usual. The waters of the Guadalaviar were running cold, and from the bulrushes along its banks the herons were taking flight. Their prey on the wing, hawks were circling. In town, there were hawks of a different feather who answered to the curate —and told him all the secrets in their ken.

Albarracín, town of my birth, how well I remember that day of storm clouds and shadow. The rain lingered like an uninvited guest. Inside, the embers hissed at each drop down the chimney. I arranged Magda's casserole lamps on the flagstone and lit a semicircle of light.

Carmela entered. She chose our best chair.

"I bring news of that dear friend of yours from Teruel, Brianda Besante."

"You've never brought news before. Why venture forth in this weather?"

"You were always such a prig, Sarita, feigning interest in those religious ideas of hers. Well, I am glad to say, you won't get more out of her than that heathenish book she sent."

The Torah with the fine green binding! If that was what she was after, it had gone with Reyna to Teruel.

"It's a good thing you didn't show your face at her prayer classes when you visited Reyna. Did she teach you in private?"

"It's not your business, and, no."

"That's interesting, because servants at the Teruel house said she came to dinner but the conversation was about planting trees and shopping in Calatayud. Maybe you can help me."

"I don't know what you're talking about."

"Don't play the innocent. Pour me sweet wine and slice a mouthful of that cheese your people keep. On second thought, some of the doctor's fortified spirits. Hurry, I mustn't stay in this house for long."

It seemed wrong to be serving spirits to Carmela. She peered into the cup as if it might not meet inspection.

"As I was saying, it's good you didn't attend her classes. Otherwise, you'd be called as a witness for the prosecution."

"Where?"

"In Teruel. With Garcés de Marzilla in charge, the Tribunal of the Holy Office is finally able to move ahead with the full backing of the town council. Inquisitorial proceedings are picking up speed."

"Inquisitorial proceedings in Teruel, so soon?"

"Of course. We have effective leaders now, who know right from wrong. You'd be amazed how fast everything can change."

"It does sound like a big change, Carmela."

"I'm proud to say Teruel held its first auto de fe this summer. Remember the Ruiz family, the ones who tried to keep Inquisitor Solibera from entering?"

Isaq had spoken of it, the night he eavesdropped from the ramparts. I kept quiet.

"Our fine new leadership in Teruel is doing away with them. Splendid bonfires. The ones who fled were burned in effigy. The ones from the old generation who were already dead, their bones were dug up and burned."

"They disinterred and burned the bones of the dead?"

"Rightly so. Just because those old sinners died in peace doesn't mean they should escape punishment. I say, burn the whole lot."

Without a resting place, would their souls wander the earth? And then I realised, it was about money. The Inquisition was entitled to a share of the property of convicted heretics, alive or dead.

"And Lady Brianda?"

"I know on good authority that Brianda Besante and two of her young cousins were among the first residents of Teruel to be apprehended.

Brianda is such a stubborn old conversa, attending synagogue and teaching the Law of Moses to girls who are baptised Christians. That's the worse combination of traits in a person, Antonio always says, hard-working and wrong-headed."

I sensed she might be leading up to questions, so I diverted her.

"I never knew she had family."

"Her husband's son-in-law is Gabriel Sánchez, the King's Treasurer. He'd better keep out of trouble! As for those girls, they've never paid her any mind, so she has to go find surrogates. You are so naïve."

"What are their names?"

"Brianda and Alba, two of the leading ladies of Teruel. Brianda's dowry was worth a fortune!"

"She has a namesake. Is young Brianda like her auntie?"

"Young Brianda de Santángel takes after her in name only. I have it on good authority that she has told the examiners that during her childhood, her mother Rita had ordered her and her sister not to spin on Saturday and many things of that sort, but when she came of age, she understood that Judaizing was a bad road. After all, she was about to marry an Old Christian. Four years ago she gave up some of the customs and two years ago, she gave them up entirely.

It is the opinion of Antonio that she will be exonerated. Of course, it helps that her Old Christian husband is none other than Garcés de Marzilla, of most honourable lineage and trusted by the Catholic Kings to do their bidding."

"Lady Brianda's cousin married Juan Garcés de Marzilla?"

"He is a perfect, gentle knight, devoted to the Cross and to his lady. In the days when he was subject to curfew, she took so ill she seemed near death. After sunset, he breached the town walls to spend one last night with her. He scaled a tree and came swinging on vines into town. In the dark before dawn, he was spied leaving his house and his adored Brianda. What a man! All the girls in Teruel are in love with him."

Garcés de Marzilla, soldier who burned the living and the dead, the object of collective desire?

"As for Brianda the Eldest," she laughed, "the Good Lord knows what that woman is capable of saying."

Brianda Besante, my teacher and guide. No doubt Father Solís had sent Carmela to us as a spy and informant, a *malsin* as Papa would say in Hebrew.

All I could manage to say on the spot was "Carmela, what happens in Teruel is none of my affair."

"I am not so sure. You've been building that friendship for a while now. I can't figure out what she saw in you —an acolyte?"

That was a fancy word for Carmela to use, but then she was living with a priest.

"You must have been aiming for gifts from the rich old lady. Saul never brought you anything nice from his travels. Magda always noticed, like the time he brought Reyna the pearl strand and diamond pendant, and you received nougat to share round the hearth."

She fingered her pendant, a cross of ebony inlaid with ivory squares. "My next crucifix from Antonio will be gold, I promise you. I am working on it."

"By gathering evidence from me?"

"Sarita, I don't need anything from you. The truth is, I am here as your friend. We care so deeply. Magda is worried. May I give you some advice?"

"You may, but make it quick."

"It's time to stop collecting roots and herbs, and start collecting men. Start with the smaller ones before working your way up. By your age, I was already well along. It's your future."

"Carmela, Isaq lies ill of the ague, upstairs."

A fib, but it gave me a pretext to see her out and a reason for her to leave.

That night I told Papa all but the last bit. He said there was no way to send help to Lady Brianda. The best I could do was pray for her and stand up for my faith.

"The Inquisition is prosecuting the Ruiz clan because they defied the King himself. I've heard that Gonzalo Ruiz is sending an appeal to the Pope in Rome for a Papal Bull to protect conversos. King Ferdinand and Queen Isabella are enraged beyond what you can imagine."

"Was he burned at the stake in Teruel's auto de fe?"

"No. Gonzalo Ruiz is still at large, determined to pursue Papal clemency for conversos from here to Valencia, and the Royal Monarchs are sending the strongest of warnings. In comparison, our dear Brianda is a gadfly."

"Papa, I am frightened for her."

"Don't fret, Sarita, she's just an old woman and they have no reason to make an example of her. She may have to wear the *sanbenito* robe, but she will be released. Mark my words."

Carmela's visit was a turning point. The previous year while I had cleaned the hearth and cared for Isaq, the world had changed fast in dangerous ways. I needed to start a life of my own before it was too late.

That winter, Albarracín received three blankets of snow as white as paper. Papa asked me to nurse a bedridden woman surviving on thistle soup. I bathed her under her tunic with warm water, marjoram and salt, and brought her bread from our hearth under wraps. Dueynna, who watched our loaf with the eyes of a sparrowhawk, lost her temper with me and then with Papa. There being no spare bread, I purchased soup bones from Haim, the butcher, and three times his son Judah walked me home in the snow.

$\mathcal{T}$he Year 1486, as counted by Christians

$\mathcal{I}$N JANUARY, THE SNOW continued falling day and night. To keep warm, I sang the lyrics of a song from the far north of Aragon that I learned from the minstrels.

> *"Treading the cold snow, all night long I have come walking;*
>
> *treading the cold snow, only to see you,*
>
> *my beloved girl from Ansó,*
>
> *my Ansotana."*

I always recalled that song because *ansotana* also denotes an herb with delicate white or pink petals, a most effective cure for acute tonsillitis.

Snowflakes as delicate as petals drifted past our shutters but as I dreamed, the Angel of Darkness rode out in the storm. In January, nine conversos lost their lives in Inquisition bonfires. Garcés de Marzilla sent the condemned men and women from prison to Teruel's Plaza del Mercado accompanied by soldiers on foot and horseback, in a terrifying procession. I don't think Garcés de Marzilla and the young Brianda were as happy as Carmela had said, because one of the men he burned to death that day was his father-in-law. Also, two brothers-in-law in the flesh and a third in effigy.

Papa decided it was time to remove from Albarracín.

"When the prudent man foresees evil he seeks shelter."

"Is the Creator bringing judgment upon us with a second Flood?"

"It's not for me to say. Noah entered the Ark out of prudence, sensing troubles. Saul was wise to leave Teruel when he did, before Solibera expelled our people from the city. Someday I'd like to join Saul in Navarre. The house I've inherited in Híjar will have to do for now."

"When do we move?"

"Dueynna and Isaq will go ahead of us. My cousins will look after them. I won't walk away from my patients. I'd like you with me, and you might like more time with Judah."

Meanwhile, I awaited word of Brianda Besante. In early March, news came that four of the leading matrons of Teruel had been sentenced to perpetual imprisonment. Each had been outfitted in a purple veil with a red cross, and shamed before officials, residents and strangers. Like Lady Brianda, these women had prominent converso husbands —yet her name was not mentioned. Papa urged me to keep hope.

Dueynna was keen to leave. She had fallen out with Chaya, the wife of Jacobo Catorce, who spread word that Papa had not maintained the honour of his household before her arrival. She fussed that she was not going to live in a "dishonourable" house! Who knows what she meant. Yet Papa put it on the market at a low price, found a buyer and agreed to sell.

Rain or shine, Papa and I called on the butcher's shop once a week. Afterwards, Judah walked me arm-in-arm to my door.

Starting in April, we took a new turn and walked, our bare feet in the grass, by the Guadalaviar beneath the bluest skies that ever served as heaven's veil. Thus passed April into May. More than this, I will not tell. As sung in the Seguidilla, "Silence! It is spring and they are speaking of love."

One splendid evening before sunset the goldfinches darted among the thistles. Their flourishes of song wafted through the door as I swept the hallway from the outside in, as was our custom. It was a woman's pride to deliver to the new owners an abode matchless among dwellings.

My throat started hurting. Another bout of acute tonsillitis! Fortunately just one task remained before my cup of hot water, *ansotana* and honey. I polished Papa's dragon knocker.

"Farewell, my brave dragon!" I whispered, "thank you for guarding us."

Darkness set in. Silence fell on the thistles, over the outcrop and down the cliff toward the river. I walked to the edge of the overlook and gazed across to the homes of families of different faiths. Each had lit its lamps, and the lights flickered in unison as if seeking one astral flame.

The knocker sounded. Mahoma the Youngest handed me a letter from Aunt Esther. I retreated to my bed. Other than in Papa's study, it was the only thing left in the house.

"Dear Sara,

I am sorry to write you this. Our Reyna has left her body and returned to Hashem. The fevers troubled her very much at the end and she fretted for her little birds. I regret having left them in the cellar in the Teruel house. She pined for them so in her last hours that I longed to kindle them to lighten her heart. She passed in her sleep, in time for preparations and burial before the third star of Shabbat appeared in the sky.

She always was such a gentle girl, otherworldly almost, and no trouble to me. Saul knew this was coming but he is crushed beyond even what I expected and I am worried for him. He no longer has the vigour of youth or even middle age. I will make the necessary arrangements for mourning. I know you could not perform the *mitzvah* of visiting her. She would have visited you had she been able. She was asking for you near the end.

I have written your father separately. The Florentine pendant with the small blue diamond and the strand of pearls, Reyna wished you to keep and I will send when times are more secure."

The writing then changed to Hebrew.

"I don't know if you are aware. Our esteemed

Brianda Besante and her husband Luis de Santángel have been handed over by the Inquisition to prison authorities. This means they will be put to death, probably burned at the stake. We are not sure where —perhaps Valencia. Though we will hear no more of them, I know that Brianda will go to her death with courage in her heart and defend her faith to the end.

We must always remember her and her example.

Be on your guard, Sara. You are not as secure in Albarracín as you might think. We have learned that the Inquisition has a covert tribunal in your town and Solís the Christian curate may be feeding them information. Solís has had his eyes on you since you were small, for reasons of his own, and the bailiff might issue an order for your arrest. If you are apprehended, stay true to yourself and keep alive in your heart the flame that Lady Brianda carries for us.

I embrace you, Sarita, and hold you in my thoughts.

Esther

Your aunt who loves you very much."

I dropped Esther's letter on my bed. I took some sips of water and tossed about miserably. It was night when I woke, without pain. I opened my eyes. At first I could see and think clearly, but then I felt the sensation of maternal love, a slight swoon like an ever-so-gentle narcotic.

On my bedside table by a lamp was a letter from Reyna. Why hadn't I seen it before? It had been there all along, in the open.

"Dearest Sister,

We didn't stay long in Navarre. Uncle Saul has brought me past Tortosa, to the sea. I am in a tower with a window that looks over the Mediterranean to where the sea meets the sky. Such deep diamond blue, Sara, as you never did see. I promise you, it is real.

Uncle Saul has found me a plump mother dove, white with caramel. She is poised on my wrist and cocks her head to listen. From far over the gleaming sea with its lifting and shifting of waves comes the Song I cannot learn onshore.

In your moments of trial, remember this Light. We all will see it at the end of time, the final *Tikkun*.

Give me one last hug, Sarita. I am going now.

Kisses.

Reyna

Your sister who loves you very much."

The knowledge of love lingered for a few moments. It lasted long enough for me to hold her close one last time.

Banging of doors awakened me. My mind returned to the present and my throat needled. I reached out for the water jug and found nothing —my bedside table wasn't there anymore.

I thought, "So there's no letter from Reyna, no table, no lamp. The house is empty, that's it. They all have gone to Híjar but Papa and me, and he is attending one last time to his patients, so who could be rapping at my door?"

It was the *pregonero*, whom I knew as an obnoxious sort, striding up and down pounding at the doors on our lane. "Awaken, residents of the *Judería*, you are ordered to assemble before the Town Hall by order of their Majesties the King and Queen of Aragon and Castile. Now, without delay."

I opened my window. The worthy men and women of my quarter, carrying children, were streaming into the street. I threw on my cloak and followed them to the town square.

Was this the plaza? A gap opened in the crowd and I pushed my way in. A mistake. The gap closed. Men had climbed onto the dais in front of the Town Hall, and guards were forcing people back with ripple effect. Strangers shoulder to shoulder were stepping backwards, the spurs on their boots striking blindly. I lost my footing and fell under the line. Then strong arms pulled me up. To this day, I remember the familiar warmth I felt at their touch. I turned to embrace —Bona!

"Where's Judah?"

"My brother's in the crowd. We need to reach him."

"Why so many strangers wearing spurs?"

"Listen! It's starting!" From the dais, the *pregonero* raised his arms for silence and an official, whom I could not see, began to speak.

"It is to be understood by the Jews and conversos of the city of Albarracín, and any who waver in the True Faith, that their Royal Majesties are most aggrieved by the murder of Pedro de Arbués, Inquisitor of Aragon and Canon of the Cathedral of La Seo in Zaragoza."

Murmurs rose from the crowd. "Kneeling at prayer. Stabbed in the back. Murder in the Cathedral!" I turned to Bona.

"Murdered in the cathedral?"

"Yes, in the Cathedral de la Seo, at night while on his knees in prayer. Knifed by assailants in the jugular."

"Who are the suspects?"

"A band of conversos. One has been caught. The suspected masterminds include the brother of the Royal Chancellor Luis de Santángel who is the cousin of Lady Brianda's husband, and the Magistrate, Jaime de Montesa.

Some other high-ups too. They've implicated the brothers of the Gabriel Sánchez, the King's Treasurer."

"Jaime de Montesa! He is a jolly man, the life of every wedding. I've met his daughter."

"Hush, you have met no one."

"Why would he do such a thing?"

"Because this is war. De Arbués has brought war to Aragon."

Townsfolk crowded round. "He watches conversos burn to death, waving himself with a fan."

"He ordered a woman's corpse exhumed and torched."

"Jaime de Montesa spoke out in defence of civil liberties. That was his crime."

"Silence! All residents of the city of Santa María of Albarracín of the Hebrew faith, regardless of rank, age or entitlements, are ordered henceforth to wear yellow circles cut from cloth, stitched prominently to their garments.

Their Royal Majesties order the exile in perpetuity of all persons of the Hebrew faith from the city of Santa María de Albarracín, effective in three months. Title to all fixed property held by Hebrews shall devolve to the Crown."

A man lifted his arms and prayed over the crowd, "'Hear O Israel, the Lord our God, the Lord is One.'" Judah!

His final "Amen" was drowned out by jeers and heckles.

"Murderers! In the House of God! Avenge Our Lady of La Seo!"

"Avenge our Martyr! How knelt the Saint-to-be, hands raised in prayer!"

"How his blood wet the holy stones!"

Then a chorus sounded the battle cry, "Blood for blood!"

Across the plaza, scuffles turned to brawls. From inside their cloaks, men pulled picks and axes. These they thrust from behind into men's necks and ribs to emulate the attack in La Seo. The stricken were reeling backward and collapsing in red pools.

"Death to the heretic!"

Strangers charged into the crowd on horseback, jabbing spurs into their steeds and swinging flails, aiming for the Jew who dared to pray. There stood Judah, undefended and unarmed. As the horsemen neared, a guard fell upon him. Judah turned, and before the flail struck, the guard clubbed the side of his skull.

The guard raised his arm and lunged forward again, the club aimed at Judah between the eyes. The eyes of destruction fixed on Judah seemed not the eyes of a human being. Old Haim, surging with energy, rushed the guard while his wife cradled her stricken son.

Then I saw Papa! He bent over Judah and touched his brow. As he reached forward he stumbled and fell onto Judah's breast. I broke through the crowd to join them. Papa was not breathing.

Rabbi Solomon dragged Papa and me from the fray.

Papa lay on the ground, his eyes and mouth open. I threw myself on him and did as he had taught, pressing his lungs like bellows.

"Come, my dear. You've done all you could. He'd be proud."

Bona helped me home to the empty house and settled me in bed. In a matter of hours, all our lives, mine included, irrevocably changed.

Rabbi Solomon arranged for the washing of Papa's body, and his white linen raiment and shroud. The outpourings of grief among the throngs of mourners who sang and wept took me by surprise. With the outpouring of condolences, during the week of mourning I was bereft but seldom alone.

At night, Bona brought me a dish of fish soup and olives. She held my hand.

"I never appreciated the good that Papa did. How his patients loved him.

How's Judah?"

"Worse. Each morning he has nausea, his head feels too heavy to lift and the room is spinning."

I visited Judah and the changes were painful to see.

"This is my trial," he said thickly. "I am going to a place in the back of my head where soon there will be no words."

We were losing him.

The last time I saw Judah, it was near the end. I don't think he knew me but I was there with him. "Blessed is the true judge," I prayed, hoping that Hashem knew what He was doing, that it was time for Judah's soul to leave this world. Personally, I thought his soul was needed here more than ever.

On the way home I took a turn and walked alone towards the Guadalaviar.

The streets were crammed with families, crying children, carts and livestock, heading in all directions. Rabbi Solomon, unbending in old age, refused to leave Albarracín and so did thirty families who vowed to stay with him. Perhaps to save face, the Town Council announced a grace period of another six months and held open the offer of a warm welcome to the parish of Santa María. How generous of them.

In any case, Rabbi Solomon and his thirty families said they were not going, and no guards stepped forward to enforce the edict. No one knew how long this truce would hold.

§§§

An ill wind rose. It set off across town, driving disunity before it. Haim was accused of cheating customers on weights and measures at his butcher's shop. Walking to his hearing he was pelted with eggs. Carmela had been partially correct. When violence against a group of people is condoned from above, it is amazing how fast things can change — for the worse.

The troubles were delaying the settlement of Papa's disposition. Upon a death, the rabbinical court would send officers into the deceased's home, and order inventorying and assessment. In most cases this was done at once. In Papa's case, by the time of his death most of his estate was in Híjar: the Albarracín house had been sold, and emptied except for his study.

Papa's scribe, preparer of Papa's final disposition and his executor, refused to travel. He said this was no time to leave his wife and children. As a Jewish resident of Albarracín, if he left town he might not be allowed to re-enter.

Isaq was heir to most of Papa's estate, being the only son, but he didn't seem to notice. He had departed Albarracín without regard to possessions except for the shards of my green lamp wrapped in a kerchief. He was working as a builder's apprentice in Híjar, counting his paces. They had never seen such intensity!

How well I remember the Synagogue of Híjar, built in the days of Papa's grandfather. I worshipped there as a child, on a night in mid-February. It was the festival of Tu B'Shevat, New Year of the Trees. In Israel, sap was starting to stir in the orchards but in Aragon the fruit trees stood bare against the cold. Bella and I climbed the stairs to the balcony. When the third star rose in the sky, we lit oil lamps. How our fingers sought the warmth from those plainest of clay vessels!

What I remember most, aside from evening prayer, were the arched doorways shut against the wind. Also, the arched windows. Each shuttered rectangle, nicely vertical, was crowned by an arc with vectors radiating outwards like sunrays, or the fanlike tracery of a lemon. Next, the arched ceiling that ran the building's length. In my child's mind, I turned it over and it was the keel of a ship that held us safe. I learned later, that was the night Reyna was born.

Isaq found work at once because new buildings were being raised in Híjar. To my surprise, the book-making trade was driving prosperity. Books were being made a new way, with blocks inscribed with letters. Eliezer ben Alantansi, a physician, had something called a "press." He already was "printing" the Arba-ah Turim by Rabbi Jacob ben Asher and planned to "print" the Torah in Hebrew. Papa's hometown, with its Talmudic school, was one of the leading centres in Iberia for printing and an illustrious future was predicted.

There was no one to anchor Isaq to Albarracín, anyhow. His esteemed Mahoma the Eldest was gone. Uncle Arabi had apprenticed him to the prosperous *de Rey* clan in the mudéjar quarter of Huesca, where he was bound to their landed property division. Bella remained overseas. No doubt she corresponded with Aunt Esther.

Dueynna felt it was not safe to return to Albarracín, where I was lodging with a widow. Eventually she relented, and we met at the scribe's office in Albarracín, without Isaq. She handed me a folded sheet —a letter from Esther that had been sent from Navarre. I opened it with a sense of foreboding, but instead of dire news there was news of a birth:

"Dear Sara,

I want you to know that I have received word from Bella. They are settled in Salonica after an arduous journey. Vidal has set them up in a fine house with servants. Jonah is a miniature of his father in every respect, which endears him greatly to his paternal clan. Bella has given birth to a second child, a girl named Miriam, who seems to take after Vidal's maternal grandmother around the eyes, though it is still early to tell. In Salonica, they are more free to worship and they have returned to the faith of our ancestors. That is all their news for now.

Sarita, for many years Magda has been keeping a letter for you and with the death of my brother-in-law Simon the time has come for you to read it. As you know, she never learned to read or write. The letter is in the hand of Orovida, who wrote and sealed it. I have never found Magda to be reliable in facing the truths of life. Even the disreputable Aldonza, her distant cousin, sees things for what they are better than Magda, but I advise you to retrieve the letter. It is rightfully yours.

I have not received word from you since Simon's death, may he rest in peace. Perhaps with the troubles our letters have been intercepted. I believe that despite the troublesome delay, Simon's disposition will be read soon. Simon intended to name Saul as your guardian until you are wed. Simon also indicated you might have marriage plans. If you do plan to wed, write me everything! If not, I will send for you whenever you wish. Send me your reply via Arabi the trader.

Always remember that I am your Aunt Esther. I love you very much.

Esther"

The scribe summoned Dueynna for a private audience. It should have been quick, because our laws forbid the widow to inherit: she was entitled to the return of her dowry and whatever share she had brought to the union. In fact, it lasted a long time. I was starting to care more about my lunch than Papa's legacy, when the door opened and Dueynna re-appeared, regal as usual.

The scribe called my name. I entered his chamber and took a seat. He adjusted his spectacles and read,

"I name my brother, Saul, resident of Navarre, to serve as guardian of Sara, bastard daughter of my former servant Magda Cruz and my nephew Aaron, deceased, until she marries. To the aforesaid Sara I bequeath my medical texts, apparatus and utensils, apothecary inventory including oil of myrtle, a pewter pomander, and my medical table and stool."

"The good doctor was most generous towards you," said the scribe. "Girls often receive only a few *sueldos*, and for a girl to be bequeathed books of any sort is unusual. Unless it is challenged before the rabbinical court, you are likely to receive your bequest."

On my return, the sitting room was spinning. I feared I would be sick to my stomach. I trained my eyes on Dueynna, seeking solace or at least affirmation, but she stared at her deerskin gloves and fingered her locket.

"My dear Reyna," I thought, "Where are you when I need you? You would have comforted me today. I miss you so much."

I retreated to my chamber at the widow's house. It was hard to comprehend. I, Sara, who had longed for a mother all my life, had lived my life under my mother's nose and never even noticed. I wondered who knew. Papa and Dueynna, certainly, and Aunt Esther and Uncle Saul. Was that why Aunt Esther came to inspect me as a new born, seeking family traits to link me to her Aaron? Perhaps even Bella. Would that explain her attitude? Carmela certainly had always known. What a nasty thought. And what did this make me? A fosterling, a serving-maid? Hadn't they always used me as one?

Who else would have known? Chaya Catorce, of course, whose business it was to know everything. The night in the season of roses, while Magda by the embers sang of lust, a scene had unfolded by Chaya's hearth as she revealed the secret of Simon's second daughter. The child of a promiscuous servant with uncounted lovers! It was what Dueynna needed to rid herself of me. She had removed to the house in Híjar. She had ordered Papa to leave me behind, and in his testament to deny paternity. Papa, smitten by Cupid's arrow, would do that much for her.

I took a breath and thought of Papa, I meant, Simon. What would he say to me now? No doubt, that my relationship with Hashem is my most important relationship. All that happens is for the best, even if we can't see why. The full intent of Hashem is never revealed. Simon would want me to feel gratitude. I recalled him saying, *"He who gives should never remember, and he who receives should never forget."*

I did not feel gratitude at that moment, neither for my parentage nor for the loss of Judah. In an ill-fated move, I gave hard kicks to my bed stand with my shoe. They must have been ill-fated, because moments later there was a knock downstairs at the door.

The widow's adolescent daughter clattered up the stairs. "They are not asking for us, they are asking for you, Sara. You are to receive them now, with no delay. Pay me first, and do not tarry packing your things. In good *sueldos*, please."

I pulled out my purse and placed some *sueldos* in the girl's palm. The smooth bits calmed her spirits.

"You didn't tell me who it is."

She didn't reply.

"Who is waiting at the door?"

"Miss Sara, waiting downstairs to escort you away, is the Holy Brotherhood."

§§§

Two constables of the Holy Brotherhood brought me to a staging post where they engaged four mules. Their haggling took time, which gave me the chance to watch them. One was tall and one was short, and neither had much intelligence about him. I realised each was calling the other Jesus. For whom was the fourth mule? Resting against a post, stuffing her mouth with fried egg as if she had no care in the world, was Granny Bigmouth.

It had been years since Granny Bigmouth, born Aldonza, had rapped on our door in her failed attempt to be our housekeeper. She hadn't changed a bit. She had reached that plateau in a woman's life between fresh and decrepit, which can go on for decades. I wasn't sure why she had been singled out for interrogation by the Inquisition in Teruel. Perhaps what goes round comes round and her meddling had come home to roost. Or, perhaps she had proven such a rich source of slander that she was wanted as a resource. What surprised me was the relish she showed for this journey.

"Aay, there you have it, I am being led off to Calvary by Jesus the Tall and Jesus the Short," she exclaimed as we were riding mules out of town.

The first afternoon, our guards drank watered-down wine from wineskins and ate bread from their satchels. There was scant water and no food for us. I supposed that delivering us in weakened condition might make us more pliable. As the road stretched on, my hunger and thirst grew and I slumped on the mule. My indefatigable companion rode alongside singing,

> "Of the four muleteers, the one on the mule with spots is my husband."

She kept egging me to sing, but I refused.

We stopped overnight at an inn. Granny Bigmouth and I were led upstairs under the eaves to a vile loft. It was stuffed with stinking straw crawling with fleas. Our guards raced down the stairs in such haste that we didn't hear them turn the key in the lock.

"Follow me, Sarita, and watch my cues. I will soon be the most indulgent granny you ever had, and we'll fill up your tummy, all right" whispered my new grandma.

The thought of food got me going again.

She led me downstairs and into the tavern. The guards were nowhere to be seen. The first thing she did, was to give all the customers a looking over. The men with women at their tables, she passed by. Then she paused. In a distant corner, poorly lit, sat a man hunched over his cup. Probably a carter, I thought —a large man big enough to control a team of oxen.

"Watch and learn. The quicker you follow my cue, the better we will fare on this trip of ours."

Granny took me by the arm and sauntered in his direction. She leaned against a wooden pillar looking twenty years younger, glanced at him sideways twice, and winked.

"Hello, good mother. What brings you here?"

"Hello, my son. My daughter and I, may the Virgin shed her grace on us both, are on our way to Santiago to bathe our Christian bodies in the holy waters of Our Lord."

The Virgin shed her grace? I hadn't heard every Christian expression in the book, but that one sounded odd.

Granny approached the table in a way that placed me to the man's left. She sat across from him. "A little bread and wine would be just the thing. Be a good gentleman, now, and order us some."

The bread and wine, after a day without rations from the Holy Brotherhood, were a revelation. I ate and drank heartily.

Refreshed, I decided it was the perfect time to sing. I broke into a Moorish ditty from Magda.

"Let me climb up to your cart, cart driver of my dreams."

My voice wobbled on the drawn-out notes. At this, my friend pressed his corpulent arm against mine.

He said with a smile, "Hello dear, look right here, have I a surprise for you!" As I glanced down, he pulled up his trouser leg to reveal a fleshy stump and a stick of dark wood. He watched my reaction.

I recognised the prosthesis from several of Papa's clients. The thought even weirdly occurred to me that I could examine his stump for signs of rot, but fortunately I didn't. Instead, I mumbled jovially, "I've seen these before, you know. This isn't my first time."

He grasped my thigh, proffered cheese and refilled my cup. The food tasted so good, I filled my mouth to overfull. "I've gone days with no satisfaction," I mumbled.

Whatever I said had immediate effect. He ordered fried meats and bread and helped me stuff my mouth. Then I remembered Papa's warnings about the perils of wine. I tried to steady myself, but I was already well supported by my friend's left arm.

I realised that his right hand was advancing considerably up my thigh. I tried to object, but only produced a hiccup.

At that point, our guards Jesus the Tall and Jesus the Short re-entered the tavern. Jesus the Tall pried me loose from the tightening embrace of my companion.

He shouted, "But I bought meats, cheese, bread and wine for them. Pay me back!"

Granny Bigmouth entered the fray. "The problem with you men is that you carry your organ around on the outside and that's making you stingy."

The carter retorted, "The problem with you women is that you carry your organ around on the inside and that makes you conniving."

"I'll pay you back," said Jesus the Short. He delivered our companion a kick in the pants that left him in need of a medical exam.

That night, I went to sleep in the stinking hay with bugs crawling over my stomach, without a care in the world. When I woke, I tried to say the morning blessings in that pile of straw but couldn't remember them. I had a headache and was in dire need of potable water, of which there wasn't any. I turned down the proffer of some soured wine from Granny Bigmouth.

"Ay, Granny Bigmouth, I am ground to bits. I can barely manage."

"Keep your spirits high, girl. You never know, there might be hearty food and wine around the next bend, or a firmly built man."

"I think we are finished with firmly built men. We are, after all, in the custody of those two," I said gesturing toward Jesus the Short and Jesus the Tall.

"Girl, what we are having, is an adventure."

§§§

My interrogator had a mole on his cheek. Beneath the mole, where his barber's blade had passed, a black shadow. Hair, I knew, but I couldn't help thinking it was poisoned blood under his skin. Like the bad blood between us. But I mustn't show it. As I waited I gathered my wits.

Granny Bigmouth had given me a piece of advice the night before. "Whatever you do, act stupid. Never act smart before authority. Act stupid, and men will value you for making them feel smart. It is the same with the examiners. Good luck."

He commenced in the name of the Father, Son, Holy Ghost and the Holy Catholic Church.

"Have you learned something of the Bible?

"No Sir, I mean, yes Sir."

I was trying my best to imitate Susana at her servant interview.

"What have you learned?"

"Proverbs, Sir. I can recite them, Sir."

"Everyone knows the Proverbs. Anything else?"

"The Psalms, Sir."

"Can you recite any?"

"No Sir."

Telling him I had committed to memory the Psalms of David through the years with Solomon the Aged was not going to help me.

The Dominicans conferred among themselves.

"If you read one to me, Sir, it might help refresh my memory."

My interrogator began to recite a Psalm in Castilian.

"Can you finish it for me?"

"No Sir."

This was close to the truth, as I knew it in Hebrew.

"Do you know your Christian blessings?"

"Yes Sir."

"Recite one for me."

"May the Virgin shed her grace on our Holy Bodies, Amen?"

"We will try again. Tell me, how did Our Lord Jesus Christ ascend to Heaven?"

"Lord Jesus climbed to Heaven on a ladder, dressed in red."

"Who taught you thus?"

"The old woman who milked our goats."

The Dominicans conferred.

"For a baptised Christian, your Christian education is sorely deficient. Can you explain why?"

"Yes Sir."

"And why is that?"

"My father, Sir. He beat me in the head."

"Your father beat you in the head?"

"Only when he was drunk, Sir. There's also another reason."

"What is that?"

"I received baptism only last week. I mean, I only learned I was baptised last week. Growing up, I was deprived of a Christian education. Deprived most sorely, Sir."

They conferred once more.

"Why did you buy meat from the Jewish butcher?"

"Because my father, Sir, he drank and lost the money he collected from his patients. The Jewish butcher gave us credit."

"Do you trust in God and believe in Heaven?"

"Yes Sir, with my mouth and my heart and the rest of me."

"Then we will concern ourselves with your soul. Guards, you may remove her."

I was almost home free. I should have left things alone. Instead, my confidence and my curiosity since the night at the tavern got the better of me.

"May I ask you a question?"

"What type of question?"

"Regarding the salvation of my soul."

They conferred. The examiner warned, "Before you speak further, I must advise you that if you do not accept Jesus Christ as the Messiah, if you lack the wisdom to acknowledge the Christian truth, your soul is lost and damned."

"My question is about the apple."

They raised their eyebrows.

"Is the fruit of the apple tree just the fruit of the apple tree?"

"What else do you think it could it be?"

"Something splendid that could bring us joy."

This was met with a stunned silence. "My child, this dialogue will determine the future of your soul. I must make sure you understand the import of your question. Can you tell me the meaning of the apple tree in the faith of the Hebrews?"

"In the Torah, the apple tree grows in the Garden of Eden. It brings the knowledge of good and evil."

"You may restate your question."

216

"Is the knowledge of good and evil and of the pleasures of the flesh consistent with the knowledge of God?"

A rush of whispers ensued among the Dominicans. One announced, "My instincts are correct. This young rose of youth that we have here is not a human child. She is the Temptation Incarnate, the work of the Devil himself, come to pervert our Christian men. In these extraordinary circumstances, we must call a halt to this proceeding."

But first, they covered the eyes of the statue of Christ with a cloth. I had a sense bad things were coming.

Then they did what the carter never got the chance to do. Holding a leather whip, the guard forced me onto my stomach and pulled up my robe.

"You see this stripe of black hair across her shoulder blades? Scribe, make official note of this. This is the mark of the Devil."

I don't recall anymore, beyond rage and regret at my foolishness. They threw me back in my cell, to await no doubt the auto de fe at which my name would be called from a roll. In fact, my fate had not gone unnoticed, and special arrangements were made for me.

$\mathcal{A}$MONG THE DOMINICANS

The Year 1487, as counted by Christians

$\mathcal{I}$N AUGUST THE INQUISITION released me into the custody of the Dominican Sisters of Santa Inés de Zaragoza. I arrived in the city with two nuns on a sultry morning in summer. We passed near the Plaza de la Seo, venue of the bonfires. I smelled smoke from oak logs burning, the same as Christians use to smoke their pork. Was I inhaling human flesh? I buried my face in my gown.

The elderly nun said, "Jaime de Montesa is to be burned at the stake today, a just punishment for planning the murder of Pedro de Arbués, Inquisitor of Aragon and Canon of the Cathedral of La Seo."

"So is his daughter, Leonor de Montesa. All her life she donated oil for the Shabbat lamps and fasted on the Hebrew fasting day. She will not be given burial. Her ashes will be thrown into the River Ebro."

"God be praised, twelve judges of the Inquisition will sit on the dais under the banner of the Holy Office, and Saint Dominic himself will preside in spirit."

"The executioner's lad is stoking the flames! Will the Saint weep with mercy as he watches Jaime de Montesa burn?"

"Yes, Saint Dominic in this life was the embodiment of mercy. He pleaded for the souls of sinners who rejected the salvation of Christ. Even now in heaven they move him to tears."

"Leonor's death is merciful, is it not?"

"Our revered Canon de Arbués, may he rest in peace, taught that in separating the wheat from the chaff we must administer the most severe justice. 'It is a medicine of mercy ordained for the health of delinquents.' So that others may live in Christ, Leonor must die."

"More than die," tittered the younger nun, her eyes widening as she leaned across me. "She must go to Hell!"

"Sister, control yourself." For a few moments, the elderly nun reflected. "'The light shall be dark in her tabernacle, and her lamp shall be put out with her.'"

Silently I promised, "No place of rest, no home, no hearth. I'll hold you in my heart."

We followed the riverbed till it ran dry and the city wilted into fields. There in the brutal August sun rose the pile that housed the Convent of Santa Inés. I was sickened by the sun, the prattle of the nuns and the burning of the pavement through my esparto soles.

My thoughts turned to Leonor. With each step I felt the flames that would lick her feet, catch fire and shoot in streaks up her skin as if galloping along the King's Road.

Leonor sat in a leather chair. Her gaze unnerved Bella. She was speaking. Yes, about the Plaza de la Seo and its storm clouds of dirty birds. I felt sick. When the door of the convent opened into darkness, I did not know where I was, and I fainted.

§§§

How Adam suffered for an apple that he took! The people of Teruel suffered too, and it was for a letter, a letter that they wrote the King. The townsfolk likened themselves to grains of wheat being sent to the mill. The Monarchs and Pope were acting as the millers, and in so doing they did wrong. Separating the wheat from the chaff is reserved for God at the end of the world. Amen, I say. The Monarchs and Pope must not serve as scribes in the Book of Life, much less judge our souls.

Life inside the convent was like being nailed to a millwheel that turned relentlessly, day into night into day into night. Driving this wheel were Holy Mass, the Liturgy of the Hours, recitation of the Rosary, and dedication to personal prayer. We rose before dawn and had prayer sessions and Mass before breakfast. Afterwards came work period, mid-day prayer, devotions to Mary, noon dinner, private prayer, work period, and more devotions. Finally, supper and evening prayers.

What saved my sanity was the Liturgy of the Hours, devoted completely to recitation of the Psalms. The Psalms were a solace though they were corrupted with an ending called the *Gloria Patris* which praises the Father, Son and Holy Ghost. We recited these Psalms several times a day, and with the addition of personal prayer, I kept a channel to Hashem. I hoped He would forgive me for the rest of it: the prescribed prayers to their Messiah and Holy Trinity, crossing myself, genuflecting, candle lighting and endless bead counting in honour of the so-called Mother of God.

So much *hevelayud* —such a lot of nothing!

Mother Inmaculada ruled the convent. She had a smooth, practical face that belied her large body. Her spiritual and physical energies prevailed over the Sisters. She believed in the Holy Book of the Christians, of course, and took literally their teachings of the miracles wrought by Jesus. What came across strongest was her sense of identity and purpose: her relationship with Jesus Christ, Messiah and her Saviour.

At mealtimes I wished I could hide. I often gazed heavenwards, though the heights of those pillars gave me vertigo. I took to fancying that there was a little ship that waited beneath the arched ceiling vaults, well-armed, on which I could sail away! In fact we sat in rows with our feet firmly on the ground captained by Mother Inmaculada herself. There was, we all knew, a place at table for her pet novice, whose task it was to watch us with eyes of a hawk.

The bread was of dark flour and millet. In my mouth, it lay down and died. The daily stew of rabbit, I spat into my serviette. Not to mention the sausages of pork offal. This followed from the Dominican vow of poverty, but I never saw the virtue in their dining. No one was fooled by the in-the-napkin trick —it was one of the first things the hawk-eyed girl watched for —so I suffered with each swallow of unclean food. The cooks put pork in every main dish, as if on purpose. Each day it was a ghoulish reminder I was unfaithful to *kashrut*.

How I esteemed Lady Brianda, who had stood up and fought. I had vowed to be that sort of person, but the moment I found myself outnumbered, I donned a mask and hid myself behind it, salvaging my faith in secret.

The nuns gave me the name María Encarnación. I didn't like the name, in part because my very own stomach was busy making pork into flesh and that was an incarnation too vile to contemplate. At least the name might not stick. I was a postulant, at the lowest rung, and the name was temporary. So, I hoped, was my confinement.

"I see you are coming along well with your Psalms and prayers, María Encarnación, particularly the Liturgy of the Hours. This sets you apart. Few of our novices worship as devoutly as you through the Psalms, or show as much fervour in their personal prayer which is a fundament of the Dominican way of worship."

"Yes, Mother."

"Worship is a central tenet of our Dominican philosophy. For us, one's personal relationship with the Creator is the most important aspect of spiritual development. I expect to see more reverence at the Holy Mass and fervour in recitation of the Rosary.

With those two elements, you will come to understand that this nunnery is an earthly paradise."

What irony. Mother Inmaculada, like Lady Brianda, emphasised the primacy of developing a personal relationship with God through prayer. However, I would never walk her spiritual path. I would never forgive the

Dominicans for burning our faithful and our holy books. Nor could I understand why they place so many intermediaries between man and God, starting with Jesus.

Everywhere in the convent I found the image of their suffering Christ. He jumped out at me in the chapels and the churches. The first thing I saw when I looked towards the East, where the Torah Ark should be, was Christ on the Cross. There he was, between God and me, painted and made of wood by men, which is idolatry.

The Church was saying everywhere I looked, "Here is your personal Saviour. Believe in Him or your soul is damned." Weren't those the words of my interrogator?

I wished I could speak freely to Mother Inmaculada. Of more interest than Christ, is how the Dominicans believe the connection with God comes about. She told us of Humbert of Romans, an early Master General of the Dominicans, who first admitted women as members of the Order. He taught that some Sisters will never feel the connection because God does not choose to reveal Himself to all of us in this life. Even if there is none, we should go ahead with our devotions and content ourselves with our cloistered earthly existence.

I understood this, in part. As Papa taught me, no amount of yearning can connect us with the Almighty. Only Hashem can reach out to us humans and bridge the gap between Him and His Creation.

But why Jesus, Mary and the saints? Why this cloistered life? How I yearned for my freedom. How I yearned for things that were so near and yet, at the same time, so far. Above all, the city's Great Synagogue with its congregation of thousands.

The Christians of Zaragoza have their Virgin of the Pillar whose fame is spreading across Iberia. We have our own pillars in Zaragoza. Inside our Great Synagogue are three aisles lined with colonnades. Aunt Esther says the pillars rise to a ceiling rendered in delicate detail. Just beneath, the walls are adorned all round with sacred inscriptions in calligraphy of blue and red. Above all, in letters of resplendent blue.

Oh, to see the Synagogue of Zaragoza and its letters of blue. May it endure throughout all generations!

§§§

I am ashamed to say I allowed the Church to have its way with me. Outwardly, I professed to love their Christ. I told them I believed. So naturally, did the Sisters accept such an unnatural thing!

I was especially clever at their mass. I knelt when they rang the bell for prayer and when they elevated the Body of Christ. This, I knew, was important because Donosa Ruiz of Teruel was denounced for not doing it. I recited the oration of the Salve. I faced the altar and took care to watch as they raised the host and the chalice.

With outward reverence I received the consecrated host. I swallowed the wafer but not the miracle. How could the Eucharist be transformed into Christ? To me, the host was only a piece of dough. A small one.

My secret comfort, unbeknownst to the Sisters, was envisioning the wafer as a tempting treat. *Buñuelos* at Hanukkah? Haman's Ears at Purim? Not quite. These wafers were circular and flat like those thin, sandy biscuits served by Bella at Calatayud. I imagined the Sisters in their black and white habits lined up along the altar rail, eating bite-sized anise rounds.

Each time the priest raised the host, he praised the Trinity, just as Lady Brianda had explained to me.

Inwardly, I affirmed the presence of one, indivisible God. When I saw the host, I said to myself, "I see the piece of bread, I believe in the Lord instead." And when I saw the wine, I said to myself, "I see the wine and bread, I love you, Lord, instead." My simple verses reassured me. When making the sign of the cross, what I really was doing was whispering "Adonai." So easy. A child's game.

One morning, Mother Inmaculada had me summoned from prayer. This was unusual. I wondered what nonsensical thing she had up her sleeves.

"María Encarnación, do you know the meaning of the sign of the cross during mass?"

"Yes, Mother, we accept the mysteries of the Eucharist."

"I will demonstrate. Watch carefully."

She brought her right hand up to her forehead, then lowered it to her shoulders and down to her ample breasts heaving under the folds of her habit.

I mirrored her movements.

"Sanctity, María Encarnación. Connect with the Divine."

I thought, "It is Hashem who reaches out to us, not the other way round."

"Reach out to the Divine."

"In my own way," I thought.

I closed my eyes. I was a child again, back in Rabbi Solomon's home with Papa. The frontispiece of the Zohar. This time, I touched the parchment with my fingertips, spread wide a concealed curtain and went into the picture. I touched the marble pillars and the grapevines.

"You are trying, María Encarnación, but you have not made the leap. Prepare yourself for the great joys in store for you."

"I don't understand."

She smiled. "Your Celestial Husband to be. Think of the mystical marriage of Saint Catherine. The first time you reach out to Him. Yes, it is time I start preparing you for this. Awe in each motion, every touch."

No, I would not think about touching their Christ. I fought it while she came close and stared fixedly into my eyes.

"Reach out to Him as Your Betrothed. Imagine your holy union. Saint Catherine extending her finger. The clove pink of betrothal. The touch of consummation.

Stroke your crucifix."

She placed my finger on the wooden effigy, smooth and hard. I vowed not to feel it. I sought refuge in the strictest memories of childhood, the vineyards of Yom Kippur.

"Stroke it with your fingers. Feel it. It is there inside you."

Long minutes passed. With her fingers guiding, I stroked absent-mindedly. Then somehow my mind went searching for grapes on the vine. Greedily.

There is something intimate in a grapevine when you push the leaves away. Especially where it bends with the weight of a cluster. The vine flesh looks smooth and tender. I stroked up and down without nicking my nails.

"Yes, I see it in your eyes now. Make the connection longer. Stroke my crucifix."

My eyes on Mother Inmaculada, and hers on mine, I lengthened my reveries. My mind started glowing with carnal flame. After stroking that crucifix, what I did at her urging I prefer not to remember.

I crossed the cloister mindful of the clanging of bells, striking again and again, and as they peaked they seemed to say, Come, Come, Come to Jesus."

I had not wanted to come to Jesus.

In chapel I positioned myself by the wall. My right eye, visible to all, shone with devotion. I heard droplets to my left. Were raindrops falling from the ceiling? No, those were my own tears. They flowed from my other eye and down my shoulder.

Those tears from my left eye were the most painful of my life. They hurt more than my tears when Papa died. My tears of mourning had flowed freely. Everyone mourns who has a heart, and in our tears we are not alone even if we think we are. These tears were different. They flowed from hurt to my soul.

At mid-day I arrived at the refectory for our main repast. Mother Inmaculada stood in the doorway holding a basket of peaches and white grapes.

Grapes, sign of the coming redemption of Israel. The Talmud says so. I felt faint.

"Make the sign of the cross, and then you may have a peach with the rest."

Slouching from hunger, I brought my hand to my forehead —my left hand. I did so deliberately. Our souls do not come down to life on this earth to be damaged.

"For shame. To use your left hand is to scorn the cross."

"I am hungry, Mother. I didn't think."

"We know how you are when your stomach is empty, María Encarnación. Weak. Your mind and your stomach walk hand in hand. That is how it is with you.

Here is your penance. Make the sign of the cross one hundred times. Before each meal."

She looked me in the eyes. "You know why I am doing this, don't you?"

The words sprang from my mouth, "so no one will ever know."

"Correct. So no one will ever know that your Christian upbringing was less than perfect."

"Weak," I thought, "that was her word for me, and she is correct. If I had courage, I would have defied her with words."

For the rest of that year, I awaited with foreboding a summons from Mother Inmaculada. She did not call for me. My left-handed signing must have cooled her ardour. Instead, convent life taught me the sign of the cross. I could make the sign of the cross at any time, even when roused from dreams of peaches and sugar at Sukkot. Criminal dreams! Sampling our fruits and candies was punishable. In Teruel girls stood accused.

I heard tell of plazas in Italy where stooped Sisters tied sugar candies to trees, on silken threads. They cradled small girls in their laps, and placed confits in their mouths. A foretaste of earthly paradise! How a glutton like my infant self, ravished by sweets, would have craved the convent. Our Sisters saw nothing wrong. I disagreed.

The convent might have been an earthly paradise for some —but only for believers in their God, Christ Jesus the Messiah, the Holy Ghost, and the Virgin Mary. That was absolutely fine for those who chose to pray the beads and marry Christ, but not for the rest of us, Christian or Jew. Believe me, there were many Christian girls who didn't want to be there either.

As Uncle Arabi had taught me from the Qur'an, "there is no compulsion in religion." Arabi the trader might have traded in opium and silks from a store front, but he had a better grasp of religion than these people. I dreamed of escape. Naples. The passage was cheaper than to the Levant. I would minister to the well-to-do in Naples with medicines and wise maxims. I intended to put into practice, as a pharmacist, the best of Papa and my grandpa. I also intended to taste those pastries Lady Miriam had talked about.

The Year 1488, as counted by Christians

I SERVED MY DUTIES in the convent apothecary, which was stocked with as wide a range of remedies and ingredients as anywhere in Europe. The sole item for which they could not match Papa and me on quality was opium. Theirs didn't come from Uncle Arabi. As in Papa's practice, opiates were used only for the dying. Other pain relievers and calmatives were widely used as many of the Sisters were old.

Soon I was wedded to the mortar and pestle. No one would believe how much pounding and grinding I did each day. At least I had company of sorts. In the cupboard, I found an old lamp with four spouts, each painted with eyes with lashes. They watched me as I pounded.

At last, work with meaning! The Dominicans valued pain relievers because they didn't believe in pain. They thought it distracted from the study of the Christian texts, hence our well-stocked dispensary. The Franciscan Sisters were said to view physical suffering as one of their main pathways to God. This gave me shivers.

One summer evening, Mother Inmaculada called me to her cell. I lit the four flames of the lamp and they flared as I walked down the passage to the dormitory. I prayed "Thy Word is a light unto my path."

The Mother was formal, as if nothing had happened.

"I see you have brought me my lamp, María Encarnación. I carried it here as a girl."

"It reminds me of home."

"Do I understand correctly that you have medical knowledge?"

"I was trained by my father, a respected physician, to prepare and give medications. I visited patients with him, women and children."

"Have you cared for patients?"

"Yes."

"Including the dying? Are you skilled at giving narcotics?"

"In fact, yes."

"Look at something for me. I am not at ease summoning the male physician, as you will understand, nor do I wish others to hear of this.

These walls have ears. Do you promise discretion?"

"I promise."

She revealed her breasts. I lowered the lamp upright so as not to drip oil, and by its four flames, its eyes and mine spied a glowing flesh-coal.

"I first noticed pain while kneeling at prayer. At first I dismissed it. Last week, though, I mounted a mule. Each jolt told me something was wrong."

Her version left out much of the story. Evidently she had been tending that rotting tumour day and night, masking its smell with oil of sage.

"Nausea?"

"Yes."

"Do you have tenderness on your left flank?"

I palpated her side and found a mass. The same illness had taken Orovida. On our rounds, Papa had taken care to teach me its symptoms.

"I can prepare a salve to bring down the inflammation, and a tonic to regulate your female humours. Most important, whenever you need it, a draught to ease discomfort."

Poor Mother Inmaculada, it was only months before she would leave her body and this illness would be painful. I could see that she knew.

"I must depart for Cuenca on church affairs. I do not desire a large entourage. You will attend to me." Church affairs when she was dying? Perhaps she wished to ride under the sky and sun before she returned to God.

"We will take the Aragonese route, down to Teruel, continue to Albarracín, and cross the mountains to the city of Cuenca. This is not the usual route, but I insist. We will stop in Teruel on the way."

A stroke of luck, but I needed a plan of escape. I didn't want to jump from the skillet into the fire.

§§§

No one suspected me of nurturing dreams of flight. In fact, no one thought of me at all, which was good, except for Mother Inmaculada herself. She was becoming clingy. After all, I was the one who brought her the medicinal draught each night. At times, there was something more. I hoped to use this to my advantage.

One night, when she called me to her cell, she wanted to talk.

"I harbour no illusions as to my prognosis, not for an instant."

I lowered my gaze and nodded.

"Dying is like anything else in life. It must be done well."

"The Rabbi taught that we must bring life's warmth to each task we undertake."

"Nonsense. I have a duty towards you which it is time to discharge. Now is the time, before we advance to a more potent arsenal against the pain which I bear in the name of Our Lord, Jesus Christ.

As you may know, I was born in Albarracín and raised in Teruel. I have a first cousin who entered the Seminary, Father Antonio Solís, may he rest in peace.

My dear cousin served God all his days and was a distinguished cleric. Father Solís as your parish priest cared deeply for you, María Encarnación."

I struggled to keep a straight face.

"He has included you in his bequest, to receive a small item of personal property. After his death, it was delivered to me here for safekeeping. Now I give it to you."

In her palm was a box lined with crimson velvet. Inside lay a cross of pale gold, softly scalloped at its four extremes, a double tracing around its edges —Father Solís' own priest's cross.

"There must be some mistake."

"Trust me, there was no mistake. I read his instructions in his own hand. I myself have done my best for you, María Encarnación." She handed me the cross and looked at me with feeling.

"I remember when you first crossed our threshold. I saw a girl of high spirits, intelligence." She paused. "An entrancing beauty."

Had it been love at first sight? Cupid hovering in the convent's entry hall, with his arrow pointing at the Mother Superior? Or did she see in me her own youthful self?

"I also saw defiance. Many girls have come and gone throughout my lifetime, and the age you were then is the most difficult to teach. I preferred you to learn by immersion."

I fingered the cross.

"Father Solís already had written me of your exceptional intelligence and abilities. You are literate, at least in Hebrew, and you learn fast."

I thought, "So that's how I ended up here. Solís intervened. And primed her enthusiasm."

"Ours is the first Convent that the Dominican Order established on the Iberian Peninsula. The Founding Sisters came from France two hundred years ago. While there are

236

many facilities for men, we have few for women. Our Order is expanding to embrace women and girls.

We have need of capable and diligent Sisters to direct our growth from the highest ranks of our organization. Also Sisters who can write tracts in the vernacular. Your Faith must also be refined. There are teachers who can guide you in Zaragoza, but I feel your future lies in Cuenca. An illustrious future."

She assumed I believed in Christ! Was she like Papa, preferring not to face inconvenient truths? Or was she set on making me into someone of note, like Aunt Esther with Bella?

"Your Vestition Day will wait until Cuenca. The Bishop will preside, of course, and I will plan the festivities."

"Oh no, not my betrothal to Christ," I said to myself, "I wish she didn't look so happy."

Her face was radiant. "I think in your case, a feast is appropriate to welcome you as a novice. On the other hand, I do not approve, María Encarnación, of the postulant who walks in procession to the church dressed in silk. Sobriety is in order."

I had heard of girls parading down the path to their Vestition ceremonies, dressed for the occasion in silver brocades and pearls, their hair loose round their shoulders. At church the nuns changed their robes quickly to novitiate black, and they turned pale as death. I shuddered. In any case, I had no intention of becoming a convent bride and hearing the clang of iron gates closing behind me. We would depart in two weeks for Teruel, where I had dispensation to visit my sister, Carmela.

§§§

Riding out of Zaragoza we passed an auto de fe that lent a grave symmetry to my arrival and departure. It wasn't people they were burning this time, it was books. In the plaza, logs were laid out criss-cross, and an elegant youth tossed in one after another. Beside him lay volumes in gold-tooled calfskin binding, black, chestnut brown and ivory. One lay on its bed of coals, its pages open to the sky. A great volume of the Zohar gazed at the Light one last time.

All round stood worthy men and at the forefront, two tonsured Dominicans in black and white. One held his hands in prayer and the other pointed his hands toward the flames like their Christ teaching a lesson, and so deep was their piety that their faces looked innocent. I could imagine those gold halos of Christian painters encircling their heads. It amazed me how people doing something so wrong, could think they were doing God's holy work.

We left the city and rode down a long, hot road into the hills. Overhead two columns of geese were flying south. Farmhands were combing blond tresses of flax, and the close-cropped fields were gold. From time to time we stopped at the roadside to buy peaches. The peaches with yellow flesh ripened in September just after our New Year, and I thought sadly that I would miss the blowing of the ram's horn three years in a row.

Mother Inmaculada and I were accompanied on our journey by two tonsured monks. Fray Anselmo was a determined man who wore spectacles. He was assisted by Fray Vicente, who was young and soft-hearted with a taste for the open road. Though he was distant in manner, his eyes were attentive to my needs. Sometimes when Fray Anselmo wasn't looking, Fray Vicente brought me peaches, exactly as I like them, a touch over-ripe.

Fray Anselmo had matters to attend to in the town of Daroca. We arrived on a Friday. As we rode down a street in the Christian quarter I detected the savoury aroma of *hamin* wafting through the shutters. I swallowed hard despite myself, and then glanced to each side to see if either of my Dominican guards had noticed. Perhaps Fray Vicente —with him, I could never be sure. I worried for the inhabitants of the house.

Papa had told me that following the Disputation of Tortosa, the Jewish community of Daroca was obliterated. This was in Grandfather's time. To the Christian organizers of the Disputation, it was a victory. Then, after a while, new Jewish families began moving into town, where they became neighbours of converso families who began relearning our traditions. For the past several years, the Inquisition had taken aim at the judaizers of Daroca.

Each morning, Mother Inmaculada and I entered the Church of Santo Domingo where she would kneel in devotion before the altarpiece. At its centre, a golden-robed Saint Dominic with merciful eyes presided from a throne framed with niches and spires. In each gilded niche stood a young woman, miniature yet regal. These beauties, seven in all, nested round the Saint in robes of umber, hunter green and ruby, cut and coloured like stained glass.

The brightest wore a skirt more vermilion than red, her fine neck set off by a dark fitted jacket, white collar and velvet snood. She gazed at a book, her eyes averted. She reminded me of Bella.

"Look upon this work with awe, María Encarnación. It is the work of Bartolomé Bermejo, the foremost artist of our land. It is said to be the finest painting of Saint Dominic in all Iberia. He fills my soul with gladness."

"Yes, Mother, most impressive."

My eyes were overcome by gilt, brocade and ornaments.

"Inspirational," she corrected. "Such love in the eyes of this most merciful Saint. Stay here with me. You will do well to contemplate the founder of our Order in all his glory, and also the Virtues Personified."

"So that's who those girls are," I thought. "Better to end up over the altar as Faith, Hope or Charity, or even Prudence, Justice or Fortitude, than the Adulteress Woman. Poor Bella."

This altarpiece, rendered expertly, must have cost more than the one at the convent in Huesca where our Bella presided. It was quite an investment. Was the money spent to win back the hearts and minds of wavering conversos in a town where the church not long ago had declared victory over Judaism? I sat next to Mother Inmaculada secretly counting the gems on the saint's crown. When I tired of that,

I stared with apparent reverence at his throne, imagining the pinnacles of agate of the future Jerusalem.

In October we left Daroca and rode south down the valley, following the river. We stopped in a grove of pines and rowan trees, the pinnate leaves turned creamy yellow and their branches weighted with red sorb apples. They were more beautiful to me in their praise of the Lord than the gold and garnets of the altarpiece. I laid down a blanket of brown homespun and settled Mother Inmaculada to sleep. The rowan trees, fully fruited, made me giddy.

Magda had taught that sorb apples from the tree are sour and in ancient times had stood for prudery, but with putrefaction attain the sweetness of unbridled passion. Curious, I began pulling down branches. I was plucking sorb apples and cradling them in my skirt as they tended to roll about a bit, heedless of propriety. Fray Vicente, who had tarried in Daroca, rode up to us.

"María Encarnación," he hastened, "those sorb apples are too astringent. They will make you ill."

"I am storing them in my satchel to rot, as these become sweet only when corrupted."

Fray Anselmo did not seem to be listening. He was examining the bark of the pines with a glass lens.

"Fray Vicente, these hills offer better prizes than sorb apples. By my observations, they are rich with truffles and mushrooms. While Mother Inmaculada is sleeping, ride down this trail and ask the local folk to find me truffles."

"The peasants are not likely to gather truffles. They are viewed with suspicion hereabouts."

"If truffles are not to be found, ask for the fungus that grows on pines, aspens and the silver fir. Make haste and do not take refreshment. We need to make progress before nightfall."

"In Albarracín, my mother used to dry sorb apples and soak them in wine. Not truffles. She always said that truffles are manifestations of the Devil."

"Nonsense. They were much prized by the Greeks and Romans," corrected Fray Anselmo. Then I remembered. Truffles can be useful in remedying deficits of a masculine nature.

Fray Vicente gestured for me to follow him till we were just out of sight and I willingly left off collecting sorb apples.

"Take some morsels from my satchel, María Encarnación," offered Fray Vicente with a hint of a smile.

I put my hand in the satchel and to my delight found *rosquillas* from Daroca, cruller puffs with a hole in the centre and delicately fragrant with sweet olive oil.

I ate two straight away.

"Delicious! And now you must tell me why you do me these kindnesses."

Fray Vicente looked both ways for Fray Anselmo, and not seeing him, spoke openly for the first time.

"I was born on a country estate on the outskirts of Granada. My grandfather was Muslim, from the Taifa.

He raised horses for the emir's stables. Then we ended up on the wrong side of palace rivalries. We removed north into Castile and lost everything. When I was a boy my grandmother favoured me. She said I had the looks of the Arabs."

I didn't know what he was talking about, as in Albarracín everyone looked the same, but the cruller puffs demanded decorum so I held my tongue.

"I am a reluctant Dominican, María Encarnación, and have no ambitions with them. To tell the truth, I pray for all the faiths." He looked me in the eyes.

"María Encarnación, do you dance?"

"No."

"From the way you held the sorbs in your skirt, you know something of the moves."

"My sister, Bella, dances. Danced."

"I don't wish to dance with Bella. I want to dance with you."

"You had sooner dance with a horse."

He approached. "The finest Andalusians dance. Didn't you know? They prance to music. We taught them, for the emir."

"Fray Vicente, you forget yourself. Remember who we are."

"If I may be so bold, you have something of the girls of Granada in you. If I were a man of courage, I'd take you away from here, but alas, I am not. As things are, I assuage my soul by riding under the skies."

Fray Vicente, who had drawn close, stepped back. He handed me more crullers and went in search of fungus.

The nearby banks of the mountain brook, beneath yellow aspens, seemed the perfect place to savour cruller puffs. I picked my way over the embankment of pebbles and autumn crocus. Fray Vicente was not of my faith, and the Dominicans forbad us from speaking. All the same, I couldn't help thinking that Fray Vicente was a coward. He would not have impressed Magda. I lingered over the last crumbs, then cast off my clogs with cork soles and sank my ankles into the water. I stretched my arms behind my head and lay back on the rocks.

Through the arms of an aspen in its autumn finery, Fray Anselmo spied on me. Then I heard his glass lens hit the ground. He made rustling noises. He seemed to have a hard time searching. At length his face reappeared wedged among the willows, his round black spectacles giving him an owlish look.

Fray Vicente returned later bearing a large sack of turnips, which grow with vigour in the valleys of Daroca, and a few paltry specimens of tree fungus.

Fray Anselmo made a great show of my transgression.

"Do you know what this child did in your absence? She bathed her legs in the stream! All the way to her thighs! Those are parts of a woman's body that the Lord in his wisdom requires to be covered."

Fray Vicente's eyes widened for a moment, but he said nothing. As for me, I lisped the lyrics of Magda's pastorela.

Fray Anselmo gave me a scolding that lasted for hours, and assigned acts of penitence. I was supposed to fast for two days, but Fray Vicente made sure I wasn't hungry. It was a relief things hadn't been worse, alone there by the stream with those men. No doubt they would soon forget all about it.

§§§

I sounded the knocker on Carmela's door. It was opened by a girl smartly attired for a servant. I looked at her again and my toe stubbed the iron rim of the threshold. Susana hadn't changed a bit since she had left us years before.

"Sara, it is good to see you. You are risen so high in this world!" She cast an admiring glance at my Dominican postulant's garb and ushered me into the receiving room.

A fire blazed in the hearth, casting light up to the plaster between the ceiling beams. Carmela was seated with embroidery in her lap, looking as healthy as always, but there was a difference. She was slower and more careful as she rose to greet me. As her gown straightened I discerned a fullness.

"Welcome, Sara, it has been a long time."

"You are changed, Carmela."

"I would say you are more changed than I, with a new appreciation for black and white," she smiled. "It's amusing to see you dressed as a Dominican."

I blanched with longing to escape the robes. Soon, I promised myself, if my plan succeeds!

"And you have a new appreciation for the colour green."

Even her coif was trimmed in olive.

"Green, the colour of the Inquisition! Hurrah for the Green Cross!"

"I don't see what the Inquisition has to do with it."

"The green cross, the olive branch, and the sword of justice! Surely you know its insignia."

"To me, green evokes Magda with bare feet in the grass. How is she?"

"Laid to rest, one year ago. She passed while sleeping. Mother never wished to live into decrepitude, as she used to say. She had comforts in her last years of life. I made sure of it."

"I appreciate that, Carmela. Beloved Magda, may she rest in peace."

"Above all, I made sure she received a proper Christian burial. Her bones lie under the floor of the Church of Santa María, thanks to the intercession of Antonio."

So Magda ended up under those suffocating tiles. She had such a horror it would end this way. So much for her dream of being buried in a meadow in virgin soil.

"Speaking of burials, did you ever hear of old Belenguer and his wife Clara? Surname was Acho."

"The Acho family is from Teruel, but I never hear of those two."

"They were before your time. Died almost thirty years ago. Anyhow, their former serving-maid has come forward to the Inquisition, God bless her. Thirty years after she left their home. Her mind is still razor sharp.

Those conversos hired the rabbi in Albarracín to teach their children to read Hebrew, at their house in Teruel. For Sabbath, they cooked a Jewish dish with hidden stuffing. And when the old man died, they sent a coffin to the Christian church with a log in it, and buried him in the Jewish cemetery. After thirty years, justice has been done."

"Surely they let him rest in peace."

"Solibera led an exhumation in Teruel's Jewish cemetery. Bravely he entered that unhallowed ground, invoking Christ and sprinkling Holy Water.

You can imagine their long faces. Their caretaker pulled up the rotted coffin, forced it open with a pry bar, and there lay that old fox, Belenguer."

What jurisdiction did the Inquisition have over the Jewish cemetery? Belenguer's baptismal record no doubt had been the sword, and even so they must have forced the arm of Rabbi Simuel.

"At least Solibera didn't force Belenguer's own son to dig him up. The Inquisition does that sometimes.

You need to understand how necessary this is! Antonio said bearing punishment in public for his wrongdoing, even dead, is the best gift Belenguer Acho can give mankind. We dressed the coffin for his bonfire."

"And his estate, confiscated?"

"Of course. His descendants don't deserve one. They will never hold public office, either. Solibera has seen to it.

Sara, there are more glad tidings. Brianda Besante is dead. I can speak with you frankly, now you are with the Dominicans. The only way to preserve the purity of our Christian flock is to kill every last Judaizer now.

Brianda poisoned the minds of our young. She is dead and, just as important, discredited."

"How did she die?"

"She shuffled to her execution, her head bent in remorse for the pain she had caused to Jesus Christ, our Lord and Saviour."

"Not bloody likely!" I exclaimed to myself.

"Sarita, I can read your face like a book. It's in the official transcript. All converso convicts executed on that day, walked to their deaths the very picture of contrition, heads bowed in shame, weeping with love for Jesus."

I thought, "They drugged her or they lie, or both. They well know the dangers of creating a martyr to the converso cause. They deny us the consolation of her heroism and the strength of her example."

For one last moment I saw Lady Brianda at the Festival of Lights, backlit with flickering stars, poised to guide our souls. I knew she had died nobly. I prayed that as Reyna had foretold, her flame would be a beacon for centuries.

A wave of sleep washed over my hurt, and I sought a place to rest.

§§§

When I woke, Carmela was at her sewing. Susana brought refreshment.

"So much family news! I'll bring you up to date.

Jaime is living down in Frías. He is a married man, you know. Mari Pilar. She was quite the surprise. Their eldest son is three years old now and they have two more."

"Tell me, Carmela, did you send Susana to us as housekeeper?"

Carmela smiled, "At first, to tell the truth, it did please Mother and me to see your household adrift after her dismissal. But as time wore on, no one presented herself to take Mother's place aside from dear Granny Bigmouth, a noble soul but advanced in years, so we conferred with Father Solís on your behalf."

"With Father Solís?"

"Of course. He thought it would be a fine arrangement if Susana went over to you, for a while at least."

"Did Father Solís pay you, Susana?"

"Every week, equal to what the doctor paid. You don't think I would work for nothing, do you?"

"And Father Solís paid you to spy on me? And to forget to shop at the Jewish butcher?"

Carmela broke in, "Now Sara, that isn't fair. Father Solís was always so concerned for your Christian soul."

"I suppose, Carmela, that you will ask the purpose of my visit. I admit, I have come to Cella on an errand."

"An errand? Something that concerns me?"

"First, tell me the story of our mother and Father Solís, from the old days."

Carmela's face assumed a faraway look. "When Antonio Solís was a youth, he did not aspire to the priesthood. He came from a long line of master builders. His interest was construction of foundations and that sort of thing."

I smiled, thinking of a youngster with the same proclivities.

"Antonio possessed an intelligence beyond his years and, how do you say it, an aesthetic sensibility. He was impressionable to beauty, and at risk because he fancied no woman of flesh and blood could ever capture his heart."

"Pride comes before a fall."

"Yes, it was then that he met Magda at age seventeen. She was a beauty, such as neither of us has ever seen. One that comes only once in a generation, and beyond that, she was always one for pleasure, to put it frankly."

This much was plausible.

"She had perfect skin, dark eyes the colour of violets, and hair that shone and rippled like wine. Antonio Solís, the youth, fell deeply in love, I think for the only time in his life, and I should be a good judge of that.

Magda, on the other hand, was always wary of Antonio. It was an instinctual thing. There was something cold about him. The bottom line was, she didn't trust him."

"Yet he persisted?"

"A more single-minded man you never did meet.

Finally, Magda agreed to marry Antonio, but on the condition that the marriage ceremony follow the rites of the conversos. The detail is, for two generations Antonio's clan had passed as Old Christian."

"She was an unfortunate choice for an aspiring Old Christian."

"Antonio was so smitten with Magda that he wrote her a letter promising that they would have two marriage ceremonies and that the second ceremony would be in the Hebrew way. Magda agreed, pleased by Antonio's yielding on the wedding. Soon afterwards, though, Antonio's dreams of marriage dissolved."

"What happened?"

"Oh, a handsome young blade rode into town on his fine horse. The youth belonged to one of those wealthy families from Castile. The story goes, that early one morning in spring this young blueblood was riding his steed along the banks of the Guadalaviar some distance from town, returning from a night of pleasure, when he spied Magda bathing in the river."

"The water at that time of year? It must have been refreshing."

"He spied Magda, with her long hair the colour of wine from Rioja gleaming in the pink light of dawn, her hair caressing her rounded shoulders rising innocently from the water. Her lacy white chemise lay tossed on the rocks like the river's own foam. Beside it among early snowbells and primroses lay her best lavender skirt, beneath plum trees in bloom and the skies of Albarracín."

"Let me guess, the man cast spells and the dawn had vigour?"

"How do you know?"

"Oh, it was just a song she was singing to herself one night in the kitchen."

"Well, our young lord dismounted, knelt at the water's edge, gazed at the swellings of her upright tits so enticingly concealed by the water, pronounced her lovely in the Queen's own Castilian, and offered her his sweet white wine."

"And the rest?"

"The rest is village history, because they were spied in the act by a plain young woman on her way to work in the fields who had always hated Magda for her looks. Her name was Aldonza and she lived by the ramparts."

"The young Granny Bigmouth?"

"Yes, who later would deliver the goat milk to your home before Magda was hired. She assumed she would get the housekeeper position and never forgave Simon or Magda."

"She might have spread word around, Carmela, but I doubt that it's village history."

"You'd be surprised. The pen is more powerful than the sword. She composed a couplet that I promise you is known to every twelve year old boy in Albarracín today."

"Tell me."

"Do you really want to hear it? It's in poor taste."

"Certainly."

"Well, you asked for it:

'When the river runs high, we can tell by its foam,

The knight and Magda, they made their own.'"

"That's bad. I had no idea she was so handy with words."

"She's not called Bigmouth for nothing."

"Was there a child?"

"Funny you should ask. No. But Magda was disgraced and her value went down on the marriage market, so to speak, like the stained Moorish cloth of song. That is why in the end she accepted Juan Sordo, whose propositions she had always rejected. When Jaime and I were approaching maturity, Juan Sordo died suddenly. Your Papa took Magda in as a housekeeper out of respect for her grandfather whose Torah was burned at Tortosa."

"And Antonio Solís?"

"Antonio broke off the engagement and entered the Dominican seminary in Zaragoza. He never trusted a woman again and his manly appetite was insatiable, until he met me, of course. His only requirement was that his bounty be implausibly beautiful."

"That must have disqualified many women."

"Yes, but his bastard children are mostly good looking, and that says much."

"He supported you and Magda in his old age?"

"Beyond old age. He has bequeathed me full and free title to irrigated fields in Cella. Wheat, rye and barley. Grazing land and sheep for our child when he is born."

"When Magda settled in as housekeeper to Simon the Doctor, what happened? Why were there so many rumours about her in the market when I was growing up?"

"My mother was at that stage of life where she was enjoying a late summer, if you see what I mean. My father had died, and she felt full of life. Juan Sordo used to beat her, Sara. She deserved some pleasure."

"Why did Juan Sordo beat Magda?"

"Juan Sordo insisted he had married a Christian, not a Jewess. He said it was her Judaizing that made him violent. He beat her and when she confronted him, he said she deserved it. It worsened with time. Towards the end, he refused to eat any cooked dish resembling *hamin* and more than once he broke the casserole."

"Did he ever beat you?"

"No, Sara, I have always taken care to be a good Christian."

"And Father Solís came back on the scene, assigned to the Church of Santa María?"

"Perhaps. She was understandably vague on the subject with me."

"What about young Aaron, Saul's son?"

"Aaron was only sixteen. He had got himself in a scrape at home and Uncle Saul had sent him to Simon till things cooled down. The problem was, there was no cooling down Aaron. Magda was old enough to be Aaron's mother but still attractive in a ripe sort of way."

"Would Aaron at sixteen really sleep with the housekeeper?"

"Wake up, Sara. He got Esther's kitchen girl with child."

"Why did Father Solís assume I was his natural daughter?"

"A man with unintended offspring at every stop between here and Navarre would never doubt his own virility, even less when fulfilling his desires from youth. Not for a moment."

"It was Father Solís who arranged my baptism?"

"Yes, he did baptise you, by his own hands. But your Christian progress stopped there."

"Why?"

"Mother said it was because of that letter Antonio had sent her years back promising a second wedding by Hebrew rites. She went to Simon and fell on her knees, revealing her transgressions with Aaron and begging forgiveness. She gave the letter to Simon, and pleaded for his help in saving you from the Sisters of Christ. Simon went to Saul and then they both went to Rabbi Solomon. That was the end of it. You stayed where you were, as a sister to Isaq."

"Why was Papa Simon so sure I was not the child of Antonio Solís?"

"Silly, the same reason as the other. Every man to his own virility. I mean to say, Simon would have assumed that his nephew, in the prime of youth, was more vital than old Antonio."

"Why did Orovida accept me as one of her children?"

"Orovida was a saint. She would have accepted you from a basket on the doorstep. Perhaps she saw you as her son's companion."

"I imagine Isaq was odd from the start."

"His infant cry sounded like a cat yowling. How Orovida worried, hearing that incessant sound from her son."

I winced. My former role as Isaq's nursemaid sister still pained me, I guess because I had wanted Papa Simon to love me for myself, the way he had loved Bella. Then I remembered the object of my visit. I turned to Carmela.

"Speaking of old letters, Esther told me that years ago Magda entrusted you with a sealed letter addressed to me, of a confidential nature."

Carmela let out one of the unbridled laughs that must have attracted Antonio Solís in the first place.

256

"Yes, confidential, certainly!"

"Do you know what happened to it?"

"If I tell you, how will you thank me?"

I reached inside my habit and produced with a flourish the solid gold priest's cross of Father Solís.

Her eyes widened, though she retained composure.

"Agreed," and she reached forward, snatched the cross, and swept it towards her across the table as if winning at a game of cards.

"Now, tell me, the letter. Where is it?"

"I don't have it. I promised only to tell you what happened to it. Those were your words. Anyhow, it was burned."

Why did Magda burn it?"

"Magda didn't burn it. I did. It was the night when Jaime brought Magda home from being dismissed by the doctor. Such a kind doctor. You should have seen how defeated my mother was. Yes, she was my mother too, you know, but I missed her all that time while she cared for you and those people. I found my own way while she cared for you, haughty Miss Sara."

"I'm sorry, Carmela. I didn't know."

"It's over now. A year ago, I would have avenged myself, but now, with a child of my own on the way, I feel more forgiving."

"If you keep that gold cross and don't tell me what was in that letter, you are certainly still avenging yourself. Tell me now, you must have read it."

"True enough." She yawned. "I tossed the letter into the fire, but of course I opened and read it first."

"What did it say?"

"Sara, I was more upset than curious. I wanted it to burn. The truth is, I just glanced through it."

Carmela yawned again, and moved closer to the fire.

"You are not the child of Father Solís, at least Magda didn't think so, and a woman has her ways of knowing." She resumed her needlepoint. The silence stretched into minutes. She was thoroughly enjoying herself.

"You are not Aaron's child, either, and certainly not Saul's. Uncle Saul was always so shabby towards you, Sara. That ridiculous fuss over a nougat tower pieced together by his cook, the night he brought Reyna the blue sparkler from Florence! Broke my heart."

"Save your tears, Carmela. Though to tell the truth, I've always wondered why Saul treated me, well, differently."

"Short of Bella, Saul is the most adroit social-climber I've ever seen. So gallant when he chooses. A perfect Sir Roland at Roncesvalles when he wooed Esther, so Magda said."

"Magda would say that."

"You know what I mean. Fancy a humble man from Híjar marrying into Esther's clan, as rich as any in Aragon, as rich as an Abravanel!"

"What difference did that make?"

"The ones who climb the highest draw the strictest line beneath them. The line had to be drawn, so to speak, and as your mother was Magda, he drew the line at you. Saul saw you as a servant."

"Never mind Saul. Who is my father, Carmela?"

"There's the detail. I can't recall the name. Why don't we both rest by the fire, so I can think. By the way, have you eaten?"

Carmela ordered my mid-day dinner. A savoury dish, legumes stewed with saffron from the nearby hills of Jiloca, and I observed with satisfaction now that Carmela bossed Susana, there were no hairs in it. As I ate, she stitched a crown of daisies onto a russet ground, reversing the wool and pulling at the knots.

I sang , "*They worked and worked their needles, the daughters of the king,*" followed by "*One hundred damsels spinning gold.*"

Spinning gold? Of course! Carmela was spinning tales. It dawned on me that she didn't read the letter because she had never learned to read! I wanted to see how she'd weasel her way through.

"Do you remember?"

"Remember what? Have you had enough to eat?"

"The name of my father."

"It was a name commonly used among the Hebrews, a given name. I think it was Simon."

"I don't think so, that was Papa's name, well not Papa, Simon the Doctor."

"Did you ever consider the possibility?"

"No, Carmela."

"Why not?"

"I knew him well and you didn't."

"With a man, you never know. There is a detail I omitted from my narration, out of delicacy for your feelings. Simon also was intimate with our Magda. Aaron might have been, ahem, a fig leaf."

"Are you sure the name was Simon?"

"Not at all. As I was saying, I can't quite remember."

"I've got it, Carmela! I know how I was fathered!"

"How?" She looked baffled.

"By Rumpelstiltskin, the Jumping Dwarf!"

I realised there was no need to guess. I was free to name my own father.

"I choose Papa Simon, the one who chose me."

I thanked Carmela and was rising to leave when she took my arm, not unkindly. "I remember the name now because it struck me as odd. Magda told me herself. The name was Solomon of Toledo."

260

Seeing me out, carrying the weight of her pregnancy, Carmela stood in the doorway clutching Father Solís' cross. I could envision that priest's cross passing from generation to generation, proof that the Father loved them.

§§§

I was returning to the convent, on the streets of Teruel, when I came face to face with a familiar figure. Arabi the trader, in the city on business. He almost walked past without noticing me. Then I remembered. My habit!

"Hello my teacher, peace be upon you."

"A hundred hellos!" We said nothing further in the street. He led me down an arcade, entered a shop, and closed the shutters.

"You are with the Dominicans?"

"Not for long, I hope. I need a plan of escape. But first, tell me, how fares Isaq? Does he continue in Híjar?"

"Isaq has inherited your father's house and is pursued by a widow with five daughters. They are immune to his tantrums."

"And Dueynna?"

"Dueynna will have nothing to do with them. She remarried and resides in a handsome townhouse in the Jewish Quarter of Belchite."

"Mahoma the Eldest?"

"He is a property dealer in Huesca, branching into Islamic finance."

"I often wonder about Azizah."

"Azizah's husband had the temerity to depart without warning for Cádiz, and the wisdom not to return. He is no doubt ready for a younger wife or two, and prefers to remove to his ancestral Morocco. Azizah is too high brow for him. It was always a mismatch. She didn't have much choice of whom to marry."

The incident in the stable! After my year at Santa Inés, I understood Solís' power.

"Azizah has decided to start a new life in Túnez, her ancestral home. She will travel soon. I cannot accompany her, but I am making arrangements for her to travel to Valencia, her port of departure.

Valencia is crowded with families of Jewish origin desperate to board outbound ships. Azizah, with her tendency to panic, will need a nurse to calm her nerves. You will be perfect."

"How can there be an exodus of Jewish families from Valencia? The Jews were expelled from that city long ago. Uncle Saul did his business outside the gates."

"The conversos are the ones trying to leave now. The Inquisition in Valencia is working on a much larger scale than in Teruel, with hundreds of proceedings under way. They are setting up for more. I would not be surprised if during my lifetime one thousand die."

"Oh no, Uncle, surely not that many."

"Do you recall when I first taught Isaq, seven years ago? Since then, hundreds of conversos have burned to death in Seville. The Inquisition in Valencia is systematic and can easily overtake Seville. The best plan of action for you in Valencia is to board ship.

"Do ships sail from Valencia to Naples?"

"Of course. Why Naples?"

"I have a mind to go there. If I ever escape the Dominicans, there will be a bounty on my head."

"Don't always assume the worst. As a sage once said, a comb has myriad ways to part the hair on a head. That includes your head, too," he said with a smile.

"Where is Azizah now?"

"In Albarracín. In a matter of weeks, she will depart. Her first stop will be the village of Terriente. Amir will attend to some matters there for me."

"If I manage to meet her in Terriente, may I join her entourage all the way to Valencia?"

"You are more than welcome. As I always say, prayer rugs can face in any direction. My team will supply you with a travelling outfit, and you will change from one robe to another. Do you remember your Arabic?"

"Enough to get by. But there is something I need from you, if I am to break to freedom."

"Your wish is my command."

"I need three packets of a small quantity of opiates in a medicinal preparation. They must be hidden in a concealed pocket stitched inside the burka, and delivered to the inn at Calomarde, to be held for my arrival. We are a small party of Dominicans and we are not travelling fast. Is Mahoma the Youngest still with you?"

"Yes, but this should be entrusted to Amir. All will be done as you ask. In return, you undertake to care for Azizah and do everything in your power to ensure a calm and secure trip for her."

"Uncle, I promise."

"Is there anything more?"

"Would you send word to my Aunt Esther in Navarre that you have seen me? Without interception?"

"No sooner said than done."

"I have some questions, about the past."

"My time is precious, and so is yours. Be quick."

"Did you ever do business with Solomon the Aged?"

"Yes, we imported works of art from the Levant."

"Where did you first meet?"

"Many years ago, in Túnez. We were in related lines of trade and he was seeking finance. He was interesting, a Jew from Toledo who quoted Shia poetry. But that was that. When I set sail from Túnez, I never expected to see him again."

"But you did meet again."

"It was very odd. I was visiting your Uncle Saul at his home in Navarre. We also did some deals together. I stayed in his home, a well-built house with a huge hearth. His children were charming."

"His children?"

Saul did get around. I doubt you knew the extent of it. He kept a wife and two young sons in Tudela, blonds like your Reyna, and another nest just outside Valencia in Paterna with the sister to your Dueynna, brunette. One snowy night at his home in Navarre there was a strong rapping at the door. Saul opened it, and a stranger enquired for Saul in Hebrew."

"Did Uncle Saul know Solomon the Aged back then?"

"No, he didn't. That was the odd part. The Saul whom Solomon the Aged was seeking turned out to be a different Saul entirely, who owned the house next door.

They were standing at the entry, and his voice sounded familiar, so I approached and we recognised each other from Túnez. With Solomon's characteristic affability, he treated me like the oldest of friends."

"How did he come to live in Albarracín?"

"At my invitation. Albarracín is at a safe distance from the Teruel duty office. I gave him discrete connections to the wealthiest Muslim traders in Valencia. He was old and broke, but full of dreams. Perhaps there was some business we could do."

"Would you tell me how Solomon met Magda, our former housekeeper?"

"Of course. He was in high spirits the day we managed to close on the sale of a Persian miniature. I remember it well. A huntsman in a tunic the hue of mustard seed with a falcon on his hand, astride an astonishing white Arabian. What exquisite brushwork! The horse was dappled with cream."

"I don't mean the miniature, I want to know how they met. When was this?"

"Almost a year before your time. Solomon, who had been penniless for weeks, received a windfall of *sueldos*. He went to the pawnshop to redeem his ebony walking stick, and asked the pawnbroker to recommend a comely matron."

"Was the pawnbroker old Jacobo Catorce?"

"The same. Solomon made a little joke about having endured months without satisfaction. Jacobo joked that it had been years given the time the ebony cane had been in his shop. He recommended in the household of Simon a certain Magdalene, proficient, discreet, and not too dear. Enough! My child, what's the use of these stories? Do not search in the past to find out who you are."

He smiled as he opened the door. "Go in the protection of Allah."

"Uncle, *Shalom aleichem.*"

As I wound my way through the arcade, I thought about how Solomon and Magda met. This was how I was engendered, most probably. Cash paid for the act. I pictured Solomon. He would have been old but perhaps with more hair on his head. I felt so low, like a trash heap. And then I recalled the words of Hillel the Elder, "If I am not for myself, who will be for me?" My beginnings are not my fault, nor do they define me. My soul can find joy in Hashem just the same.

The church bells rang and I realised it was time to return to Mother Inmaculada. She was overdue for her unguent and medicinal draught. Nor could I be late for Fray Vicente. He had been tasked with standing guard over me all day. I had told him it would not be necessary. I had promised to meet him outside the convent before the third star appeared in the sky.

When I reached the convent archway, Fray Vicente emerged from the shadows with a basket of peaches and black grapes. He extracted from inside his cloak a thorny rose the colour of a blush. I don't know where he found it so late in the year. He placed it delicately atop the fruit, mumbled something about this being the last of the season, and offered the basket to me. When I extended my hand he shifted his fingers and our hands met, within mystical orb that encircled us both. We stood silently for a few moments. He then rode off on the orders of Fray Anselmo on a long journey somewhere to the north.

§§§

Mother Inmaculada and I arrived at the inn outside Calomarde, the last town before Frías. The corruption was gnawing deeper, for she was wincing with every jolt of the mule. In our chamber I arranged her beddings, her cross and her beads. I also lit her lamp with the four flames, which I had carried with me from Zaragoza.

As I watched her lying on the cot with the stillness of the very ill, I wished I could bring her a steaming cup of Arabi's Syrup of Good Cheer. Unexpectedly, she turned her face towards me with her eyes shining, but she did not speak.

"Mother, are my ministrations enough, or has the time arrived for something stronger from my arsenal?"

She smiled but her breath was laboured. "I am ready, María Encarnación, for the next stage of my life's journey and the draughts it may entail, but don't give me much. I must arrive at Cuenca in possession of my faculties. I must still have the mental acuity and energy to command respect. Your path will be distinguished, María Encarnación, but first I must open the way." Her head fell back on the pillow.

"I will be direct with you. I have treated this stage of illness before. You have reached the point where a small dose of narcotic will help."

Her eyes widened and her pupils constricted with fear. I took her hand.

"Don't be alarmed. The dispensary at the Convent did not stock the active ingredient. I took the liberty, while we were in Teruel, of arranging in advance the delivery to this inn of a small quantity of opiates in a medicinal preparation. The packet should be with the innkeeper downstairs. If you will permit me, I will fetch it now and administer relief. You will sleep only until dawn, I promise you that. I will add it to your wine only with your consent. "

She lay with her eyes closed and then clasped my hand. I felt a gentle swooning, an inner warmth. I felt as I had upon seeing Reyna's letter on the bedside table. I wondered if Mother Inmaculada was hearing the Helmsman from the shore. Perhaps not yet, but soon. He was calling.

"Your answer?"

"Yes."

I fetched the package from the inn keeper. All was as requested —one burka with a pocket concealed in a sleeve, and three doses. Plus three *sueldo* coins, courtesy of Uncle Arabi.

The Mother was resting. I poured a small stream of the preparation into the cup of wine, careful with the dose. I brought it to her lips and she drank.

She requested that I recite the 23d Psalm, which I managed in Latin. She closed her eyes and slept. I recited it once again, in Hebrew.

"The Lord is my shepherd. *Adonai Ro'i.*"

I changed into the burka and walked to the door. I stopped to look at her one last time.

There she lay, struggling with pain and exhaustion, when she would have been more at ease at home at Santa Inés. She was fighting to remain in possession of her faculties till she could set me on the path to an illustrious future in Christ. And here I was, pretending to have procured the opiate out of solicitude for her, when I was planning to walk out that door and abandon her. Yes, Fray Anselmo would return her to Zaragoza, and she would most probably live to reach there, but I would break her heart.

"She has her path to God, I have mine. There is no compulsion in religion, not even for reasons of sentiment."

I imagined her wake when her time came. The room would be lit by elongated tapers of white wax, and nuns would say the rosary. Their prayers and supplications for her soul wouldn't be directed to God, or even to Jesus, but to the Virgin Mary. I wondered why the Christians need intermediaries to help departed souls reach God. I snuffed the flames of the lamp and left the room.

Outside in the courtyard the moon waxed high, bathing the well and corral in silver. This was not a good sign. Hunched forward, I followed the frosty hedgerows across the pastures to the forest edge, avoiding the road. In the forest I breathed freely the fragrance of the pines. The needles would do well inside a pillow for Mother Inmaculada and the frozen juniper berries for her salve.

Why was I thinking this? I had to make my way to Frías by this forest path, to the second-to-last house before the road to Cuenca.

An arm grabbed me from behind and a hand clapped my mouth. I was trapped by highway men. They must have watched me leave the courtyard in the moonlight. There were two of them, one big and one slim.

"What's your name?" The big one spoke in Aragonese.

"I am called Zahara," I replied in my best Arabic which wasn't very good.

"Zahara, shut up and come with us." The other led a captive Christian boy, a farm lad of about fourteen.

The path veered upward. Wet walls of rock rose to one side, and down the other was sheer cliff. This trail followed the gorge and was hewn from the rock face. As I progressed, it grew steeper. Often, I had to grasp an overhang and hoist myself to the next ledge. My captors did not help me. The light of the moon overhead revealed chinks for my footing. The waters roared.

There were moments when I feared that my life would end on those rocks. Well, going on an adventure doesn't mean a happy ending, I started to think, and then I recalled Uncle Arabi's verse about the comb.

"There are a myriad possible outcomes to this night," I said to myself. "One might be death, but even if I fall into the water below, that might be a beginning. As Papa taught me, Hashem does not reveal the full reality to us in this life."

The rushing of water was near. The larger of the captors, who was behind me, forced down my head and gave me a shove. I landed at the entrance to a cave — the same cave as the day of the picnic.

The big one frisked the boy. His boss called him "Fats." They spoke the Arabic dialect of the high Sierra of Albarracín. They were angry because the boy had no money.

"No coins, I kill you. That's the law around here."

Fats sliced the youth's throat and dragged him away. The boy fell to the depths with a plash.

I was next. Fats frisked me. I held my breath.

Fortunately the *sueldos* were in an outer pocket. On finding them he stopped searching. He never discovered the secret pocket Azizah had stitched inside.

"How many *sueldos*, Fats?"

"Three. Lousy yield. What do we do with her?"

"Slave trade," he yawned, "take the torch and look her over."

Fats held the torch up to my face and pulled off my veil.

"Is she plump?"

"No, thin as a pullet."

"Is she blonde?"

"No, brown hair."

"Maybe she has blue eyes?"

"No such luck."

"They got plenty of those on the other side of Gibraltar. She won't fetch two camels in Tetuan."

"Do you want her tonight?"

"No. Do you?"

"Me neither."

Fats raised the torch one last time and held it to my face. I almost jumped. In the light I recognised the face under the flesh and the beard. It was Jusef Pacheco.

In the back of the cave, his boss pulled a rug out of a saddlebag and a pipe for hashish. He lit and inhaled, stretched, and closed his eyes.

"Jusef," I whispered urgently in Hebrew, "It's me, Sara, the doctor's daughter from Albarracín."

"I don't know you," he replied dully.

"Yes, you do. Don't you remember Jaime and Isaq whom you used to tease?"

"No."

"Remember the Tenth Plague?"

"No."

"He's playing dumb with me," I thought, and then I saw in his eyes that he was addicted to opium.

"I can tell you what your own mama used to say to you every morning up on Crow's Peak."

"How dare you speak my mother's name? You shall pay with your life!"

I gave my best imitation of his archaic Hebrew.

"May the milk of goats be sufficient for your food."

"Sarita!"

"Jusef!"

"You need to get me out of here. Now. I need to get down to the village of Frías."

"No way. He'll kill me."

"I can get you opium."

He was suddenly alert. "I don't believe you."

"Listen, Jusef. I started as an apothecary but switched to dealing. I have access to Arabi's finest from Ifriquyah, of medicinal quality."

"How soon can you get it?"

"In as long as it takes you to get me to Frías."

"You swear?"

"By the milk of your mother's goats."

And so it came to pass that I road horseback down to Frías with the most feared bodyguard in the sierra.

We dismounted by the gate to Jaime's pasture. I folded my arms inside my burka, slipped my left hand into the pocket sewn in the inside, and opened my palm, placing under his nose a small packet of opiates.

He snatched it.

"Now I have to kill you."

"No you don't."

"Yes I do, I need something to take back to my boss to show him you're dead." He stroked his jowls. "At least your ears."

"I have a better idea. Here is my last dose of opium. Give it to your boss and tell him you traded me to some thugs. He'll be happy. Anyhow, you owe me a favour."

"Favour? For what?"

"For the fritters in the hay crib, the Ears of Haman."

Jusef shrugged, took the proffered opiates and rode away.

A single light was shining from Jaime's house. I crept toward it across the sheepfold, to the barking of dogs. In the yard I was accosted by an odd-looking pup with an exuberant tail. Mari-Paws leapt forward from behind her offspring, jumped high into the air and licked my nose. I pushed open the door.

Jaime was seated at a kitchen table, holding an infant, lit by familiar casserole lamps. In the lamplight, his face looked older.

"Jaime! My brother! It is good to see you at last! I have travelled far for this moment."

At first he did not recognize me dressed as a Muslim, ringed by Mari-Paws who was circling frenetically.

"Mari-Paws must be seven years old by now. Remember when Saul brought her home?"

Then he laughed. "Sara, you do look odd in that burka. How did you get here?"

"I have escaped from a small party of Dominicans at the inn at Calomarde."

"Escaped from the Dominicans? From a comfortable life with a full belly? You always were original. There is hunger in Aragon and many would like to be in your place. But come, what is your plan?"

I felt proud to have an answer of my own.

"I plan to travel to Valencia and from there set sail to Naples."

"What will you do in Naples?"

"Support myself by dispensing powders, as always."

"I am glad to see you have found courage, Sara."

Jaime was terse as always. "Is there anything I can do to help within my power, which is limited these days?" He looked fondly at the sleeping infant.

"Deliver me from Frías to the village of Terriente, without detection."

"That much I can manage, but you need to know the danger. It's a rough ride for a girl. Between here and Terriente are steep mountain paths, and bandits."

"Jusef Pacheco and his boss?"

"How did you know?"

"Never mind the bandits, they are asleep in the Land of Nod."

276

As I waited by the hearth, the church bells struck midnight and I realised my escape had occurred coincidentally on the last day of the year as the Christians count. This year the Dominicans certainly had counted out my year day by day, like a hand dealt by Fate, but there I was, about to taste my liberty.

Among Muslim Friends

The Year 1489, as counted by Christians

In TERRIENTE WE RODE along the river past dark blue ice, black branches and marsh-grass singed in the fires of sunset. Jaime halted under the archway of a door shot with iron studs. It opened onto a spacious room with the largest hearth I had seen since Bella's manor. I was led to the women's quarters.

"In the name of Allah the Beneficent, the Merciful.

Welcome, Sara, our home is yours." Azizah rose in welcome, wrapping me in her ample arms, and I embraced her with my puny ones.

"'Praise be to the Lord of the Universe, who has created us and made us into tribes and nations, that we may know each other.'" Azizah beamed.

"Sarita, what a lovely surprise!" Fatima came dancing to me.

Then I noticed a figure by the hearth, silhouetted in the firelight. It was Xemci, Mahoma the Youngest's sister. I didn't know if I was glad to have her along on this trip. Xemci was unpredictable, and I didn't need any surprises when caring for Azizah.

"Why is Xemci here?"

"She insisted on coming along to keep us girls safe.

Uncle won't pay her passage to Túnez, so we will leave her behind in Valencia when we set sail. Don't worry, Sarita, she won't be on the ship with you and me."

"I'm not going to be on the ship to Túnez with you, Azizah. I am going directly to Naples."

"Of course, Sarita, of course you are. Túnez will be just a stop on your way."

"I'm going to Túnez?"

"My cousin Arabi has everything arranged, including passage paid in full. We are forever grateful to you for reviving me in the square, and besides, I need you with me on the crossing."

"How long does Uncle Arabi plan for me to stay in Túnez? I don't want to live in a harem!"

"One month, more or less, and then Fatima's brother Amir will come to collect you. You won't stay with us in a harem. Arabi has arranged for you to stay with your own people, in a prosperous family. The same is true in Naples. He has found you a position with a merchant who used to trade with Saul, who needs a nurse for his daughter."

I was about to protest, when Fatima broke in, "Praise Allah —I am to be married! I am sailing to Túnez to meet my betrothed!"

"Will he bring you gifts of striped silks and rose water?"

"He is wealthy. As for you, I have a very special gift — unfold it!"

I unfurled a small prayer rug in blue-green and pale orange, with the interlocked quatrefoils and eight-pointed stars of the Muslim weavers of Cuenca. Inside each leaf of the quatrefoil was a tiny fleur-de-lis.

"On the road, you will pray at the same times as we do, to your Adonai, of course. My rug matches yours. We will be sisters."

Fatima and I climbed the stairs to our sleeping quarters.

"Sarita, do you have clothes for the wedding?"

"Your wedding?"

"No, the wedding in March in Mirambel. My cousin is marrying her sweetheart. We will travel up to Mirambel and attend the wedding, before crossing the Maestrazgo to Castellón and the Valencian plains."

With nostalgia I recalled my silk frock from Bella.

"Nothing but the outfit I am wearing."

"We will attend to that tomorrow. I suggest velvet in hazel and chestnut brown with a fitted bodice, sleeves slit to show your chemise, and ribbon trim round your skirt."

"And my sash? We mustn't forget my sash!"

I was in jest but she took me seriously.

"Perhaps a belt enamelled in red, black and gold. We wear them mid-waist, you know, and wider than you are accustomed. Your cap and veil should be hazel with a crimson border."

"Will you wear a dress of similar cut?"

"My inspiration is Granada. I will wear a robe of yellow damask patterned with carnations, light yellow on saffron, with purple trim at the sleeves. Underneath, a crimson tunic, white silk pantaloons and velvet slippers with silver thread."

She paused. "Can Azizah hear us?"

"No, she is still downstairs, but she will come up any moment."

"Azizah has a necklace from Granada with three golden acorns. Let's see if she will lend it! I think my veil will be aquamarine and of course I will wear dangling filigree earrings."

"You will be wearing such finery in Mirambel? Shouldn't you save it for your own wedding?"

"My nuptial outfits are secret and will be a surprise. You must wait to see my red velvet from Samarkand. Promise not to sail for Naples from Túnez till you have seen me wed!"

"That depends on when Amir fetches me."

I shouldn't have said that. Amir doted on his sister.

Azizah joined us. "Are you handy in the kitchen?"

I hesitated, recalling the cabbage I served Papa. "Yes, in the kitchen I serve well enough. Better yet, in the dispensary

I am a marvel to behold. No one can pound roots, leaves and seeds with such dexterity."

"Is that what you did, in the Christian convent?"

"Absolutely. I was first in the dispensary of the Dominicans for pounding in the mortar. My calluses, from years at the pestle, are the hardest in Aragon!"

"You should show me sometime, my darling," purred Xemci from her corner.

"Xemci, what you need is a husband," replied Azizah, "the sooner the better. I'll arrange for one in Mirambel." Fatima laughed.

"Girls," said Azizah changing her tone. "I am charged with oversight of the wedding feast. I will depend on you for support."

"You can count on me, at least with the mortar and pestle."

"The desserts are a weighty matter. I am thinking we want something special."

Fatima made a gesture for me to settle down and sleep. Azizah was famous for her discourses on food. This one could go into the small hours of the night. I had better not sit up for it.

"I am thinking of salvers of *sukkariya*, the joy of Baghdad, a confection of sugar, rose water and split almonds."

"A nice change from nougat, I agree."

"As for the savouries, your pounding will be needed for the eggplant recipes, simmered with beaten eggs and flavoured when hot."

"Azizah, your eggplant recipes are famous in Albarracín."

"These eggplant dishes will be my best ever, with cinnamon, lavender, powdered cilantro and cumin, and I shall put you in charge of the rose water julep for syrups."

"Will there be roast lamb?"

"Yes, but the men will do the roasting, so it is no concern of ours. We will prepare all dishes boiled, simmered and baked —partridges with quince, tagine with cheese, lamb with prunes and mint, green olives with meatballs and chard —girls, are you listening? You need to know this!"

The others in our party were snoring softly, but I lasted longer than the rest thanks to my love of treats, which endeared me to Azizah.

"Stay awake, Sarita dear, and I will share how to prepare a white flour crust for lamb pie. You will grind Chinese cinnamon for the minced meat filling."

I drifted off to sleep to a recipe handed down in Arabic as "a dish of Jewish Partridge," which called for stuffing the bird between its skin and meat, browning it on four sides in the pot. It took me back to my childhood. Aunt Esther always said a bird must be stuffed between the skin and the meat, and browned on all sides, above all for Rosh Hashanah.

§§§

One cold morning in January after the Prophet's Birthday, we departed on a north-easterly route toward Mirambel. On the first leg of our journey, Amir chose to follow the road to the village of Bezas. Bezas was home to many Muslim and Jewish families, and a growing number of conversos of wavering faith.

I was happy to be on the road and didn't mind the cold. Ruddy cliffs glowed in the dawn, crowned with savin junipers. We halted below a cliff of sable sandstone as luminous as dark sherry. In front a waterfall stood frozen, the torrents turned to pillars and its ledges to frets. It seemed to me a heavenly ladder such as Jacob saw in his dreams at Bethel.

The muleteers lit a fire. They raised a canopy and we unrolled our carpets. Inspired by the stony hollow, which seemed a sacred place, I prayed in a hushed voice for Hashem's protection on my journey. We womenfolk received a visit from Amir.

"Uncle Arabi has explained your circumstances. We are happy to extend our protection, but there are certain rules you must follow on the road."

"Yes, Amir."

"You will travel as one of us. Your name is Sariya. As long as you are in our entourage, to the temporal world you are a Muslim. You must not mention to anyone that you are of the Jewish faith, or that you are known to the Dominicans and the Holy Office."

He paused. "You must not speak in the Hebrew tongue. It is a risk to you and to us, given your circumstances."

Azizah and Fatima exchanged glances.

"You will pray only when we pray, alongside us, and always under the canopy. You may pray according to your own custom, but your prayers must be silent. We must not listen to the prayers of other faiths."

"I promise."

Actually, this was good news. I had returned to my devotions in Terriente. It was liberating to recite my beloved *Mizmorim*, which the Christians call Psalms, free of the *Gloria Patris*.

"How many times daily will we stop for prayer?"

"Azizah, I defer to you with respect to the girls' prayer."

"Five times." Fatima shot Azizah a pleading glance, and she relented. "Except when the weather is bad."

Azizah toasted slices of flat bread, sprinkled them with salt, and passed them round with a skin of sweet must.

When I had swallowed a morsel and sipped some juice, she announced, "Now that you have broken bread and shared salt with us round the fire, Sarita, you are under our protection for as long as we travel."

"Azizah, I thank you. Is this a custom of yours?"

"Yes, from the Bedouins. And there is something else that you must remember."

"Tell me and I will do my best."

"You must never look back. This tradition harks from Mecca itself."

"Don't worry, Azizah, I know better than to turn my head."

We reached Bezas at night as snow began to fall. For the first time, I was to play the role of Fatima's sister in a Muslim home. I intended to fade into the background, but I was too thin for the part. To our hostess, big was beautiful. She seemed worried by my bony frame.

"How would you wed, and you a wisp of a girl? Eat, or your dowry will bankrupt your uncle."

What to say? My stomach was empty and my mind was walking with it hand in hand. I hadn't dreamed that she'd address me instead of Fatima.

"May it be the Will of Allah! I will gain weight to please the Lord of the Universe."

She peered into my eyes. "What do you mean?"

Anxious, I raised my right hand to cross myself, a reflex well embedded at the Convent of Santa Inés.

The wrong gesture! My hand stopped at my nose. I stood for a moment like an idiot. Then I sniffled loudly and wiped it four times with the back of my hand, from left to right each time, exactly like Isaq.

"You poor thing. A half-chick. And hungry, too. We'll start you on garlic soup with thick slices of bread, and afterwards, sautéed turnips."

"Sprinkled with cinnamon? The turnips, I mean."

Fatima's dark eyes were shining.

"Fatima, you are a beautiful young lady, and I can tell you are a good eater."

"My Fatima here likes cinnamon on everything. When she was a girl, I always sprinkled cinnamon on her toast and creamy curd."

"And what about this skinny one? What did you feed her?"

"Miss Half-Chick was odd from birth. She was lazy to latch on my tit and she never liked to chew. Only ate soft foods, jams and jellies, and she slobbered my milk. But she was sly, too. Dough went missing from the pan."

After dinner, I still faced a plate of turnips pureed just for me. Our hostess, tender-hearted at the story of my infancy, offered to sing "The Ballad of Count Olinos" while I supped. Finishing the puree of turnips was obligatory and so, it seemed, was listening to her song.

"Count Olinos? I haven't heard his name before. Are you sure it isn't Count Arnaldos? Or perhaps, Count Ayruelo?"

She laughed. "No, my poor dear, to you these names sound the same, but I know Olinos from Arnaldos and as for Ayruelo, he's a scoundrel. Hush and listen while you eat your turnips." As I listened, I did feel half-witted, because it sounded like Magda's songs melded together.

A princess heard a strange and seductive singing on the shore of the sea, and even the birds stopped to listen. Then the Queen heard the song and said the mermaids were singing, but her daughter said no, the Count himself was singing to woo her. A princess could be wooed only by royal blood, so the Queen ordered her men to kill the Count. They speared him dead. The Princess died of grief, and from her tomb there sprang a white rose, and from his a briar, and they climbed and climbed into the sky where they entwined in a true lovers' knot. When the Queen learned, she commanded them to be uprooted. The Princess turned into a heron and the Count into a hawk, and together they flew across the sky, side by side.

"Now it's your turn. One of you must sing, or I will not turn down your beds."

Fatima and Azizah exchanged glances. "Our skinny one can sing. Not as well as you, of course. Sariya, don't be shy, sing our hostess a song."

"She thinks I'm an innocent," I thought, "I'll enjoy this. There's no harm singing one of Magda's lively ditties."

I sang the pastorela true to Magda's phrasing but in a piping voice, as if I were seven years old. Our hostess was delighted and when she learned I knew enough well-seasoned ballads to sing for weeks by the hearth, she urged us to stay until the snow melted. In a month, she would take us on a picnic to a lake in the mountains to gather flowers of spring.

288

She promised me a basket of honey candies, and narcissus, violets and hepatica in bloom, under the pines by the melting lake.

That night in bed, Fatima threw a pillow at me. I smothered a laugh.

"You were so funny singing with a straight face, of your bare feet in the grass. And your slender, pointed breasts! Yours aren't, really. You know what I mean."

"I like Bezas, and I liked most of my dinner. Spring will be here soon. Can't we stay, Azizah, till the violets and hepatica unveil their sweet faces?"

"What a golden tongue you have, my daughter, sweeter than your voice, but honey will not induce me to stay."

"The hepatica will be good for your liver." Truth be told, Papa Simon always said that hepatica seemed to do more harm than good.

"Just long enough, Aunt, for the ice to melt?"

"And an outing to their lakelet, a silver and lapis broach set in granite. They say it is a perennial pond that glistens even in summer. Have you ever seen such steadfast waters?"

Azizah was not convinced. "We should be on our way. The cold won't hurt us."

"What if there is no bread in the hamlets?"

"We will eat all the bread we wish, baked with the black olives of Aragon, in Mirambel."

"Why the haste? Are we in danger here?"

"Perhaps you had a careless moment, but what a ridiculous thing to say. Gain weight to please Allah? I know you didn't mean it, but you sounded disrespectful." I hung my head.

"I thought you were convincing, at least."

"Don't think she's fooled. She was just playing along. That's probably why she invited us to stay, to figure you out. She means well enough, for now, but these days even friends can betray. We must go."

And so we said our farewells and set off again, in the month of February, on a dreary morning. Many times on the road I imagined Bezas in its April finery, but outwardly I was true to my word and never once looked back at my beloved Sierra de Albarracín.

§§§

Beyond Teruel, we climbed into a new hill country, the Sierra de Gúdar. Years earlier, Christians had fought other Christians, spilling their brothers' blood, and the earth had received it. We wound past fields sown with vetch, and crags where vultures made their nests. Even Fatima was silent, as our mouths were wrapped against the wind.

One morning, far into the hills, we stopped by a river to pray and break our fast. The pine forest encroached so close to the icy shore that we had scarcely anywhere to sit. We finished prayers and the complaints started.

"These branches tickle my back."

"Then rouse yourself, niece."

"It's colder when I stand up. The wind hits my middle."

"Azizah is right, Fatima. Moving about will warm you."

"There's nothing to do."

"Gather some juniper berries for a hot drink to thaw our noses."

Fatima seldom did anything I asked, but it was worth a try.

"Let's sizzle juniper berries in the fat of roast lamb," said Azizah, "when we reach Mirambel."

"Speaking of fat, your middle looks big enough to keep you warm," Xemci whispered.

Fatima picked baubles of ice from the bushes. They had twigs and buds inside. She tossed them onto the river. I watched them scatter. A stone's throw from the shore, a trickle of black water snaked down the centre. The sun pierced the clouds.

"Do you think the sun will warm us?"

"What happened to the juniper berries for our hot drink?"

"I dropped them in the grass. My fingers are numb."

The ice-blue berries lay nested in the reeds. She gathered them up, wincing. The sere grasses glowed russet, but were cold to touch. The sandstone bank across the river, bathed in the blond light, looked warm too, the way Bella used to look. Looks can deceive.

I never have understood how something cold can look warm in the winter sun —the sun must be a tease. It was teasing me that morning by not warming me at all. The cedar and the holly, the king of winter and his squire, wore velvet sleeves with ice cuffs that were warmer than mine, and as for my underside, the earth's cold breath cut through my prayer rug.

The sun rose higher as we sipped our steaming juniper water. After a while I smelled pungent resin in the steam. Xemci discretely took wine from her own wineskin. We waited with growling stomachs for breakfast to arrive, but Amir returned from the nearest cluster of farmhouses with nothing more than toasted peas of the chickling vetch.

"No bread, Amir, not even three days old?"

"None. These will have to do." He poured us each a handful of the dun-coloured peas.

"Not even pease porridge? Not even ground into meal?"

Amir shook his head.

"He may as well pass round stinking hellebore. It grows hereabouts," I whispered to Fatima.

"That's a poison, Sarita."

"Yes, deadly. I was in jest. The tiniest dose of hellebore will induce retching. Chickling vetch lingers in the gut and causes flatulence. It's the flatulence that's deadly, to others."

"Poisons the cattle," added Xemci.

"If eaten for long, it will paralyse the anus. At least, that's what Papa Simon said."

"Stay upwind of Azizah." Fatima rolled her eyes.

Raucous caws sounded from the cedars —ravens.

They spied the vetch peas and wanted them. I was not overly careful handling those peas and let many roll to the ground. The ravens landed beyond our reach and walked toward us faster and faster till they hopped along on one leg. They snatched the peas and flew away.

"This land is so empty. I don't like it. And now these birds. Stop feeding them, Sara, that's my breakfast," scolded Azizah.

"It is empty due to the old wars. Too many dead."

"Last night, my cat stared up at the sky and her fur stood on end."

Since Terriente, Fatima had been riding along with a wooden cage strapped to her saddle. Inside wrapped in fleece was a black kitten.

"A comet. Perhaps she saw something that we can't. Magda used to tell of the Phantom Host, the souls of soldiers who ride across the sky in a ghostly army. They start their parade years before a terrible event."

"Sarita, you are superstitious for a doctor's daughter."

"I am not so sure, Fatima. Jacob himself saw the Army of the Otherworld, so he called the place Mahanaim."

Anxiously the small cat mewed and flicked her ears. Large oval ears.

"Was she a gift from Uncle Arabi?"

"Yes, from the summer litter. We think the father is Noor's old flame, the black Tom."

"What will you name her?"

"For now, her name is Leyla, Arabic for night."

"In Hebrew we have that word for night, and also an angel." I recalled Old Solomon mentioning that the angel was in charge of conception, a detail he need not have shared.

"Sarita, what is the word that the churchmen use for dusk?" asked Xemci.

"Crepusculum," I replied with misgiving.

"Her name shall be Crepus."

"What a horrid name for my darling. I won't have it."

"It's decided, then. She will be Crepus. She's such a pathetic little puss, wrapped in soiled fleece, lapping soup. A mangy fox has more spirit than that cat."

"Girls, we should be kind to one another and think warming thoughts. Fatima, remember when you were small, and I used to tell you the story of the crow and the fox?"

"Oh yes, Aunt, at bedtime. And a nice, snug bed it was, with a canopy and feather pillows. Not to mention the warm toast on a plate."

"Yes, I warmed your toast every night. Do you recall how the fox flattered the crow, and how she retorted?"

"Tell me again, Azizah, as in the old days."

"'Oh fast-flying bird of the coal-black wing.'"

"'Oh coal-footed fox of the sootiest tail.'"

"'My darling eagle at break of day.' Isn't that the silliest compliment to give a crow?" Azizah laughed.

To my surprise, Fatima wiped away a tear. "I detest those birds."

"You are not alone. Athena envied their prophetic powers."

"I don't care a fig for Athena. It's their horrid croaking that bothers me."

"Have you seen the mountain goats on the ridge?" Xemci pointed to the chaparral.

"They look warmer than we are, and better suited for the wet."

"Better looking than that he-goat of yours, Fatima, who wooed you in Terriente at midnight. Don't think I don't know. I heard him rap at our chamber door, and saw you rise to open."

"Impossible."

"It was a full moon. I followed you. I saw him thrust you forward with his elbow, onto his breast. You did it standing."

"You lie."

"Really? I heard you warbling with pleasure like a bird. Fatima, I heard him take you. Twice."

"That settles it. When we arrive in Mirambel, you are not staying under the roof of my cousins' house."

"I can't blame you for fancying a young buck. You are marrying a toothless greybeard who can't get it up."

Azizah put her arm round Fatima. "Hold your tongue, Xemci, or you will shame Allah with your insolence. Fatima never left my side at night and you know it. I trust Fatima as I would my own daughter."

It did rain, all day, rivulets running the length of our wool cloaks. The muleteers rode in front and behind, listening for wolves. It was hard to hear any living creature above the roaring of the torrents in the ravine.

Azizah's mood had shifted —whether with Xemci's words, the weather or the chickling vetch, I wasn't sure.

"I hear the voice of a ghoul in those waters."

"Calm yourself, Aunt. This road is bad enough without you imagining things."

"I am not imagining things. There —I heard it again! In the water and the wind. This wilderness is truly the howling land, haunted by demons."

"Sarita, you're supposed to be the sensible one in this group. Tell her there are no demons about. When we stop next, do you have a calming draught?"

"I have my own worries, Fatima. I agree there is no ghoul calling to Azizah, but for me, the Seven Evils lurk round each bend."

"Say again?"

"Our Torah says so. Pestilence whom we call Resheph, plague, famine, the teeth of wild beasts, and the venom of crawling creatures, that sort of thing, because each week I violate the Shabbat."

"You left out the flying serpents."

"I fear worse than that, Xemci. Old Solomon knew the secrets of the Canaanites. The sons of Resheph are flying demons who hover over us in the sky, invisible, and strike us down from above."

"I hope I never live to see it."

"They are as old as mankind, Fatima. Apollo shot down arrows of sickness and disaster at Troy."

"That doesn't mean they will come again."

"They will come again and again, for as long as we break God's commandments."

"Sarita, you need the same calming draught as Azizah."

"My daughters, these are troubling thoughts. Clearly what is required is more worship."

"More worship? Aunt, this journey is hard enough."

"I have been soft with you, skipping prayer sessions in bad weather. From now on we will pray regularly in the frozen rain. It will please Allah, dampen ardour and promote chastity."

At that moment, Azizah put her hand to her heart and collapsed on a bundle of poles. Heartburn from the chickling vetch, which she had dusted with spices! Something gave way with a loud crack.

"Oh no," whispered Fatima, "the poles to the prayer tent!"

"Broken or not, this canopy shall bear witness to your prayers. Silent prayers, Sara, because sometimes you forget."

"A spoonful of fennel seeds," I thought, "might promote clemency."

But there was no stopping Azizah.

"Girls, as you pray in the rain, banish untoward thoughts. Remember that a woman's honour is precious to Allah and more important to man than bread and salt."

"Her words are intolerable and so is her wind," moaned Fatima.

"This spells trouble," I added, "for us both."

Day after day, Azizah made us pray beneath the lopsided tent. It was sustained by two poles and the rest of it draped over our backs. The waterskins of heaven drenched us, and after a prayer session spent kneeling on a sodden carpet, I rode along with fever. My breath was short and my bones ached.

The words kept resounding in my head, "Like a lady she is stripped and carried off. Yea Nineveh is like a pool whose waters are ebbing away." In my confusion, I couldn't tell whether the taking of Nineveh was in the past or future.

When Nahum died down in my fevered brain, Mica started to speak instead. Would the Lord cast my sins into these running waters, or the sea once we set sail? How many lives will be lost in the seas of Carthage?

Winter eased by our journey's end. Snowdrops pierced the dead, wet leaves and catkin-lamps lit the poplars. The white willows burst into yellow fuzz.

They could help me break into sweat.

"Have the muleteers strip willow bark for me, Azizah, to dry by the fire," I whispered painfully.

"What do I do with it?"

"Make a decoction —boil it. Make a beverage to bring down my fever, if I am delirious."

"May it be the will of Allah, may Allah cure your illness. I will pray for you five times a day."

"Not prayer, Azizah, medicine! Promise, Azizah, if I lose my senses —you will give me a decoction of willow bark."

"I promise. You also must take our remedy. A cup of thyme infusion, five times a day." She winked.

I grabbed her hand.

"Don't worry, Sarita. In the glory days of Al-Andalus, your doctors learned from ours."

We reached Mirambel on a day that was grey like the others. I was sick for weeks. I do not remember my illness, except for Azizah tending me. She was repentant of our prayers in the rain, and vowed never again to travel in cold weather.

§§§

The bride gave Fatima three bracelets with gold charms shaped like barley corns. The dangles were supposed to whisper to each other and put ghosts and demons to flight. I wasn't sure about that, but the gold was pure and of good colour. Fatima fastened one of the bracelets round the cat's neck. As for my gown for the wedding, it did not materialise. Truth be known I was happier without it, having learned in Calatayud the folly of donning finery to please another. Nor was I allowed in the kitchen. Azizah would not permit me to exert myself.

After the ceremony, the newlyweds tossed sweets into the crowd, and while the others gathered them up in their skirts, I had the foresight to bring along an ample pouch, which I stuffed for the long ride ahead. The feasting and partying ended eventually, but we lingered there for more than a month, and the candies were gone.

"Azizah, when are we departing for Valencia?"

"It is too cold for you to cross the mountains. We must wait for spring."

"As the minstrels sing, '*in balminess the apples bloom, their petals blow away.*' It's time we start."

"Not at all. I want you all beautifully plump before we arrive in Túnez, and you, Sara, are the one holding us back. I need to see you eat, like our Fatima here."

Fatima beamed. She had put on so much weight that I hoped she had enough fabric for her bridal gown.

In April we bade farewell to Fatima's cousins. It was a Christian holy day, and a line of dancers was wending its way to the plaza. In a dance known as the "Rolde of Mirambel," couples were arrayed in a circle, the girls dancing from youth to youth. To the piping of clarinets we rode out the gates, towards the mountains of the Maestrazgo and the plains of Castellón.

Fatima and I each wore a robe that veiled us from head to toe, the *almalafa*. Azizah, vigilant of our modesty, insisted that we wear our winter travel cloaks on top.

"Aunt, I am too warm in this double layer. I feel hot and prickly."

"At least no one will notice us."

"Oh no? Look who's here!"

A flamboyant female approached astride a donkey. Judging from her outfit, Xemci was as handy at the womanly arts as Carmela. She wore a tunic of peacock blue, crimson pantaloons and headscarf, and a striped sash with pom-pom tassels that matched her new saddle bag.

Fatima rode up face-to-face.

"What did I tell you when you gave me that insult?"

"Don't worry, you are forgiven. I wouldn't let you girls travel without me. I'll make sure no men are lurking about!" Xemci eyed Azizah.

There was a pause. Then Azizah nodded her assent and Fatima shrugged, so we fell into line. Amir rode up front and behind straggled four muleteers, guiding pack mules overloaded with bags bound for Túnez.

"What do you think of my dark blue cloak, Sarita? Is the colour severe?"

"That tone of blue is mute in the shadows but sings in the sunshine, Fatima. It helps that the dye is good and the wool, very fine."

"I just love the midnight blue and yellow stripes that run the length of my *almalafa*."

"It is clever, I agree, how the blue stars are woven on the yellow background and vice versa. What I like best of all, Fatima, is your saddle cloth with its matching horizontal stripes."

"The saddle cloth was the very best of Uncle Arabi's collection."

"I wonder where Xemci got hers."

Xemci's saddle bag was adorned with pom-poms of crimson, white, blue, green and ochre, in the style of the weavers of Morella.

"Don't think about it or you will sully your mind."

"Why did she say that about you to Azizah, at our winter breakfast with the ravens?"

"To put in Azizah's head that she's indispensable as an extra pair of eyes. And it worked!"

"I'd feel safer with her gone. Where are your gold bracelets?"

"With Amir for safe-keeping. You should give him your valuables, too, for the trip."

"That's a good idea."

I tried to keep a straight face. She still thought I possessed things of value.

"By the way, Sarita, I am glad we chose you that camel hair cloak. The leonine shade favours you."

Magda used to sing a song, a Peteneras, about a beautiful Jewish girl who wore camel hair. I sang,

> "Oh where do you go, my lovely Jewess
>
> In finery so well composed,
>
> At this unearthly hour?"

I sang in a second voice.

> "In search of a camel hair shawl, it is in a synagogue."

I sang in a third voice.

> "You, the Lord's missionary,
>
> If you should find her out there,

Tell her I die contented

If she remembers me,

Each day for a moment."

"This one is scary. What comes next?"

"So many men meet their end in this song that it is seldom sung."

"Enough!"

We stopped in time for mid-day prayers. As had been our custom since leaving Terriente, Fatima and I prayed side by side, on our Cuenca prayer rugs. I imitated her manner the best I could, while reciting silently the first Psalm that came to mind.

"You tested me — You found not. My thoughts do not transgress the words of my mouth."

These lines worried me. I remembered the convent. My mouth had transgressed, and worst of all, my thoughts. I recited,

"The judgments of Hashem are true, altogether righteous. They are more desirable than gold, than even much fine gold; and sweeter than honey, and drippings from the combs."

"Psssst, Sarita, your hijab is slipping off your head. It is lopsided again."

"I have centered it on my head. Does it look right now?"

"Shhh!"

304

To cheer myself, I recited,

"Also from intentional sins, restrain Your servant; let them not rule me, then I shall be perfect; and I will be cleansed of great transgressions."

But my mind was intent on transgressing. Fray Vicente as a Christian and Dominican was twice forbidden. The harder I tried to forget the peaches, cruller puffs and his glances, the more I remembered.

I thought of his eyes. The kindness in the eyes of that Dominican. And his lips. To me, his lips were perfect, though ours had never touched. And then, I recalled our fingers touching round the basket.

"You are so clumsy at arranging the hijab, Sarita. If it looks wrong to me, others also will take notice."

I nodded. The Muslim girls are very particular about how they cover their heads during prayer and their method seemed to elude me. My hijab always shifted on my head, even more because I had to pray with my head bent toward the ground, Muslim style. Perhaps it sat crooked on my head like King Solomon's crown because I had strayed from the Laws of Moses.

We rolled up our carpets and climbed onto the mules. At least, Fatima tried.

"I don't know why this mule is so much harder to mount than the one I rode to Mirambel," moaned Fatima after another failed attempt.

She had gained so much weight since the wedding and didn't realise it.

"Maybe you should call Amir to help you up."

At that instant, Fatima slipped off, bringing the cage to the ground. The wooden pin that secured the latch shot into the bushes. Crepus proved her feline worth by bounding up a tree. While I treated Fatima's bruises, the muleteers snared a thrush to tempt the cat. Fatima was too worried to eat. I quietly thanked Hashem for giving us bread, not chickling vetch.

Azizah and I then sat on a blanket and chewed like ungulates through our entire supply of loaves and rolls, savouring the dough amid the tannic fragrance of the oaks.

§§§

By evening, Crepus back in her cage, we had hardly progressed. A commodious farm house stood nearby but the farmer kept pigs. We rode on. We had to make camp in a shepherds' hut in a copse of hawthorns and thistles.

"This is a miserable place to stop. I wish we were back in Mirambel."

"Cheer up, Fatima, at least you are on your way to your wedding."

"You also need to cheer up, Sara. You haven't been yourself since you sang that ghastly ballad."

"Will your cat let me pet her?"

"I don't know. You may try."

Crepus didn't like me. Fatima then put her in her own lap and she purred at once.

"Keep her close to you in the dark, Fatima. She is growing up fast and might attract a dangerous suitor —a mountain cat. He would sire strange kittens impossible to tame."

"How does he look?"

"Yellow-grey with a bushy tail with black stripes. Jaime saw one at Frías. It stared straight into his eyes."

"Let's change the subject. I don't like those cats."

"Anyhow, if Crepus escapes again, the weasels will eat her first," said Xemci placidly. "She would make a good dinner for a large and hungry mother weasel."

She eyed Fatima. "Especially the polecats. There is one hereabouts, you know."

"Why do you say that?"

"One was living in this shelter over the winter. I found a mound of scat outside that explains the fetid smell."

"Well, it is springtime now, so she is gone," replied Fatima with forced cheer.

"Not at all. She probably has a nest of hungry kits nearby. They have powerful jaws and kill by crushing the neck. She is down by the stream listening to us right now!"

Fatima shuddered. "How do you know so much about polecats?"

"My brothers and I used to steal the bittern's eggs down by the Guadalaviar. The polecat was our rival at raiding the nests. Each spring we would go searching for her lair."

"The polecat is the companion to Hecate, the Greek goddess of witchcraft and dreams."

Actually I had never seen one, but Magda, who believed in spirits, used to tell of Hecate and her polecat by the hearth.

"According to the ancients, Hecate's shrines ward off the restless dead. Barking dogs signal her presence."

"Amir, what if the wolves are about?" interjected Azizah.

"The muleteers will rotate watch tonight, with their own canines of flesh and bone. I cannot make any promises. Next time, keep moving along so we don't have to pass the night in places like this."

Xemci and I finished sweeping out the shepherd's hut and laid down carpets and blankets, but there was nothing we could do about the putrid smell. I groped about in the saddle bags for Fatima's magical lamps but did not find them — instead, out popped Azizah's travel lamps of brown clay. Each looked to me like the head of a beast.

After prayers, I passed round some dates as cold as the blankets.

"Xemci, I smell fat on the fire and hear it hissing. Go see what meat is cooking at the camp outside," ordered Azizah. Xemci took her time in returning.

"The head muleteer is an animal, and I mean a complete animal. The mother who bore him must have had hair on her ankle bones. Anyhow, they have slaughtered a goat and are roasting a haunch on the spit. Want some?" No one replied, though Fatima wrinkled her nose.

"Did you do it standing?"

"Listen, Fatima, the animals are singing for you tonight. They sound hungry." It was true. A rising nocturnal chorus was engulfing us.

"Stop it, Xemci, we don't want to listen," scolded Azizah.

"I hear the polecat! How horrible!" Fatima moaned.

"Not that sound. That's just a bird."

"Is it the owl?"

"No, the hoopoe, who spoke to King Solomon."

"Hoopoe nests stink worse than this place. The mother polecat is singing too. Listen!" Xemci threw back her head and caterwauled.

"Hiss! *Kik-kik-kik-kik*, hiss!" retorted the polecat.

"Crepus, darling, that settles it. You are sleeping with your mama tonight." Fatima swept the cat, cage and all, inside her cloak.

"Fatima, that bump of yours is the last straw. You look pregnant, you really do."

"Out my door, you witch. Go spend the night with your muleteer, or I'll tell Amir to send you home."

Xemci shrugged. "You are safer with me inside, I promise you," and so she stayed.

Nestled in my prayer rug and camel hair, I felt cold in my bones. I woke in the dark seized with fear it was an ill-fated hour. The shrieks of the owls were unearthly. Finally I entered the world of dreams. The bittern nested in the reeds. Weasels hissed at cats and one satyr called to another. I settled to toss restlessly on the forest floor, half nightjar, half woman, luring men to their deaths in the desolated Edom of Isaiah.

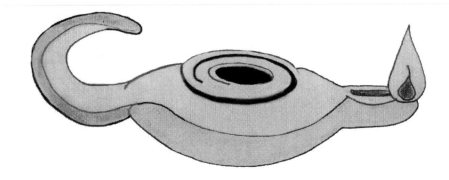

§§§

At daybreak I cleansed my hands and wrists in the fastest running water in the brook and recited the prayer Papa Simon had taught me to say upon waking from night terrors. *"Lord, I am Yours and my dreams shall be Yours also."*

We departed in the early light. Gray-blue shrubs rose up the hillsides and merged into inky outlines along the ridge. Above, a hint of white, then a blue firmament so vast I feared the Lord who created the heavens.

Amir rode up beside me. "Peace be upon you."

"The same upon you."

A hundred goldfinches flew past. They folded their yellow-striped wings and soared like arrows.

"Goldfinches! My sister loved the sight of them."

"The one who travelled to Navarre, where the winter was too cold?"

"Yes, she was the one. Reyna."

"I remember playing my oud for her. That poem was about a garden. Here, in her honour, are lines from another.

'I am the garden that appears at dawn with adornments.

Think upon my beauty, and understanding will shine in you.'"

"Reyna always said the first light of day is the most resplendent."

"There's a reason. The master Ibn Ma'udh, who lived in Al-Andalus centuries ago, taught that moisture refracts the rays of the sun. The angle of sunlight is different at dawn than at twilight. He measured them mathematically."

"Go on, Amir, this is interesting, more interesting than the teachings of the Dominicans."

"Another master, Abu Rayhan al-Biruni of Persia, taught that light travels from a luminous source, and that light travels much faster than sound."

"You should go to Toledo to study. Uncle Arabi told Papa Simon that if I were a boy, I would study the classics of King Alfonso the Wise."

"Be content with what Allah has given you. As for me, this is not the time for me to pursue studies and turn my back on my people. Almería is in danger of falling to the Catholic Kings. The residents of Almería will be exiled."

"Will they be forced out?" I thought of our edict of expulsion from Albarracín.

"If they convert to Christianity, they will be free to settle anywhere in Castile. If they choose to remain faithful to Islam, they must find a Taifa to accept them —yet only Granada remains, and its fall is inevitable. I fear that Islam will be driven from this land."

"Islam swept from this land? So many people? It hardly seems possible."

"The Catholic Monarchs are amassing power. They or their descendants will use it against Muslims. It is a matter of time.

For you, it is more urgent. Last year the King and Queen set up the Supreme Council of the Inquisition, to govern all Castile and Aragon, and elevated Torquemada to the new post of General Inquisitor.

They have created an institution with royal sanction that needs victims to finance itself. It will endure for generations."

I shook my head. Pestilence, famine and ruin, inflicted upon his people? Upon mine? Not even in my feverish dreams had I imagined such a thing.

"Are we are headed to a safe place?"

"Since the death of the mighty Caliph 'Uthman, there has been strife in Túnez. The years of peace and prosperity on which Azizah has built her dreams may be over. There are internal feuds, and feuds with the Maghreb to the west. But these feuds will pale before what is to come.

The Muslim traders of Valencia have ships that ply the seas and they see changes on the horizon. Vaster empires, faster ships, terrible battles between the Ottomans and Catholic kings. The old order and all that we know will fade."

Changes on the horizon. What ominous words. They made me think of the Phantom Host flying the night skies.

"Surely, Amir, things are not as bad as you say."

"I would prefer that our faiths live in peace."

"Are you worried for Azizah and Fatima?"

"Yes. Azizah has many fanciful illusions. Promise not to tell either of them."

"I promise."

"And I digress. I called you to ride with me for a reason. Uncle Arabi has entrusted to me a packet, containing a pewter pomander handed down from Doctor Simon, which I will give to you now. It also contains something of value, which I will carry with me on your behalf until you reach your destination.

The widow of your Uncle Saul, who had dealings with my uncle for many years, sent it from Navarre hidden in a blue clay lamp. It is a gold pendant, sized for a child, on a short strand of pearls with a blue diamond in its centre. Such a pendant must have had a chain or necklace of considerable value. I am afraid it came to me without it. I need you to have faith in me, and believe that if I had received the chain I would pass it to you."

So Reyna had been with me, all the way, and also her blue light. I recalled watching her lamp's many-pointed star. What were her words? *"Its foundations shall be sapphires."*

"Amir, what have you said to her? When this child needs good cheer, you make her cry. Just like a man, to have such bad timing. Leave her to me."

Truth be told, it was our pilgrimage to Túnez that broke my heart.

"For all your dreams of Túnez and castles in the sky, you are truly one of us, Azizah. We are Aragonese."

"We hail from the mountains of the southern frontier. We are *serranos*, mountain folk."

"Yes, but Aragonese. Why are we leaving the place we belong?"

"Sit straight in the saddle, Sarita. Aragon does not believe in tears!"

"Just leave her a while."

"Fatima, I have just the thing. We will play a game to pass the time."

"Oh, no!"

"Oh, yes! Each of you will take turns describing things in Albarracín you think you will miss in Túnez. Just wait till you hear how much nicer everything will be in your new home!"

The words "your new home" did not cheer me.

"I'll join in the game, Azizah, but remember that my new home is Naples."

We halted at a patch of mud. At that point the stream crossed the trail and fed puddles as cool and grey as potter's slip. The muleteers pitched stones at an untended herd of cattle. They moved to our right but did not fall back.

The rest of the way down that trail, we rode more or less abreast with the herd. Over the exchange of insults between cows and muleteers, I could scarcely hear Azizah. Worse, something about Azizah was attracting a spotted heifer. No matter. Whatever we mentioned, she managed to explain why the equivalent in Túnez would be infinitely superior.

Fatima and I were soon running low on things from Albarracín that we would miss.

"The salmon pink gesso of our houses in Albarracín."

"The houses in Túnez are white, a white that dazzles the eye. You'll see!"

"Our clove pinks, the *clavellinas* of my Teruel, are lovelier than the gifts that Abel offered to the Lord."

"Don't be silly, girls, in Túnez Fatima will have a proper garden laid out in squares. Fountains, pavilions, and date palms tall as sentinels."

315

"And the dragons on our doors that protect against the evil eye? I wager they don't have those in Túnez."

"In Túnez, to ward off spirits, the doors and grillwork are painted blue, brighter than a bird's egg."

"Our Turolense tiles of green, black and white with stars with eight points, and flower-stars."

"Hush, Sarita, you have spoken out of turn."

"Then it's my question. Answer it!"

"Fatima, in the mosque of my ancestral home Al-Qayrawan you will find tiles with ribbon-stars and quatrefoils. The *mihrab* is more resplendent than in Córdoba."

"The crispy borage fritters of Aragon are the best in the world."

"I'm sure they are very good in Túnez. The borage grown in the fertile fields of the town of Amdoun is famous."

"If that is so, why did you pack the sack of borage seeds that is strapped to the mule?"

"I want to guarantee our borage will be of the highest quality. I am Aragonese, after all."

"What will you miss the most from Albarracín?"

"Our tagine," sighed Fatima, who was getting hungry.

"That is the silliest comment yet, girls. The tagine in Túnez is so rich, you slice it like a pie. Such a tagine, you cannot imagine."

With that, Azizah won the match. Fortunately, our superior Aragonese cattle had faded from view. We asked Amir to tell our muleteers to find a shady spot for a picnic but he said it was early yet and he needed to reach the next town to buy bread.

Azizah passed round some crumbled white squares with sultanas and green bits that tasted of pistachio. I admired how she managed to hide sweets about her person, tucked away in her scented handkerchiefs.

After a while she started to doze in the saddle, and I decided to play a trick on her.

"Azizah, wake up! We are almost at Carthage!"

She sat bolt upright, such was her fascination with Carthage. "Amir, where are we?"

"Approaching Cantavieja."

"Just as I said. The town of Cantavieja was founded by a Carthaginian general who named it Cartago Vetus.

Papa taught that during the Punic Wars, all the lands of Teruel were ruled by Carthage."

"Allah be blessed! You make me feel closer to our destination. Long live Carthage!"

In Cantavieja Amir bought provisions and the plaza inspired Azizah. "This is a handsome town, Amir, and well appointed. Let's stop and try their dishes and cakes. I smell pastries baking, scented with anise."

"Me too, and it smells delectable."

"How I adore the scent of anise from the oven, and the thought of biting into that hot pastry, and after I swallow, the uplift of anise perfume in my throat, as if inhaled!"

Azizah closed her eyes and took a deep breath for effect. "As the poet wrote in Persian, a fruit cobbler to save your soul!"

I was convinced. My nose, as discerning as Galgo the hound's, had whiffed a hint of hot fruit jelly.

"No stopping yet, Azizah, we have to make up for lost time."

"We can't leave now in any case, because the muleteers have not returned."

"I hope the cows didn't drive them to drink."

The men reappeared a short while later and our expedition got on the road, in the direction of Castellón.

§§§

We rode down the face of a mountain into a valley where eagles and the break-bone vulture floated high overhead.

"The muleteers were told in Cantavieja that this is a good place to stop, as there are pools of water in this river bed," said Amir. "You may eat and take a short rest, but be quick about it or we will spend another night in the wilderness."

"I think we are not going far," observed Azizah. "Those same muleteers are missing!"

In fact, our muleteers were nowhere to be found.

"Stay together till I return. I need to water the animals. They are skittish." Amir set off downstream to water the remaining mules.

"How am I to find a thrush for my cat, without men to set snares in the bush?"

"Fatima, I am more concerned about those round loaves with thick crust that have gone with the muleteers."

"And the flat breads with parsley. It's a good time for a nap if we can't have a picnic like yesterday." Azizah settled down on a blanket and fell asleep guarded by Xemci, or so I thought.

"I am going to bathe my feet, Xemci. This is the perfect moment, as the men have gone. Don't leave Azizah."

"Watch your step, Sarita," Azizah called out, "there are stones lying about, strewn by jinns when the earth was young."

"I think there's an old ruin in the bush. I guess the ancients were here before us. Don't worry, I'll be careful."

The twisted oaks and pines, under a canopy of ancient holly oaks, hid a pool of dark water. They fought me with their branches but I pushed through.

"There must have been baths here once," I said to myself, for the spring-fed fount was lined with stones. "Better than a tomb. The ancients thought water helped spirits to rise."

Perhaps it was the spirit of that place, or my years of longing for a Shabbat bath. Maybe it was the dancing of the midges in the shaft of light, or the briar in flower in the trees above. Whatever the reason, I did something I should not have.

I stripped the white petals off a branch of the blackberry briar, which pricked my arm. I cast off my cloak and stepped out of my robe. Step by step, I immersed myself in the wine-red water.

Afterwards, my eyes were weary. I dressed and lay on my cloak. I pulled up the hem of my robe just above the throat of each foot, exposing my ankles and their bracelets and henna flowers to the sun.

Pines laden with mistletoe, the golden bough of Aeneas, towered over me. I wanted to sleep but two doves sent by Venus were pulling and tugging at the golden berries with a flapping of wings. They turned into rooks and led me down a path to the Underworld.

The birds of the blackest wing converged on a rowan grove where Faunus and his revellers were feasting. At last, the sorb apples of putrefaction! I tried to resist, but soon I joined in the feast. The corrupted fruits tasted of custard, and peaches when their flesh is brown as sugar, and slightly of sulphur. I ate one, and then another. I succumbed to one more.

My dreams of that long day came together. Half nightjar, half woman. Death in the ruins of Edom. Then down, down to the orchards of putrefaction. Peaches, sugar, sulphur, an acquired taste. There the two of us would share our pagan god. The two of us?

"Psssst, María Encarnación, wake up."

"Who is there?"

"It's me, Fray Vicente." He was kneeling over me, his face close to mine, and my hands in his.

I was still half asleep. My hood slipped back and my hair fell dishevelled over my face.

"You are in danger. We were waiting in Cantavieja and rode ahead of you this morning."

"But I have been in disguise!"

"Fray Anselmo has just identified you most affirmatively, by your ankles and feet, which he has committed to memory as surely as brands on a sheep. He has gone for some rope."

"That explains Fray Anselmo, but how did you recognise me?"

I blushed, realising the possibilities.

"I got here before he did. I'd know you anywhere without your habit."

"I don't understand."

"I mean, your ankles, uncovered."

"My ankles?"

"I didn't leave straight away to look for truffles, that day in October. I didn't want to leave you, and I wouldn't leave you with him."

He paused. "Sarita, if I may address you thus, let me help you."

He bent forward and raised my hands to his lips. I reached up and placed one arm around his neck, and then the other. I kissed Vicente. He kissed me. I recalled the firm strumming of mandolins and the swaying of the dance in the plaza at Torres. I lengthened out his kiss the way the singer drew out the *copla* till we both were suspended in air.

Then, I heard it. A rustling in the bushes on the far side of the pool. Something had dropped to the ground.

"Taking me captive is not enough! First, you make a spectacle of me for Fray Anselmo!"

"No, Sara."

"Anselmo is there, in the bushes. I heard him. The same as that day by the stream in Daroca. Only this time, you love me for his amusement. Then he will bind me with rope. What a thrill he will have. Something he can control."

"Sara, I have come here on my own, to take you to freedom. Believe me."

"Tell me the truth" I whispered, pulling away from him.

"Fray Anselmo set a bounty on your head, and your muleteers have agreed to split the reward three ways. Your fourth man is bound and gagged."

"What do I do now?"

"Come with me. I have a mount."

My eyes fixed on his crucifix and fear tied a knot in my throat. I shook my head. He sighed, and watched me for a few moments. He then collected my pouch from the ground, and looped it over my shoulder.

"Get out to the main road as fast as you can, and run downhill to the fields on the other side. The field hands are

Muslim and they will defend you. Hurry, you have no time to spare. I will delay Anselmo."

I raced barefoot to the road. Xemci came running after. She set a fast pace, and soon outstripped me. "Faster, Sarita, faster!" We followed a bank to a meadow where field hands were tending white lupine.

At that moment, a bespectacled Dominican friar overtook me and dismounted. He was wearing a new black cloak over his white habit, but it was Fray Anselmo, no doubt about it, at his most impetuous.

"I have orders to apprehend you in the name of the Holy Office!" Fray Anselmo produced what looked like a warrant, and moved forward to bind my hands.

Xemci scrambled up the sides of a stone shelter of the sort that abound in those hills. She stood tall in her tunic as blue as the sky's cloth, adjusted her crimson scarf to show a gold halo of hair, and threw back her shoulders. She called to them in Aragonese and then Arabic in her rich and powerful voice well known in Albarracín.

In my heart I gave thanks to the Lord that Xemci had imitated our town's muezzin all those years. The field hands, Muslim to a man, came running to assist from the sea of white flowers. Within minutes, Fray Anselmo was accosted from all sides by men wielding picks and shovels. They surrounded him completely and then we lost him from sight.

Another field hand came running, not to my aid, but straight to the stone hut to help Xemci down. He sank on one knee with an armful of lupine, peppery-sweet and buzzing with bees.

"These white blossoms on their bended stems bow low before your beauty. On my knees I beseech thee to accept my offerings, my Star of the North, you who guide me on my path."

"Come with me, then, and be my knight."

"I am yours, as far as the city of Valencia, the Balensiya of the Muslim kings, whose walls conceal secret pleasure gardens."

"Shall I bathe in a fountain, serenaded by the lute?"

"Your wish shall be my command."

Handsome in his shirt, trousers, and jerkin, the youth fingered a scarlet pom-pom dangling from her sash.

As graceful as dancers they moved from view.

Amir rode up with Azizah, Fatima with Crepus in her cage, and our one faithful muleteer. This taciturn giant turned out to be Xemci's uncle. Azizah was mumbling a prayer in Arabic to ward off unholy spirits. I looked for something to revive her.

Fumbling in my pouch, to my surprise I touched something warm —a bundle of turnovers filled with medlar conserves from Cantavieja, neatly packed with a skin of red wine, and candies.

"Where can I eat these without being seen?" I thought. "Nowhere."

Medlars, like sorb apples, are sweet only when corrupted. The rose-coloured preserves on my tongue were sweeter than drippings from the honey comb. Sweeter than my dream of the Underworld. I recalled the melody that Magda had sung, that last night together by the hearth.

"He took her by the hand,

To a lush bower they go."

Vicente. The two of us as man and woman, under the roses in the shadow of the cypress.

"Sarita, what have we here? Small fruit pies!"

"I can't hide these from you, Fatima, can I? Here, take one." She took a bite.

"Medlar jelly, with anise in the crust!

Tell me the truth. You had a Dominican friend with you by the water."

"It wasn't what you think."

"If not, too bad! Whatever! These are truly fruit pies with soul! What else did he give you? Come on, confess! Isn't that what the Dominicans always do, confess?"

"Wine from noble Aragonese grapes. It tastes of Cariñena, near where Bella used to live."

I passed the wine round to their delight, as they weren't supposed to imbibe. Azizah in particular was able to take in a large volume at one go.

"Easy, Azizah, or there won't be any left for me," scolded Xemci, who had returned carrying her bouquet. She snatched the wineskin and stuffed her mouth with pie.

"My favourite filling —dog's arse conserves!" The peasant name for this fruit.

"Medlars do have such round bottoms," agreed Fatima.

"And arse holes too, when you pull out the stems."

"Don't listen to this, Fatima," warned Azizah.

"I want to know everything that happened between you and that ugly-tit Dominican you were kissing."

"What?"

"Azizah woke just when things were getting good. I want it step by step!" She emptied the wineskin.

"Come on, out with it."

"No."

Xemci winked and sang in Arabic a couplet from the muleteers.

> "Oh, the butt of that boy that receives me
>
> Like the buttocks of no other lad."

"If you don't talk, I'll drag it out of you."

"Nothing happened."

I realised my mistake. I had heard Xemci in the bushes, not Anselmo.

"Your loss, then. As for me, I don't wait for life to give a second chance."

"Do Dominicans have tits?" giggled Fatima who was not used to wine.

"Tits and more, woman, and our Sarita here would know all about them already if she had any of her own."

"Xemci, why don't you ride at the back and be the North Star to your knight. He awaits by the pack mules, unaware the hulk beside him is your uncle."

"And your own father."

"What?"

"You mean to say you haven't figured out by now that our faithful muleteer is your father? You know, the man in the alcove with Magda."

"Shut your mouth, Xemci, I'm fed up with your stories."

"Godspeed, I'm going for a ride in the rear. More fun than you'll ever have, cousin dearest."

As we rode along in silence, I began thinking of the lovely Petenera who went out into the night alone. Maybe I also was the kiss of death and it was just as well for Fray Vicente that I had fled. I dried furtive tears that Amir didn't notice and pretended to listen to Fatima. Eventually, I started eating the honey drops, which I refused to pass round. They brightened my eyes.

The Zohar teaches that each day of one's life has spiritual tasks assigned to it. Even on bad days, the spiritual assignment remains. I decided first to give thanks to Hashem for my rescue by reciting the *Amidah* with special concentration. What else? Thank my travel companions! As Papa Simon taught, gratitude is the most important and difficult of virtues.

When we stopped that evening, there was no sign of pursuers. I expected a visit from the police of the Holy Brotherhood, but they did not appear. After prayer, I prepared Azizah sage infusion with dates by way of apology.

"Not now, I am sleepy." She pushed them aside.

Next, I tried to thank Xemci.

"Xemci, I am grateful for what you did today."

"This episode had served me nicely, Sarita. I have proved that I am needed. My passage to Túnez is secure, and my uncle's as well. He will sell me upon arrival, you know, out in the main square."

"Xemci, how can you consent to being sold?"

"I will cause a commotion. 'Blue eyes and gold hair. Muslim. Speaks Arabic.' A rich man will pay a fortune. If I were a comely lad, maybe more, but still a fortune."

"He pays a fortune, but then what?"

"I will be worth it. As I have told you many times, apparently in vain, Sarita, I know how to please."

"Have you been planning this the whole time?"

She laughed. "We did the calculations in Albarracín. My uncle has promised to share the proceeds with my mother. His take will exceed the bounty of that miserly Fray Anselmo. Our share will feed my siblings."

"Money. He was faithful to us, only for money?"

Xemci thought for a moment. "He knows you are Magda's daughter. He wouldn't give you back to them. Not for all the money in the world."

"Xemci, why you? Don't you have an older brother?"

"My older brother is a no account. I will provide."

"I can't see you as a slave in a harem."

"Don't cry for me. You are the one who needs help. Wherever I wind up, I will rule the roost, and if I tire of it, no walls can hold me."

I then tried to thank Amir, who was playing the languid melodies of Al-Andalus on his oud. He stopped long enough to reply, "Muslims and Jews are brothers. The Prophet rose to the Heavens after the Temple Mount." That night I heard him from afar, singing the phrase in Arabic.

By morning, his mood had sobered. "Your antics will be the end of you, Sarita. Today we start our march to Castellón, and then on to Valencia, military style."

"I don't like the sound of this," whispered Fatima.

"Listen to me, all you women."

There were rumbles of discontent, but we listened. We didn't have any choice, as without Amir there would be no expedition, and we all knew we had pushed him to his limit.

"No weddings, no picnics, no naps, no stopping to feed cats, and no kissing Dominicans."

Fatima poked me in the ribs, but I ignored her.

"Cover your faces, your ankles and whatever, and look sharp if you want to reach your destination."

From that day on, we ladies rode hard from dawn to dusk to the imaginary drums of an Ottoman marching band.

§§§

Amir chose an inland route for our journey south through Castellón. The Christian dialect had changed, so we spoke Arabic. We rode wide loops round Old Christian towns and halted where the muezzin called to prayer. In the hills, families shared couscous from their cooking pots. Some said Túnez sounded good and they wished they could join us. Too much pressure to convert. Times were changing.

We avoided Castellón de la Plana and had passed south of it, when we learned that the Holy Brotherhood was searching for a band of Muslims who had kidnapped a Christian girl. These fierce Muslims also were wanted for the disappearance of two Dominican brothers. I doubted the truth of the latter. Fray Anselmo struck me as indestructible. He was probably following us to win the prize himself.

We rode west toward the Serra d'Espadà and disappeared into ancient forests of cork oak. Fatima fancied a visit to Ahín, Arabic for freshwater spring. We reached as far as Eslida, where the springs flow from sandstone and are said to heal the stomach, but Fatima was sick and had no appetite. By this point, I couldn't eat either.

"What worries you, Sarita? At least you're not sick like me."

But the truth was that since the lost kiss my heart had been a lute that could not keep in tune, my strings wound tight or slack. I said nothing.

"He might still be around, for all you know."

"I don't think so. It's over."

Fatima shrugged. I searched in vain for honey drops.

"Forget him, Sara, there will be others. I promise. Who wants a Dominican, anyway? And Xemci says he has ugly tits. Like mulberries."

"That's not it."

"What is, then?"

"Valencia."

"Why? You can tell me, no one else can hear."

"The Inquisition has a tribunal in Valencia, and I'm drawing closer with each step."

"Do you have family there, just in case?"

"No. The city has been off limits to my people for a century, since riots targeted us and killed hundreds. There's a mass grave."

"I'm sorry, Sara."

"After the riots, the city expelled the Jews, not the rioters."

"Where did they go?"

"Some to Sagunto. Many other families converted to Christianity. I worry for them too. The old Jewish quarter stood empty for a while and then filled with brothels."

"Xemci's pleasure gardens."

"And worse."

Azizah rode up next to us.

"Don't worry about Valencia."

"It's a dangerous place for me."

"Amir says there are Muslim towns to the west and vast sea marshes to the south, where no one will find us."

"We're not lodging inside the city?"

"We will give it wide berth till it's time to board ship. For your sake."

"So we'll be moving from place to place?"

"Perhaps, or we'll stay in the maritime marshes."

I fell silent for a while. I recalled the lines of a poem I had learned in the convent — "Our lives are rivers which flow out to the sea, which is death."

"Sarita, you are brooding again. Time to buy sweets."

"And where are you going to buy sweets?" Fatima used a patronising tone, but then, her aunt hadn't made the offer to her.

"You girls are too wrapped up in yourselves to notice what's around you."

"Aunt, that's not fair."

"Who was the girl who waved to us at the last farmhouse?"

She was right. We hadn't noticed.

"The honeypot's daughter," she winked. "The old man was high up the hill, tending his hives. Fresh honey in spring water —an ambrosial refreshment. I'll return soon."

Fatima called after her, "Honey syrup for me!"

Azizah, cantering away on her mule, didn't seem to hear.

"With sheep's milk curd, Aunt, the creamy kind, in a little pot. I might be able to swallow some."

"Azizah is right, Fatima, we should look around us. There is magic in this place."

At the crossroads, three paths met. By each, a cork oak green with lichen stood sentinel. The silence of nesting birds rose from the bush. The sun was high but still shone from the east; overhead on powerful wings soared a Partridge Eagle.

"I feel faint again, Sara, and fain would lie down. Where is the blanket I bought in the hills?"

I unrolled row upon row of clever dots, red on dark blue, pulled into stars on a weave so fine it sang among my fingers. Against the cloth, her skin was pale.

"Let's put crimson in your cheeks. Time for smelling salts!"

"I'm tired of smelling salts. Put your pomander away. It's no use."

"A life-giving fragrance," I thought, "that's what she needs."

Here and there the bush was painted with sky blue. Rosemary in bloom. I unclasped my pomander, took a few steps into the heather, watching for serpents, and found — Xemci.

"Just as I hoped, something is hiding under these rocks!"

She stood on a tussock of rock-carnations, slender white stars. Trampling them, she dislodged a stone and pressed her fingers to her lips. Twenty pairs of vertical slits glared at us. Toads. They hopped into the light.

"Watch what comes next!"

Xemci crouched beside Fatima and lifted the latch to her feline's cage. Crepus leapt free. At once she pounced on the toads, one after another with precision.

"Look how that cat can dance! You should let her go, Fatima."

"Nonsense. She'd starve to death."

"At least she'll live her own life."

"No."

"She'll dine finer here under the cork oaks than on board our ship, on these frog delicacies. What are they called, Sara? You know the names of the wild things."

So that was her joke. We all knew the name. The Midwife Toad.

But Xemci wasn't joking anymore. "She's a cat, and she should have a cat's freedom."

That was the most philosophy I ever heard pass Xemci's lips. She had a point —at least Crepus could roam free. Not us. Why did it matter so much to others, how we dressed, how we prayed, whom we loved?

I wondered how much freedom Fatima had known. She had escaped from Azizah for an evening or two, but that wasn't freedom, just her last chance at knowledge before marrying an old man.

"She is due in a few months," I thought, "and she might not even know. I'll stay with her for the birth. With luck, we'll disembark in Túnez before then. Naples can wait."

What was worse, from what I could see, Fatima's womb was narrow. She needed soups of chicken and partridge. Warm baths in sweet spring water. Hot ointments of chamomile and anise, to make her supple for birth. How explain this to her, and keep a secret from the others?

If only I had an eagle stone, I could pass it to her and gage her reaction. We had inherited from grandpa a stone shaped like an egg from the nest of an eagle. It helped those birds to lay. For generations we had used them to help women give birth. Xemci might be persuaded to go looking for eyries but even she couldn't climb that high.

Azizah returned. "I have a surprise for you, Sarita, to boost your spirits."

"Tiger-nut milk! Pour me some too, be a good Aunt."

Fatima introduced Crepus, fresh from her first kill, to the frothy beverage. The cat spattered it on her whiskers. Fatima reached to wipe them, but the cat leapt backward and escaped into the bush. A partridge flew from her nest.

"Niece, don't annoy the cat. Xemci is right, she has fed herself."

Bird cries rose from the gorse. Crepus didn't lose any time in finding the nestlings. Xemci jumped to her feet, waving her fist.

"Atta girl, bite them at the neck. Snatch the mother in the air like your cousin the lynx. You can do it!" She made an undulating motion with her arm muscles and I could see the lynx jump.

"Xemci, this is not a cockfight, Allah forbid," scolded Azizah.

"She'll be after all the nests now. Partridges are tastier than toads."

"How do you know?"

"My brothers taught me to hunt frogs. You lie on your side and slip your fingers into the water."

"That's revolting, Xemci, those creatures are unclean."

Fatima began to cry. I put my arm around her.

"You're the one who needs nourishment. Come, let's share some tiger-nut milk. The foam on top is the best part."

More tears. I kept holding her.

"It's not what I asked for. Where's my little pot?"

"It's not creamy curd with honey syrup, but it's good."

"I don't like it made this way."

"Try some. You'll like it."

"But there's no cinnamon." Tears flowed.

"Yes. Also, sugar and candied citron carried by caravels from Crete."

"Like the dates we offered Azizah on the enchanted dish?"

"Even more special, because this is for you."

She took a sip, and then another, and then two more.

"Magda always said, that where three roads come together mystical powers are unleashed."

"We believe that too."

"Close your eyes, Fatima. Many years from now, you will have a tribe of manly grandsons. Tall Tunisians, with broader shoulders than Amir, and black hair like yours. Can you picture that?"

She nodded.

"Your cat's progeny will be chasing toads from here to Castellón. They will be exemplary hunters."

"Yes, Sarita, I can see now, but it is after I am gone. Blacker than the raven of the blackest wing, fiercer than the eagle who sails the skies at dawn."

§§§

It was the month of May, when the heat had returned to the earth, when the wheat stalks grew tall and flowers bloomed in the fields, when we arrived at the maritime marshes. We rode to the mouth of a vast lagoon. Its depths harboured waterfowl, its shallows rice, and its fringes orange groves.

"What river is this, Amir?"

"The great delta. These are the marshes of Albufera."

In flooded fields, men bending at the waist planted rice, an illicit crop, in patches midst the reeds. The lagoon shimmered with shoals of surface-swimming fish and its water mirrored the sky. This blue water-sky was overlaid with lace patterns of birds —ducks, egrets, eagles —which billowed up and down like veils from heaven. Further out, white sea-birds circled.

"I am taking a good look, because this is the last river I'll see in my homeland."

"It was also your first," Amir smiled. "This delta is fed by our very own Guadalaviar. It runs down from Albarracín, and if we had followed its course, instead of wandering north for the wedding, we would be in Túnez by now."

"I wish we had travelled by its side, Amir. It would have made a fine companion and reminded me of home."

Three white birds came sailing in, gliding towards the water on outstretched wings. With these, they beat six times, and on the seventh they landed. Heads held high, they folded their wings into perfection.

"Swans! To see these here is a gift from Allah."

As if my door to wonder were ajar, I stood outside Papa's study one last time. The fragrance of myrtle! The branches encircling me, come June, would unfold their buds into a bower of white and gold. My dreams of Naples faded. I wished to stay forever by the shores of Albufera's shining sea.

In the morning, Amir urged us on. We rode upriver to a town where mudéjar families displayed row upon row of ceramics. Never had I seen such splendid lusterware, piled as high as Arabi's carpets —glazed platters, dishes, flagons, jars, and vases —rising round each bend again and again like banks of riotous flowers at sunset.

As we couldn't stop, we whispered our preferences while riding down the street.

"I like the apothecary jars with grape leaves of blue and gold."

"Logical for a doctor's daughter."

"Bookbinder," I thought. "The frontispiece of the Zohar."

I recalled Papa's lessons to us children, not long past. The doors to our synagogue. The lamp of God.

"Naturally, I prefer the plates with the Hand of Fatima."

"So many dishes with Christian saints. It's the latest style. What's this world coming to?" moaned Azizah.

"Goodbye girls, I'm going to Valencia." Xemci was very animated. "You know what the muleteers sing in Arabic?"

Azizah clapped her hands to her ears.

"'A handful of hash, a loaf of bread and a lad.' Hah!"

"What's so funny?"

"You carry it up your sleeve. Gimme some, will you?"

"Not herb, but opium, and I don't have any."

"We'll see about that when I return. Anyhow, don't wait up for me tonight."

Xemci rode away with her man. Somehow I knew she'd be back. Amir led us into a courtyard littered with unglazed jars and bolted the gates.

"We arrive with no time to spare. Our ship has docked at Valencia. In a few days, we set sail."

"So soon? Will there be storms at sea?"

"Fatima, the corsairs concern me more than the weather. We shall sail in a small flotilla of caravels and hug the coast as far as possible. Our safe passage along the shores of the Maghreb is in the hands of Allah."

"What town is this?"

"Sarita, this is Paterna."

I said to myself, "where Papa Simon fell in love."

"You must be careful in Valencia. I advise you to remain silent while you are in the city. Stay close."

"Yes, I know."

"Your passage is paid. But if you prefer, I will bring you to a household of people of your own faith where you may take leave of us."

"Who?"

"Dueynna's family. They reside here, outside the city walls, in defiance of the law. Uncle Arabi passed me the name of Dueynna's brother and told me to give you this choice."

I thought of the Holy Brotherhood, whose police would hunt me down, and the Inquisition in Valencia. If they caught me, there would be no reconciliation. Yes, I would stand up for my faith, but how could I serve the Lord from the grave?

"Amir, I thank you and Uncle Arabi for your goodness toward me. I choose to continue with you to Túnez and stay with Fatima till she is settled. Then, onward to Naples."

Late that night, in the attic overlooking the courtyard, I lay awake thinking of Dueynna. In Valencia I began to see her in a new light. Papa was right —she was precious, the relic of a lost community. Where were the Jews of Valencia? Not in the city, and even in the inland towns, our families were far fewer than in Teruel. As for me, Teruel was far away, my loved ones dead. Even my adored river had changed.

At its source, the Guadalaviar runs between walls of red sandstone, past trees festooned with ivy beloved of the Arab poets. I closed my eyes. I tried to return to the river of my childhood, to the shallows where the dipper wades in the spring. Instead, the delta stretched before me.

In the water, I saw reflected a young woman in Muslim attire standing alone, as slender and straight as a stalk of wheat, whose eyes might reflect the faith of any of our three religions.

My reflection said to me, "Aragon is my homeland. I am as Aragonese as anyone, yet I have to leave to keep my faith. I am not the first. How many will follow?"

My heart already in exile, by the light of Reyna's lamp I wrote my last lines in Iberia.

§§§

We rode down the streets of Valencia on mules, dressed in black from head to toe. Even Xemci. Amir had procured a mule strong enough to carry both Azizah and me. The immense beast was the ogress of mules, but I felt sorry for the weight she bore. I sat behind Azizah grasping her waist, my eyes lowered.

By the water's edge hemmed in by crowds, we sat on our bags all morning. A woman was pleading with the captain of a ship. She clutched a bag of gold in one hand, and the other hand she wrapped round an adolescent. She was seeking passage for her son to Salonica. As contraband. The captain countered that her son was a criminal for adhering to the Law of Moses, and her purse was not enough. Nestled between Azizah and Fatima, under my burka I kept very still.

A small boat sailed up to us and Amir roused us to climb on board.

"That tiny boat? We'll never reach Túnez."

"Fatima, this is just the launch that will carry us to the ship. The caravel is farther out."

Amir went first and extended his arm to Azizah. She couldn't time her step to the swaying of the boat, and in the end she took a leap of faith. Once the boat had settled in the water, like a ladle in a punch bowl, we all did more or less the same.

Though we jumped an arm's length from shore, we landed in the world of the mariner. Everywhere round us smelled of new things —salt, seaweed and ropes sticky with brine. Waves rolled toward us.

"Now we will dance," laughed Amir.

"I'm going to be sick. Soon. Why don't we cast off?"

"Fatima, a personage of singular importance is joining us."

"Who?"

"My new horse."

"A horse on this tiny boat? I am getting off. Now."

"Azizah, don't stand up, or we will capsize."

I looked at launches to our right and left, and sure enough, horses were standing among the passengers.

"Why buy a new one here? Why not wait till the other side?"

"See for yourself."

Amir's horse arrived, led by an Arab groom. The Arab had a way with horses. The animal stepped into the launch more gracefully on four legs than any of us had on two.

The groom wore a black beard neatly trimmed that touched his lower lip. Beneath his mulberry turban, his eyes shone bright as jet. Grandson of the Taifa of Granada. I would have known him anywhere. Even without his habit!

"I'm not sailing with horses. I am putting my foot down." Fatima was in need of a calming draught.

"How do you think horses cross over to Túnez, by walking on water?" Xemci laughed.

"On wings like Pegasus."

The launch set course for the caravel, and we left our native shore.

§§§

My name, Sara. I am the bastard daughter of Magda Cruz, may she rest in peace, widow of Juan Sordo. I have a half-brother, Jaime Sordo, shepherd at Frías, and a half-sister, Carmela Sordo, landholder at Cella. I might hail from aristocrats who trace back to King David. Then again, I might not. I was baptised a Christian as an infant but raised as a Jew for motives that are not clear to me. I choose to live my life as a Jew for reasons of faith. I might have to die to do it.

From Teruel, I rode to Valencia. From Valencia, I am bound for Túnez and then Naples, but anything is possible. Tonight I will say my prayers, in the Hebrew way. These prayers I will not transcribe, except for a few petitions, as the Christians call them.

For the Muslims, I pray that the voice of the muezzin always resound through the hills of Aragon, and that the minarets stand proud in our towns once more.

For the People of Israel, I pray that our people and books be cherished and that joy illumine our beautiful synagogues in Aragon, always.

For the Christians, whose churches are being built everywhere, I pray that they follow their best teachings and leave space for the rest of us.

The Sage Rumi taught that there are many lamps but the Light is the same. So it is with the lamps of Albarracín. Farewell, my town on the hill, may your children always plant flowers and fruits in the Paradise of the Three Religions.

GLOSSARY OF JUDAIC TERMS
AND HISTORICAL FIGURES

Ab, Ninth Day of   Day to commemorate the destruction of Jerusalem and the Temple by the Chaldeans and the Romans, spent in fasting and mourning

Abravanel   A leading Jewish family of medieval Iberia, that traces its origins to King David

Adonai Ro'i   Psalm 23, The Lord is My Shepherd

Aleph   First letter of the Hebrew alphabet

All who thirst,
come to water   Isaiah 55:1

Amidah   In Jewish worship, the central prayer of all daily services, recited while standing

Balcony/Gallery   Area of the synagogue, reserved exclusively for females

Benjamín de Tudela   Jewish writer who travelled from his native town of Tudela in Navarra, Spain to the Middle East in the second half of the 12th century and wrote an extensive chronicle of his observations, the Book of Travels.

Blessed is He who planted trees
in the Garden of Eden   Sephardic Siddur for Yom Kippur

Blue is to the sea, as the sea
to the sky, as the sky to
the Throne of Glory   Sage Rabbi Meir, from the Menachot,
referring to the blue of the chilazon

Booths/Cabañuelas   Temporary booths or huts built to celebrate the seven-day holiday "Sukkot"

Brazada   Medieval unit of measure of approximately one arm's length

Brianda Besante de
Santángel   A female leader of the converso community of Teruel who was tried by the Inquisition in the 1480s, defended her Jewish faith, and subsequently was handed to secular authorities, presumably for execution; her daughters were exonerated

Broken cisterns
that hold no water   Jeremiah 2:13

Buñuelos   Balls of fried dough sprinkled with
honey or sugar

Candles of God   "The soul of man is a candle of God"
(Proverbs 20:27).

Casher   See Keser

Challah   Egg bread baked for Shabbat; the
loaves are often braided from strands of dough

Chilazon   Sea creature that in ancient times
was the source of the blue dye used for the blue tassel threads of
the four-cornered prayer shawl worn by Jewish men

Converso/a   A person converted from Judaism to
Christianity by baptism, by force or consent

Da'at   Knowledge of God

Day of Atonement   See Yom Kippur

Disputation of Tortosa   Christian-Jewish disputation held in
Tortosa in 1413-1414 CE, convened by the Catholic Church to
prove the truth of Christianity

Declaration of Faith   See Shema

Edom   A nation of the descendants of Esau,
located southeast of the Kingdom of Judah. Isaiah prophesied
that "in the future, the ruins of Edom will be haunted by demons" (Isaiah: 34:14)

Eliezer ben Alantansi   Printer of Hebrew books, based in
the town of Híjar, Aragon, from 1485 to 1490 CE

Flame of Thorns   The fire that did not consume, seen
by Moses in the episode of the Burning Bush (Exodus 3:1-5)

Foundations shall
be sapphires   Isaiah 54:11

Guayas   Hebrew expression of grief in wide-
spread use in 15th century Iberia

Haman   The antagonist in the Book of Esther who plotted to destroy the Jews

Haman's Ears   Cookies traditionally eaten at the Festival of Purim

Hamin   Traditional one-pot dish often eaten on Shabbat because it can be prepared ahead

Hanukiya   A candelabra with nine candle holders, lit only during Hanukkah, the Festival of Lights

Hanukkah   The Festival of Lights, an eight-day holiday that commemorates an ancient Jewish victory against Hellenistic dominance

Hasdai Crescas
de Zaragoza   Spanish Jewish philosopher, writer and expert on the Talmud (1340-1410 CE). Famous for his work La Luz del Señor (Or Adonai), he influenced modern philosophy through his impact on Spinoza.

Hashem   A Hebrew term for God, literally "The Name"

Hevelayud   Hispanicized Hebrew phrase meaning "so much nonsense"

Hillel the Elder   Talmudic sage from the first century BC famous for his wisdom

Holy Ark   The place in the front of the Synagogue where the Torah Scrolls are kept

Jacob ben Asher   One of the greatest Talmudic scholars of all time. Born in Germany, he arrived in Toledo in 1317 CE, where his father was rabbi. He is remembered most for his compendia of the laws of the Torah, abridged for practical use, including the Arba-ah Turim, printed in Híjar, Aragon in the 1480s CE.

Judería   In medieval Spain, a neighbourhood designated by secular authorities for residence by Jews

Kashrut   Jewish dietary laws governing the consumption of foods and their preparation

Keser   In accordance with Kosher dietary laws and customs

Kiddush   A Hebrew prayer recited on Shabbat and Holy days before the ritual drinking of wine, "Sanctification" in Hebrew

King Solomon   Biblical king widely viewed as the greatest king of Israel, known for his wealth and wisdom

Kippa   A small cloth circle worn on the head by Jewish men and boys, to show their respect to God

Law of Moses   As used by Inquisition authorities, these terms refer primarily to the Torah or first five books of the Hebrew Bible

Leonor de Montesa   Daughter of Don Jaime de Montesa, King's Magistrate of Aragon, burned at the stake in Zaragoza in August 1487 CE for donating oil for the lamps of the Synagogue and keeping the fast of Yom Kippur

Lions of Judah   Symbol of the Tribe of Judah, one of the Seven Tribes of Israel

Maimónides   Rabbi Moshe ben Nachman, a great Jewish philosopher, author of many works including the Mishneh Torah, a compilation of the teachings of Judaism

Malsin	Informant or spy, from Hebrew

Mitzvah — A divine commandment, either positive (to do something), or negative (to refrain from doing something). More generally, a good or noble act, as in an act of kindness

Mizmorim — Psalms from the Book of Psalms

Moses — Biblical leader of the Jewish people, who led his people out of slavery in Egypt and received the Ten Commandments at Mount Sinai.

Moshe — Moses in Hebrew

Nineveh — The principal city of the ancient Assyrian Empire, located on the east bank of the Tigris River, in modern-day Iraq, mentioned in Jonah 3

Ocho Candelitas — The eight candles or oil lamps lit over the eight days of Hanukkah; a song in Ladino about the same

Pesah   The Jewish festival of Passover, commemorating the flight of the Jews from slavery in Egypt

Purim   Holy day in early spring commemorating the Book of Esther from the Torah

Queen Esther   Protagonist of the Biblical Book of
Esther, she outwits Haman in his attempt to destroy the Jews

Rabbi   "My teacher" in Hebrew, a rabbi
serves as religious leader of his community and must be quali-
fied for this title through examination

Rabbi Solomon
of Albarracín   Rabbi of Albarracín who resisted the
Edict of the Expulsion of the Jews from Albarracín in 1486

Rabbi Yehuda Harizi   Hebrew poet and scholar, born in
1160 CE, who translated many medical books among other
works

Resheph   The Canaanite God of Plague, mentioned in Habakkuk 3:5, often portrayed as shooting at his victims with arrows of disaster and disease

Rosh Hashanah   The Jewish New Year, a time for self-examination, the "Head of the Year"

Salt   In Judaism, salt symbolizes the covenant between God and Israel

Samuel ha-Nagid   Jewish statesman, Talmudic scholar and poet, born in Mérida in 993 CE. He rose to be Vizier of Granada and was top advisor to two Muslim kings, advising on both political and military affairs

Satyr will call
to another   Isaiah 34:14

Seder   The festive dinner of Passover commemorating the exodus of the Jewish people from Egypt

Shabbat   Rest day on the seventh day of the week that is devoted to prayer and study of the Torah

Shalom aleichem   Peace be upon you

Shechinah   The dwelling of the Divine Presence, also the "feminine" manifestation of the Divine

Shema   The Declaration of Faith, a prayer
that is central to Judaism, affirming faith in a single God, as dis-
tinct from the Christian Trinity

Simon ben Zoma   Jewish scholar and teacher who
lived in the 2nd Century CE, famous for his words of wisdom

Sukkot   Seven-day Festival of the Booths,
held in the autumn. The tradition stems from Leviticus 23:41-43:
"You shall dwell in booths seven days"

Synagogue   Jewish house of worship

Talmud   This authoritative compilation of
religious teachings and spiritual knowledge, made up of more
than 63 books, is considered central to Jewish culture

Temple of Jerusalem   Either of two temples that served as
the centre of Jewish worship in Israel in ancient times

Tenth Plague   The Death of the First Born, after
which Pharaoh freed the Jews from slavery; it is written that
they fled so quickly there was no time to let their bread rise, and
in commemoration, no leavened bread is eaten at Passover

Third star in the sky   In pre-Expulsion Iberia, the appearance of the third star in the sky marked the start of Shabbat

Tikkun   Repair, as in "the repair of an imperfect world," one of the spiritual duties of a believer

Torah   The first five books of the Hebrew
Bible

Tu B'Shevat   The New Year of the Trees, traditionally marking the start of the crop year for tithing purposes

Yom Kippur   Day of Atonement, a day of prayer, introspection and fasting, the first major holiday after Rosh Hashanah (the New Year)

Zohar   A work ascribed to 13th century Spanish Jewish mystic Moises de León that expounds the traditional teachings of Jewish mysticism

AUTHOR'S STATEMENT

The Lamps of Albarracín gives voice to the Jews, Muslims, conversos, mudéjares, and Christians of Aragon at the close of the Middle Ages. Those were the years prior to the expulsion of the Jews from Spain in 1492, when the social contract that had sustained a tenuous co-existence of the three faiths was coming apart As an author, I sought to explore issues of religious belief, identity, and inter-faith friendship. The shock of forced conversion to Catholicism. The peculiar logic of the Inquisitors and those who supported them. Stories of ordinary people in extraordinary times.

While this is a historical novel, I do not claim to capture in a single story the complexity of the fragile *convivencia* of people of different religions that existed in Iberia in the 1480's. From such vast human experience an infinity of stories is possible. This work is in the tradition of the Portuguese *saudade*, a tale of nostalgic longing for a past that witnessed inter-faith friendships as well as enmity. Too often, the study of history shows us how to group people into boxes. What interests me is the fluidity of human interactions. I also am passionate about restoring awareness of multicultural heritage, in particular, patrimony that regimes have tried to destroy.

We humans have a tendency not to notice what isn't there. It is analogous in medical science to a blind spot in a patient's field of vision, which the patient doesn't notice because the mind abhors a vacuum. Regimes that enforce uniformity of religion understand this. In Iberia, thousands of synagogues and mosques were demolished. When we arrive at a site where one once stood, it is tempting to think, "We don't know for sure how it looked," and walk away. Instead, let's imagine possibilities.

Consider the Great Synagogue of Zaragoza, once one of the largest congregations in Europe. Nothing survives of the main building, but we have some clues. In 1598, the Compañía de Jesús took possession of the property and sent a certain Diego de Espés to take inventory. Imagine the scene. Espés enters and finds the interior as it had been left more than one hundred years before, at the time of the Expulsion of the Jews in 1492. Many sacred objects are gone, melted down as tribute to the Crown. Yet much remains. The "little pulpit," the "altar" set into the wall and adorned in mosaics, and the painted candelabra with its seven lamps. Round the walls at their height, sacred inscriptions in blue and red. Even Espés, a detached observer, takes note of the blue Hebrew letters. Where Espés ends his terse account, our work begins.

William Butler Yeats is credited with the saying, "In imagination begins responsibility." The novelist Haruki Murakami, who struggled to make sense of the horrors of the 20th century, framed it as a challenge for society: "our responsibility begins with our imagination." I believe that imagination, properly directed, helps shape the future and we have the responsibility to use it. If we harness our imagination to re-envision diverse houses of worship, we are more likely to protect diversity today. If we understand the thinking that led to atrocities, we can recognise warning signs and work to prevent them. The very exercise of multicultural re-creation, our informed re-imagining, helps bring us together and strengthens our commitment to a multicultural future.

The Lamps of Albarracín has a spiritual subtext. For readers so inclined it offers an exploration of the Hidden. As Reyna exclaims, there is so much more to the world than we can ever imagine. Is beauty a revelation? Do our souls shine with the same light? These were spiritual preoccupations of that time. Their relevance today is for you to decide. The lamps in this novel belong to us all.

EDITH SCOTT SAAVEDRA

Republic of Singapore, May 2018

Acknowledgements

While all episodes and dialogue are fictional, historical personages appear in the story including Brianda Besante de Santángel and her husband Luis de Santángel, Leonor de Montesa, Tomás de Torquemada, and Rabbi Solomon of Albarracín and his thirty families. The fictional character of Bella was inspired by the woman depicted in the painting "Jesús y la mujer adúltera" attributed to the artist Miguel de Jiménez, painted for the Real Monasterio de Santa María, a convent in Villanueva de Sigena, and now in the Museum of Huesca. A separate altarpiece for the Iglesia de San Pablo in Zaragoza is also attributed to Miguel de Jiménez from about this time. The hanukiya of little birds is based on a 14th century ceramic original from Teruel. Many scenes and images were inspired by paintings by master artists of the period, including Bartolomé Bermejo and Pedro Berruguete, and two masters born a century later, Jusepe Ribera and Francisco Zurbarán.

My gratitude to David Landau, author and creative writing instructor at the Harvard Club of San Francisco. David believed in this project from its beginning and persuaded me to go ahead with the simultaneous creation of English and Spanish language versions. For editing the Spanish version, poet and author Néstor Díaz de Villegas.

Special acknowledgement to David Gitlitz, former Professor of History at the University of Rhode Island, who generously made time to review the manuscript.

362

For translation into Spanish, acknowledgement to the novelist Benigno Dou, and also to Carmen Morata, Álvaro González Montero, and Elise Kendall of BookwormTranslations.com.

I thank friends and family who gave of their time: Javier Bona López, Cayetano Félix Castellanos Valencia, Judy Damas, Viacheslav Dinerchtein, Katherine Enright, Ana M. Escario Hernández, Michael Gisser, Neal Horwitz, CJ Hwu, Tedd Joselson, Paloma Julián, Hertzel Lelah, Maggi Lidchi-Grassi, Andrés D. López, Mandakini, Leslie Martin, Miguel Martínez Tomey, Sarah Monks, David Murolo, Jutta Odenwaelder, Armando and Mari Carmen Saavedra, Luis Sedgwick Báez, Albert Torel, Cynthia Torres and Devora Werchowsky.

Deanna Blacher Cohn advised on the history of Spanish music and dance; Javier Bona López, on the culture and Jewish history of Aragon; Maurice Elie Lidchi, on Persian carpets; and Carlos Zarur, anthropologist, on medieval Sephardic culture.

I am grateful to my professors at Harvard University, above all, the historian and essayist Juan Marichal, who awakened my love for the Spanish romancero, and the author and activist Robert Coles, who awakened my love of justice. Also, my parents.

ATTRIBUTIONS

All the ceramic lamps in this novel are inspired by actual lamps, and credit is due to the ceramists:

Isaq's crocodile lamp and Mother Inmaculada's lamp with eyes, by Cerámica Domingo Punter, Teruel, Spain;

Uncle Arabi's peri lamps, Fatima's magical slipper lamps, Papa Simon's swan lamp, Magda's casserole lamps, and Azizah's travel lamps by José Balmón Castell and María del Mar del Valle López, El Taller de Lucérnaga, Córdoba, Spain; and Reyna's blue lamp, Sara's green lamp, and dream lamp for Isaq by ceramist Inbal Oren, Tel Aviv, Israel, whose ancestors left Spain in 1492.

Cover photo by photographer Michael Gronow, Singapore.

Drawings by Devora Werchowsky, Madrid, Spain.

Historical maps by Daniel Hasenbros, Utrecht, Netherlands.

Poem "One, One, One," by Mevlana Jalaluddin Rumi, reprinted from *The Rumi Collection*, pp. 137-8, trans. Andrew Harvey, ed. Kabir Helminski © 1998, Shambala Publications, Inc., Boulder, CO. www.Shambala.com.

Attributions to David Gitlitz, *Secrecy and Deceit: The Religion of the Crypto-Jews* (Albuquerque: University of New Mexico Press, 2002) based on Inquisition records and testimony: sayings about heaven and hell, p. 113; Jesus climbing a ladder, p. 140; Brianda Besante de Santángel, trial details, pp. 122, 400, 475,

509, 522, 591; secret prayers and thoughts during celebration of the Eucharist, pp. 151-2; the scattering of drops in a pan, p. 192; Yom Kippur customs in Teruel, p. 359; Sukkot customs, pp. 371-4; fasting at Yom Kippur as a cure, p. 400; Sara's morning prayer, p. 447; Sara's prayer after a nightmare, p. 482, endnote 38; Conversa girls in Teruel accused of eating sweets at Jewish festivals, p. 590; Inquisition destroying trust on which human relationships depend, p. 596; and, converso martyrdom, p. 601. See also, Stephen Haliczer, *The Inquisition and Society in the Kingdom of Valencia: 1478-1834* (Berkeley: University of California Press, 1990).

Two comments from David Gitlitz: the ballad "La Torre" (in the sea, there is a tower) has not been proven to precede the Expulsion, and Hanukkah festivities in pre-Expulsion Iberia were generally not as lavish as portrayed in the Teruel episode.

Attributions to David Gitlitz with Linda Kay Davidson, *A Drizzle of Honey: The Lives and Recipes of Spain's Secret Jews*, Kindle Edition: hamin recipe from Teruel, Loc. 915-54; Rita Besante and daughters, trial details, Loc. 2948-65; Belenguer Acho, trial details, Loc. 3503-12.

For the history of 15th century Teruel and the city's resistance to the Inquisition, including socio-political analysis, see Mary Halavais, *Like Wheat to the Miller: Community, Convivencia, and the Construction of Morisco Identity in Sixteenth-Century Aragon* (Gutenberg-e), Columbia University, January 22, 2005, www.gutenberg-e.org/ham01/ham01.html. Chapter 1: Muslim property transactions in Teruel; *convivencia* and minority expectations of fair treatment; city's inclusive identity; and Gonzalo Ruiz' warning. Chapter 2: Inquisition's arrival and campaign; city's resistance; marriage of Garcés de

Marzilla; Serranía identity; and letter from City of Teruel to King Ferdinand (like wheat to the miller).

For Diego de Espés' description of the Sinagoga Mayor de Zaragoza, see Miguel Angel Motis Dolader y María Teresa Ainaga Andrés, "Patrimonio urbanístico aljamial de la judería de Tarazona (Zaragoza): las sinagogas, la necrópolis y las carnicerías", Rev. Zurita, 56, pp. 83-129, 105, I.S.S.N. 0044-5517.

The vast majority of the Spanish ballads in this novel are drawn from course materials that were taught by Professor Juan Marichal at Harvard University in his course Humanities 55, including the following: C. Colin Smith (ed.), *Spanish Ballads* (Oxford: Pergamon Press, 1971); Manuel Alvar, *Romancero Viejo y Tradicional* (México, Distrito Federal: Editorial Porrúa, 1979); and unpublished materials.

Made in the USA
Middletown, DE
05 December 2018